LOVE ME LIKE A LOVE SONG

ANNMARIE BOYLE

D1599285

DAHLIA
MEDIA

For Paul,
my partner, my best friend, and
my most ardent supporter
For over twenty years you've reaffirmed my belief in the existence
of happily-ever-afters.

CHAPTER ONE

G race O'Connor dropped the packing tape dispenser on the kitchen counter and pressed one perfectly manicured finger over the adhesive strip holding the cardboard box closed, dislodging air bubbles. Pulling the cap off of a Sharpie, she scrawled 'men's clothes' over the top of the box.

A plain brown box. Filled with the clothes of a man who had been anything but plain.

Sucking in a deep breath, she turned to the teenager hovering just inside her door. "This is it. This is the final box." It was one box out of a hundred. It shouldn't be a big deal, but if she'd learned anything over the past year and a half, it was that grief had a way of obliterating life's 'should's.'

The teenager heaved the box onto his shoulder and Grace tucked a tip into his t-shirt pocket emblazoned with the charity's logo. "Thanks Mrs. Jensen! Have a great weekend," he called, scurrying toward the elevator.

"It's O'Connor," she mumbled. It didn't seem to matter how many times she told people, they still got it wrong. For over twenty years she'd been Jax Jensen's apostrophe 'S.' First, Jax

Jensen's songwriter. Then Jax Jensen's wife. And now, Jax Jensen's widow.

"You talking to yourself again?"

Grace's head snapped up. She'd almost forgotten Annie was in the apartment. "It's the sign of creative genius."

Her best friend chuckled and tossed the magazine resting in her lap onto the coffee table. It flopped open to the center spread and Annie quickly flipped it closed. "Is it?"

Grace nodded as she tucked her clipboard under her arm, crossed the vast expanse of the converted warehouse loft, and sunk into the navy velvet Chesterfield sofa opposite Annie. She crossed her legs underneath her and forced her gaze upward, away from the magazine.

"Thanks for coming over today." Grace picked up the to-go cup from Common Grounds, their favorite haunt, and air-toasted Annie. "And, for bringing coffee."

"I would have brought something a little more appropriate for a Friday afternoon, but I have to pick up Ellie from dance class. Plus, I would have missed the barista falling all over himself to make your coffee. He asked about you three separate times." Annie winked. "With a little flirting, you'd likely have free coffee for life."

"Not really my thing. But you could try it."

"I doubt he's interested in an old married lady with two kids."

Grace gave Annie a head-to-toe appraisal. From top to bottom, her best friend was her opposite. Straight chestnut-colored hair to Grace's mass of blonde waves. Copper skin to Grace's 'have you ever gone outside?' complexion. Legs that pushed her to near six-foot compared to Grace's legs that needed heels to even hope for the middle fives. And deep chocolate eyes to Grace's icy blue. Annie was a glamazon—and, kids or no kids, likely to turn the head of every barista in a hundred-mile radius.

Grace snorted and rolled her eyes. "We're the same age, Annie. Though I feel like the past two years have aged me twenty."

Annie's expression softened, silently acknowledging the challenges Grace had battled—the kind no one wants, and no one faces voluntarily. She pointed at the dog-eared pages attached to Grace's clipboard. "Speaking of which, what's next on The List?"

Grace peered down and smoothed her hand over the wrinkled papers. The List. It read like a piece of fiction. Sell house in Malibu. Sell apartment in Tribeca. Donate guitar to Smithsonian. Donate the proceeds of "Best of" EP to the hospice that cared for Jax when he'd decided to forego additional chemo.

Her story had played out in a way she never could have imagined. One moment she'd been a shy midwestern girl from a middle-class family who, aside from an affinity for poetry and piano playing, was the very definition of unremarkable. Then, in the twinkling of a mischievous hazel eye, she'd been sucked into the swirling vortex of a musical superstar on the rise. From ordinary to extraordinary in one chance meeting.

But in the end, it didn't matter. It didn't matter how many stamps she had in her passport, or how many red carpets she'd walked, or how many hit songs they'd written, the Jax Jensen juggernaut jerked to a halt in a plain white room with a small soft-spoken man in a starched white coat. It took only two words —Stage Four—to silence the tempest.

"Grace?"

"Hmmm?"

Annie pointed at the clipboard again. "The List?"

Grace motioned toward the cup of rainbow-colored pens

sitting on the recycled natural steel end table next to Annie. "Throw me a pen."

"I will not. I will *hand* you a pen. You're distracted and no one needs to lose an eye today."

Grace shook her head and smirked. "I retract my previous statement. You are clearly much older than me. If I promise to sit up straight, wash behind my ears, and not swim for an hour after eating, will you please *hand* me a pen, Grandma?"

Annie arched one perfectly sculpted eyebrow and retracted her outstretched hand. "Grandma? Just for that, get it yourself."

Grace lowered her voice. "Annie, if you hand me the pen, we can officially retire The List."

"What? It's done?"

Grace swallowed hard and placed a hand over her belly, willing the ache away, and nodded. "Donating Jax's remaining clothes was the final item on The List."

"That's why you asked me to come here this afternoon."

A smile tweaked the corners of Grace's mouth. "You should be careful. I asked you to take the day off and you did it. No questions asked. The sheer power of that is likely to go to my head."

"You said you needed me. You never ask for help unless you really need it—and sometimes not even when you do. Of course, I'd be here." Annie extracted a neon-pink marker from the cup, rounded the table and plopped down next to Grace. She slung her arm around Grace and pulled her into a half hug. Uncapping the pen, she held it out. "Ready?"

Grace's gaze traveled between the pen and The List. She'd organized The List about a month after Jax's passing. It gave her a reason to get out of bed in the morning. For eighteen months it had given her purpose. Like a slow-release capsule, it helped her say good-bye in steps. In the beginning it was a healthy coping mechanism. Now? It was a counterproductive crutch. It was time to retire it—past time, actually.

She reached for the pen but pulled her hand back. "I can't do it," she whispered. Crossing off the final item equaled facing the future. Without The List she was a ship unmoored, floating out to sea, bobbing over the waves with no idea where she was going and no land in sight.

Annie squeezed Grace's free hand. "Do you want me to do it?"

Grace nodded and Annie tugged on the clipboard. "You're going to have to let go, sweetie."

Grace squeezed her eyes shut and shook her head. "Can't do that, either."

"Okay, on the count of three, all you need to do is take a deep breath and straighten your fingers, and I'll slide it over to me. One, two . . . two and a half"—Annie pried up Grace's fingers—"three"—and yanked the clipboard free.

Grace listened as Annie shuffled through the paper, stopped, and scratched the pen across the page. The pen's cap clicked into place. The List was finished. She waited for relief. It didn't come. It felt strikingly similar to a book with an unsatisfying ending. Hollow. Incomplete.

Annie tucked an errant curl behind Grace's ear. "Open your eyes, *mi amiga*. Tell me what you're feeling."

Grace's stomach tumbled and twisted. How did she feel? Exhilarated. Guilty. Scared. And something else. "Foolish," she blurted out.

Surprise flashed across Annie's face. "That wasn't the answer I was expecting. Why foolish?"

"I thought when The List was complete, I'd know what to do next." She picked up the clipboard and threw it, sending it clattering across the table, finally coming to a rest next to that terrible, horrible—likely truthful—magazine article. "But I got nothing. No clarity, no direction, no plan."

"I thought the plan was to give yourself some time and then return to what you do best—writing songs. Has something changed? Because, Grace, the world would be a darker place without your music."

Grace snorted and rolled her eyes. "Overstate things, much?"

Annie smirked. "All the time. But not when it comes to this. I believe in you . . . and so did Jax. He wouldn't want you to stop writing."

Grace got very interested in the nap of the couch, watching the velvet change color as she dragged her fingers over it. Is that what Jax would want? She wasn't so sure.

"A songwriter is nothing without a singer." Grace stared out the mullioned floor-to-ceiling windows recessed into the original, feet-deep, industrial brick wall and absentmindedly pulled at a string dangling from the rip in her jeans that bisected her thigh. "Who would I write for?"

"Anyone you want."

Grace turned her attention back to her friend. Annie had settled into an oversized emerald green sofa pillow and exuded every bit of confidence Grace didn't feel. "It's not that easy. The music industry is a fickle business. I've been MIA for nearly two years and a single artist recorded all my songs."

"Pffft." Annie waved off her concerns. "One artist or not, you've authored some of the biggest hits of the last decade and have the hardware to prove it." Annie tipped her head toward the line of golden gramophones covering the mantle. "Who wouldn't want to work with you?"

"Anyone who's read that." Grace pointed at the magazine taunting her from the center of the coffee table. Annie opened her mouth and Grace raised a single finger. "Before you say anything, I saw you reading it."

Annie grabbed the magazine and rolled it up, smacking it against the table. "Who cares what one hack thinks? Plus, the article is mainly a retrospective on Jax's career."

"Exactly. We were equal partners, Annie, in every sense of the word and how am I portrayed in that story? As nothing more than a footnote in his storied career."

Annie gave her a pointed look, her chocolate brown eyes flashing as she bolted upright from the sofa and stomped into the kitchen. "I'm putting this damn thing in the garbage because that's what it is." She wrenched open the trash bin and slammed the magazine inside. "I have a single question for you, Grace. Do you still want to write songs—is it still your dream?"

Grace grabbed the pillow Annie had been leaning on and wrapped her arms around it, pulling it tight against her chest. "Technically, that's two questions."

Annie frowned. "Make your jokes, *chica*. I'll wait. I'm paid —handsomely, I might add—to wait and let my opponent sweat the silence."

Grace brushed a curl that had escaped from her loose braid away from her face and bit back a laugh. Annie stood with both hands on her hips and a don't-even-think-about-fucking-with-me look on her face. This was Annaliese Santos, Esquire, in full reckoning mode.

"What else would I do? It's the only thing I've ever done."

Annie blew out a breath, sending her bangs skyward. "Not a real answer." Grace's eyes followed her as she walked, strike that, marched, into the den and started digging through the bench perched in front of the grand piano.

"What are you doing?"

"This," Annie said, lofting a Tiffany-blue journal in the air.

She stalked up behind Grace and dropped the book over her shoulder.

It landed with a thud in Grace's lap. Her lucky writing journal. The leather cover worn to a buttery sheen and the corners rubbed raw, exposing the original tanned hide from years of use.

"Open the magic book, G. Reacquaint yourself with your talent—and your dream. And, then do what Grace O'Connor does best. Write." Annie pressed her lips together and stabbed a finger at Grace, coming within an inch of her nose. "Do it."

"Right now?"

"No time like the present." Annie's hands reconnected with her hips with a thwack. "Go on, I'll wait."

"Didn't you say you had to pick up Ellie from dance class?"

Annie flipped over her phone and sucked her top lip under her teeth. "Shoot. I lost track of time. I gotta go, but my instructions stand. And, I'll know if you're not writing."

"How does that work?"

"I'm a lawyer and a mother—makes my Spidey sense very acute."

Grace chuckled and stood, linking her arm through Annie's and directing her toward the door. "I'll keep that in mind."

"Oh, and don't forget, Abbie's school play is tomorrow night."

"On my calendar. I'd never miss her debut as the Cowardly Lion."

"They're lucky to have you, Tía G."

She was the lucky one. The List may have given her purpose, but it was Abbie and Ellie's spelling bees, dance recitals, and soccer games that forced her to leave the house.

After Jax passed, she needed a break from the lights of Hollywood and the never-ending pulse of Manhattan. She needed the peace that she only found at their Minneapolis loft

—the place they'd written some of their best songs, the place where they were simply Jaxson and Gracie and the place where they could enjoy a leisurely Sunday morning cup of coffee clad in soft t-shirts and well-worn jeans. Like any other midwestern couple . . . almost.

Those were the reasons she moved back to her hometown, but they weren't the reasons she decided to stay. No, those reasons were Annie, her husband Will, and their two beautiful little girls. They'd known and loved her long before she became Mrs. Jax Jensen. They didn't care about the money or the fame. They grounded her and gave her the stability she'd never found on the road. There was only one word to describe them: family.

Annie pulled Grace into a tight hug and whispered in her ear. "You've done so much for everyone else, now it's time to do something for yourself. You're ready, *mi amiga*." She released Grace from the hug and poked at the journal wedged under Grace's arm. "I mean it. Open it, sit down at the piano, and write something. It doesn't have to be a masterpiece. I read something recently that said creativity isn't faking it until you make it, it's making it until you make it. Make it, Grace. Make it today."

Grace laughed. "If this is the way you treat people on your side, I'd hate to see what you do to the opposition."

"Promise me, Grace."

"I promise," Grace said, stressing each syllable. "Now go. Ellie's waiting—likely stomping her foot with her hands on her hips."

Annie smirked. "Can't imagine where she picked up that behavior." She pulled open the industrial sliding steel door and turned back to Grace. "You could come along. Then have dinner with Will and me and the girls?"

"And come face-to-face with fifteen five-year-olds in tutus?

The cuteness overload would likely kill me. Plus, I just promised my best friend that I would put my butt on the piano bench and see if I remember how to compose a song. Raincheck?"

Annie nodded and yanked the journal from Grace's grasp, thrusting it into the center of her chest.

"Oof. You're relentless."

"And you love me for it."

Grace rolled her eyes and gave her friend a gentle nudge into the hallway and slid the door closed. Her gaze dropped to the book in her hand. Anxiety simmered in her stomach on its way to a full boil. She promised Annie she would try. But she had a dirty little secret.

She had been trying.

About six months ago, after a year of silence, simple melodies or six, eight, ten words of a lyrical hook started flashing and flickering in her mind again. The notes and words came at inopportune times—in the middle of the night, while out walking, or neck-deep in a bathtub full of bubbles. She groaned, remembering the night she sprinted naked and dripping through the condo searching for a scrap of paper, desperate to write it down before the idea disappeared. But like most times, by the time she found a pen, she had nothing. Sometimes she might get a stanza or two, but when she tried to build on them later, nothing came. She tried blaming grief, but the voices in her head whispered it was more than that.

Doubt and fear had unpacked, gotten comfortable and were applying for permanent residence in her brain. Doubt would push back in his recliner, take a draw off his beer and say, "What you had with Jax Jensen was likely magic in a bottle. You'll probably never be able to write without him." All while Fear ran circles around Doubt yelling, "The writing is on the wall. Your career is over. What will you do? This is the only thing you know how to do. You should quit before everyone finds out that you've lost it." It was like her own personal version of that kids' movie. And, her own personal version of hell.

She could just walk away. She didn't need the money.

But...

And it was a big 'but.'

Despite Doubt and Fear's tap-dance, something buried deep inside her urged her not to give up without a fight. Likely she just needed more time. That maybe in another six months, or a year, it would come back.

She walked over to the Steinway and opened the keyboard cover. It creaked as she pushed it back. "You mocking me too, old gal?"

She laid her right thumb on middle C and her fingers followed. D, E, F, G. She depressed the keys so slowly they hissed out just a whisper of sound. In mirror image, her left fingers fell silently—G, F, E, D, C. She stared at the ebony and ivory keys, willing her fingers to move, telling her brain to disengage and let muscle memory do its thing. But again, nothing.

She sat in the silence, staring at the keys, and nearly leapt out of her skin as the chorus to "Overcoming"—the title track on their final album—assaulted the silence. She really needed to change her ring tone.

Placing a trembling hand on her chest, she paced the living room searching for her phone. The sound led her back to the coffee table. A stack of bills vibrated. She pushed them aside and stopped short. A familiar name flashed across the screen. A name she hadn't seen since the day after Jax's funeral.

What could he want? She sucked in a couple of ragged breaths and swiped her finger across the screen.

"Grace O'Connor."

"Ford Marini," he mimicked back. "I need five minutes."

"People skills, Ford. We've talked about this."

"Pleasantries take time and I'm a very busy man."

"So you've told me—a thousand times."

He sighed and Grace frowned. Even twelve-hundred miles away it took no effort imagining the music executive. Smooth olive skin, wavy mahogany hair held in place with something thick and shiny, starched Armani dress shirt, Italian loafers, and dark eyes—no doubt flashing with undisguised irritation.

"I want you here. In my office. Monday morning."

Grace snorted. "Excuse me?"

"We signed a new group that has real potential, but they've cut their teeth on covers. Can't put a group on the map without originals. We gave their writer six months to write the songs and he has summarily fallen on his ass."

Grace's breath hitched and her pulse kicked up. "And?"

"And, you're a writer and I need a writer. And, a recent magazine article made it crystal clear you're not doing anything else."

The universe really had a sick sense of humor. The ink was barely dry on The List and no matter what Annie thought, she wasn't ready to write again. She needed more time. To find her rhythm. To figure out how to do this without Jax.

She clutched the edge of the table and clenched her teeth together reminding herself that she did, in fact, want to return to the industry . . . someday. But, how did she say no without burning an important bridge? She snapped her fingers. *Got it.*

"Declining such a flattering offer is hard, but we both know that writing is a collaborative process and I no longer have a partner."

"We're not cutting out the group's writer, we're just adding you. Think of it like exchanging Jax for a new guy."

Anger bubbled up inside her. "I don't think that's how this works," Grace said, biting back a string of off-color words. Swap out 'some guy' for Jax Jensen? Not possible.

"It is if you ever want to work in this industry again, Grace."

"Is that a threat, Ford?"

"You and Jax signed a publishing deal—a contract that remains unfulfilled."

"Jax died!"

"But you didn't. You still owe us an album. Do this and we'll call it even."

"I think we both know that's not the truth. You have no power over me."

"Untrue. I am a very influential voice in this industry, and if you want to keep working, it's in your best interest to do this. Plus, you've been away so long you should be grateful anyone's still asking."

Grace squeezed her eyes shut and dug her fingers into her temple. Time to fake the confidence she wasn't feeling.

"You're willing to ruin my reputation for one new, untested group? Seems extreme. Got yourself in a bit of a financial situation?"

Ford grunted. "You sure you want to call my bluff?"

Did she? He wasn't a man to throw around idle threats. A few words from Ford Marini and her Grammy-award winning career could be reduced to a whisper in industry hallways. *'Who was that songwriter—you know the one—she worked with Jax Jensen and then just disappeared?'*

"Grace? You still there?"

"Give me a couple of hours." A couple of hours to come up with a reason why she wasn't the right person for this job. "I'll call you back before the end of the business day. Make sure your assistant knows to put me through."

"Five o'clock, Grace. *Eastern.*"

She terminated the call and hurled the phone at the sofa. The word 'disaster' flashed in front of her eyes like a four-foot-tall neon beer sign. If she said no, Ford would blacklist her. If she said yes and couldn't write? Shit. Her choice was between certain disaster and likely disaster.

CHAPTER TWO

C lutching a small carry-on containing her laptop and the most basic essentials, Grace strode into the coffee shop that encompassed the entire first floor of the Wright Music building. Facing Ford Marini generally required a tequila therapy session, but since it wasn't even noon, another dose of caffeine would have to suffice.

After pacing her apartment for an hour and not coming up with a way out that didn't involve blowing up her career, Grace had called Ford and agreed to meet with him.

That's how she found herself, two days later, standing in the middle of Manhattan.

The toe of her boot clicked against the floor, increasing in tempo as names were called and coffee was handed out. What was her hurry? A thirty-second elevator ride would put her face-to-face with her future. She'd spent the flight trying to convince herself that one man didn't have the power to take away something she'd spent twenty years building. But every scenario she conjured ended in career annihilation. Either by his hand—or her own.

"Grace! Large white mocha with an extra shot and extra

whipped cream," the barista barked out. Reaching for the hot, sweet, beautiful brown concoction, Grace inhaled and offered a prayer of gratitude to the coffee gods.

The barista winked at her. "That's an I'm-not-having-a-good-day drink if I've ever seen one."

Grace choked out a laugh. "Is it that obvious?"

"Trying to break into the business?" he asked, pointing at the ceiling.

"More like trying not to break *up* with the business."

The barista shrugged and nodded sagely. Dropping a couple of bucks in his tip jar, she rotated on her three-inch stiletto at the same time the man to her right whirled directly into her. His iced coffee—who drank iced coffee in New York in November—sloshed over the top of his cup and sprayed the front of her white blouse from neck to waist.

Grace sucked in a breath and flicked the rivulets of liquid away.

"Sorry. Sorry. I didn't expect anyone to be right beside me."

"Yeah, you're right, it's Manhattan, city of wide-open spaces and very few people."

He met her gaze and a smirk flashed across his face. Without warning, an entire colony of butterflies took flight in Grace's stomach. Leave it to her to get spilled on by the sexiest man in Manhattan.

Hard as she tried, she couldn't stop staring. Tall and lean, his dark hair just kissed his shoulders and a five o'clock shadow danced over his chiseled jaw.

Perfect. Of course, this was the moment her dormant lizard brain roared to life. She was on a one-way trip to career hell, and all she could think about was the best fitting pair of Levi's she'd ever seen.

Her thumb reached to touch the ring on her left hand and found nothing. That's right, she was single . . . and apparently still in possession of fully functioning girl parts. The parts she was sure had shriveled away into nothingness were suddenly up and dancing, wasting no time shaking loose two years of dust and cobwebs.

He pulled a handful of napkins from the dispenser in rapid succession and thrust the giant bundle at her. She ripped the towels from his hand and followed his gaze. An ice cube melted and dripped down over her left breast, rendering the fabric transparent.

"Um, you might want to blot that before it stains." His eyes darkened as he gestured to her chest and poked a single long finger to the back of her hand holding the napkins.

Grace flicked the ice cube to the floor, blotted the front of her blouse and pulled her jacket lapels together, buttoning the center button.

"I really am sorry," he repeated, and Grace zeroed in on his voice—deep, mellifluous, excruciatingly masculine, and a telltale sign of only one thing. That voice. This building. It was no coincidence. This man was a performer.

And a reminder of the reason she was here. She had a career to save . . . or a music executive to kill. The jury was still out. A great ass and butterflies were distractions she couldn't afford. Certainly not now, and maybe, not ever.

"Is there anything else I can do?"

"You can call Zac Posen and get me a new shirt," Grace muttered under her breath.

"What?" he rumbled.

"Nothing. Never mind." She shoved the heap of wet napkins into his large hands, tossed her head back, and marched through the door.

Twenty-three. Twenty-four. The digital display taunted her. With every floor, her anxiety climbed. Maybe she should have walked away, feigned retirement, rather than prove she couldn't do this. Twenty-five. The elevator dinged and the doors swooshed open revealing a dark-paneled room filled with glass-topped tables and mahogany leather club chairs—like a high-end doctor's office minus the months-old magazines.

Seated at the single desk in the room, a woman studied her computer and pushed her tortoise shell glasses up her nose with a wizened index finger. An engraved nameplate rested on the desk—Margaret Enfield, Executive Assistant. Imagine every stereotype about women in the music business and then picture the opposite. Margaret looked more like a kindergarten teacher than the woman who played sentry for one of the industry's most powerful men. Where most assistants were under thirty, having sampled their share of Botox, Margaret's dark skin was lined from laughter and a lifetime of experience.

Eyes fixed on her screen, Margaret slipped a hand into her top drawer and removed a white, orange, and blue tube. She peered over the top of her glasses and pointed the stain remover pen at Grace. "You know you're supposed to drink coffee, not wear it, right?"

Grace laughed. Never underestimate Margaret. She missed nothing. "So that's why I'm not getting the promised caffeine rush."

"Grace," she said, rounding her desk and enveloping her in a hug. Taking a single step back, she placed her warm hands on Grace's cheeks. "Even covered in coffee, you're a sight for sore eyes." She gave Grace a thorough once-over, tsk-ed a few times, and returned her penetrating gaze to Grace's face. "I was beginning to wonder if you were ever coming back."

"I wondered that, too."

"You doing okay, baby? Such a big loss." Margaret sighed and shook her head. "I know it's been a while now. I wish I could have come for the funeral, but"—Margaret pointed in the direction of the heavy double doors behind her—"he's stingy with days off. Thinks they're for the weak-minded."

Grace smiled and nodded. "Thank you, Marty. I got the flowers you sent." Grace stepped back, desperate for a subject change. Any thoughts of Jax, here in this place, would do nothing but diminish her already shaky confidence. "Is Ford ready for me?"

"He's wrapping up a meeting, asked that you wait for him in the conference room. It'll give you time to go to the ladies and put that stain stick to use." She winked and gave Grace's shoulder a gentle nudge toward the bathroom.

Grace peered into the ladies' room mirror. All the signs of this morning's run-in erased from her blouse. If only Margaret had one of these fancy pens for everything else in her life, she'd erase several things. Like this meeting. At one time, coming to the label epitomized everything. Work. Love. Life. Now it was merely a reminder of how much had changed . . . and how much was on the line.

Turning left out of the restroom, she traveled down the hallway lined with gold and platinum records. Mid-way to the conference room she stopped and turned, almost as if she could sense where it hung. Their first plaque.

Presented to

JAX JENSEN

to commemorate the sale of 1,000,000 copies of

GIRL, LATELY

Released May 2000

"It was—it is—a good song. One of your best," a soft voice said from behind her.

Pulling her attention back to the present, Grace turned to look up into a familiar face. "*Brad?* What are you doing here?"

"I have a meeting with Ford. What are *you* doing here?"

Grace let out a shuddery breath, a single thought taking shape. "You aren't by chance managing a new group that is struggling to write their first original album?"

Brad's eyes dropped shut as his chin hit his chest. "Shit. Grace. *You're* the songwriter Ford is bringing in?"

"Surprising us both, it seems."

"I'd have called you myself if I knew you were ready to write again." Brad's eyes narrowed. "Are you ready to write again?"

Wasn't that the ten-million-dollar question? Grace shrugged. "I wasn't given much choice." Brad opened his mouth to speak, but Grace cut him off. "Tell me about this group. Ford's information was sketchy, at best." At Brad's puzzled expression, she muttered, "Don't ask."

"They're a five-man country *a cappella* band —"

Grace's eyes widened and her mouth fell open. "I'm sorry, did you just tell me that a major label signed a country *a cappella* group? That *you* signed a country—*a cappella* —group?"

"It is a little out-of-the-box."

"*A little?*" Grace's anxiety hitched up another notch. This train had just pulled out of Challenging Town and was chugging its way to Impossible Station. This was no longer about waiting for the other shoe to drop but ducking and weaving as the universe threw an entire closet of wedges, boots, platforms, and Crocs at her. Wait. No. No Crocs. Nothing could get that bad. At least she hoped so.

"They're good, G. Old school harmonies—think Oak Ridge Boys or Alabama but made for the digital world."

"So, let me translate. That means they've got the whole good looking, tight pants, cowboy boots, big hat thing going on?"

"No hats." If Grace hadn't recognized the voice, the stifling cloud of cologne would have given him away. "Join me in the conference room," Ford said as he slithered by them in the hallway.

It wasn't a question. That would require manners the infamous Ford Marini did not possess.

Following the men into the cavernous room, she dropped into one of the modern black leather conference room chairs and watched as Ford arranged a stack of papers in front of him. And, then re-arranged it. He was anxious. And if Ford was nervous, he'd do whatever it took to ensure he wasn't painted a failure, including blacklisting her.

Ford nudged the stack of papers toward her—sheet music. A very large stack of sheet music.

"Group's name is Storyhill. Incredible social media following. Very respectable ticket sales."

"But, country *a cappella*, Ford? That's a huge risk."

Ford's brows came together in a frown and he sucked air in through his teeth. "I'm going to pretend you didn't just question my judgment, Grace." He stared at her and, despite the roller coaster ride her stomach was taking, she stared directly back. He'd take advantage of anything that even hinted at weakness.

"As we discussed on the phone, you'll work with their writer, Andrew Hayes—who is also the group's bass—and get this ship righted before it runs further aground."

"If anyone can do it, it's you, G," Brad said, trying to release some of the tension in the room.

Glad someone thought so.

Ford swirled his pen through his fingers and planted it in

the corner of his mouth. Likely a holdover from the days when this room was blanketed in cigarette smoke and billowing testosterone. At least the smoke was gone.

"I booked a studio for next week. And, when they go on tour in"—Ford consulted his calendar—"thirteen days, you'll travel with them."

"Whoa." Grace lifted a hand, pushing her palm toward Ford. "Go on tour? With a group I've never met? No way, Ford. That part of my life is over. You've given me no choice but to work with them, but I'll do it from the comfort of my own home with a computer screen between us."

"I have to agree with Ford on this one."

Grace jerked her attention to Brad, a hammer starting to pound behind her eyes.

"Andrew is talented"—he pointed at the mound of paper in front of her—"but he, um, tends to be his own worst enemy. Better that you're in the same room."

"Let me get this right. You need a writer *and* someone to babysit your cowboy?"

Brad cringed. "Not a cowboy. He grew up in New Orleans and is hardly a kid, he's thirty-five."

Grace rolled her eyes.

"Think of it this way," Brad said. "It's an all-expenses-paid trip to London and Dublin."

"It's an *overseas* trip?" Grace's eyes widened and she swiveled her head between the two men. "In less than two weeks? You two are certifiable."

Ford fixed his beady brown eyes on hers. "It's not like you have anything else —"

"Ford," Brad interrupted, a hint of reproach in his voice. He tapped the stack of music. "Check it out. I think you'll see the same potential Ford and I do."

Grace didn't have a choice. It was do this or commit career

suicide. "Fine." She swallowed the lump of fear working its way up her throat and fanned out the sheet music in front of her, the room falling silent.

"Why the hell is my music spread all over the table?" Three sets of eyes turned to the man leaning against the doorframe. Tall, dark, handsome—and holding a cup of iced coffee.

~

Andrew Hayes instantly recognized the players around the table. The man who'd signed Storyhill to their first big contract. The man who agreed to be their manager only months ago. And the beautiful woman responsible for his spilled coffee.

A few hours ago, he watched her walk out of the coffee shop, mesmerized by the way her hips softly swayed back and forth, unable to shake the feeling that she was somehow familiar.

Different setting and he immediately recognized her. Grace O'Connor. The songwriting genius behind all of Jax Jensen's biggest hits. Strange. The rumor mill had all but concluded her career was over, that the death of her husband was also the death of her muse.

Yet, here she sat—with *his* music spread out in front of her. Was he honored, scared, or pissed as hell? Yes.

Andrew ran his fingers through his hair and rubbed the spot tightening at the base of his neck. He'd made a promise to the band. He promised to write the album that would take them from YouTube stars to country music superstars. Failure wasn't an option. He had to be the one to write the songs. And he had to do it alone.

"Andrew," Ford said, breaking the silence, "perfect timing. Join us." Ford pointed to the chair next to Grace. No way. She might be songwriting royalty, but he was not handing over his songs. He'd started this and he would finish it. He walked around the table and slid into the seat next to Brad.

Andrew rubbed his palms up and down his long legs, trying to still the anger bubbling up inside him. "No one answered my question."

"This is Grace O'Connor," Ford said, tipping his head to the woman with the blonde waves that had stopped his heart twice today. "I'm sure her reputation precedes her."

"I know who she is, what I don't know is why she's here . . . and why she's pawing through my music."

Brad placed his hand on the arm of Andrew's chair and cocked an eyebrow. "You're surly today."

"Not enough caffeine. Someone spilled my coffee earlier."

Grace narrowed her gaze, but her face remained blank. She reached for her handbag and stood. "I need to excuse myself to the restroom. Gentlemen, why don't you see if you can pull the burr out of the cowboy's ass before I get back."

Brad's lips twitched and he bit back a laugh. "See you in a few, G."

Andrew watched Grace walk from the room before turning his attention on Ford. "I know the songs aren't quite complete, but they have good bones. I don't see why they have to be handed off to another writer."

"I haven't even told you that's what we're doing," Ford sneered.

Andrew pushed his fingers through his hair. "It's pretty obvious, isn't it?"

"I gave you a lot of rope, Hayes, and you've tangled yourself up in it. We made a hefty investment in Storyhill, and it's my job to protect it."

Brad cleared his throat. "Ford is not replacing you, Andrew. He's simply offering you help, especially with the tour only days away. Frankly, I'm surprised at your reaction. Partnering with someone of Grace's stature is a coup."

Andrew grunted. It might be if he wanted a partner. He needed those songwriting credits. He needed to prove that chasing his passion was the right choice. That music was indeed a viable profession. Having the credits solely in his name would finally make his father eat his words. He couldn't—wouldn't—let this happen. He didn't work this hard and this long, giving up everything from money to women, to just end up proving his old man right.

He needed to come at this from a different angle, make them understand he was the person for the job—the *only* person.

Collecting the sheets of music spread across the table, he counted to three and raised his eyes to Ford.

"I understand she's talented, but from what I've heard, she's never written a country song."

"Writing is writing. And, I'd never tell her this, but," Ford paused, flicking his eyes to the doorway and waiting a beat, "Grace is one of the best in the business. You're at the point of needing a savior, my boy, and I got you one."

Andrew winced. When did they go from 'keep working on it' to 'you need a savior?' Ford's words echoed his father's. *It's never going to work, son. If you're crazy enough to pursue this nonsense, don't call me when it all falls in around you and need someone to pull you out. In fact, don't call me at all until you've come to your senses and picked a real career.*

They were both wrong.

"Unless I've missed something in the trades, Mrs. Jax Jensen hasn't produced anything in the last two or three years, putting her squarely in the 'has been' camp."

"Andrew," Brad said, his voice low, "I understand you're

frustrated, but her husband died—after a difficult battle with cancer."

Andrew squeezed the arms of his chair, pushing his spine tight against the back of it. Was he being an unfair asshole? Yes. But he didn't care. There was too much on the line. "I'm not trusting her, or anyone, with my songs."

"Your songs?" a female voice growled. "You mean those poems that you've attached a few quarter and eighth notes to?"

Andrew's spine stiffened. He didn't need to turn around to know Grace stood in the doorway.

CHAPTER THREE

G race stood stock-still, hands clenched into fists. She stared at the back of Andrew's head. She didn't want to be here anymore than he wanted her help, but damn if she was going to let some no-name cowboy belittle her reputation and muddy Jax's memory.

Ford twirled in his chair, amusement dancing in his eyes. He motioned for her to return to the table. Barring a giant black hole opening up and swallowing her, she had no choice but to rejoin the meeting. Grace stalked to her chair and leveled an icy glare at Andrew.

Ford glanced at his wrist and straightened his Rolex. "I've got another meeting in ten minutes, so here's how it's going to go. Monday morning the two of you will meet at the studio I've reserved." He nudged the stack of music back in front of Grace. "Until then, Grace will go through the music and determine the needs of each song."

Grace snorted. "That's a week away!" Seven days to sift through pages and pages of half-completed songs. Seven days to completely rearrange her life for the next few weeks. And, seven days to figure out how to work with this stubborn, sexy, infuriating man.

"We don't have the luxury of time," Ford said. "You'll have the week leading up to Storyhill's weekend concerts here in New York to work on the songs, and then the balance of the tour to finish up."

Andrew's head popped up. "She's coming on tour?"

The muscles of Ford's jaw tensed, and he pointed to each of them. "You two need to get on the same page. And fast. Don't make me remind you how much is on the line—for both of you." He snapped shut his portfolio and stabbed his finger at them a final time, rose from his chair, nodded at Brad, and left the room.

Brad expelled a long breath and slumped in his chair. "That was painful, but it could have been worse."

Worse? How? In less than three days she'd found herself on an unplanned trip to New York City and face-to-face with an arrogant music executive who expected her to upend her life to help a pompous, presumptuous, pretty-boy musician who not-so-subtlety proclaimed she was unqualified and used-up—all in the name of saving her career. Never mind that he might be right.

It could have been worse. Not likely.

Brad slid his glasses off and rubbed the spot between his eyes. "Andrew, I know you have a plane to catch. I'll ask Margaret to book you a flight back here on Monday morning and have her email you the details." Andrew nodded and got to his feet, stretching out his long legs and flipping his hair away from his face.

His gaze met Grace's and damn if the butterflies didn't do their dance all over again. Who knew it was possible to be completely infuriated and turned on at the same time? She was pretty certain she'd never experienced this particular cocktail—

two fingers of hostility mixed with a splash of unwelcome hormones.

He pointed to the stack of papers in front of her. "Try to not spill any coffee on those."

Huh. It only took ten words to kill every last butterfly.

After a few subdued words with Andrew at the door, Brad turned to her. "Are you flying back tonight, or can I buy you a drink?"

Grace retrieved a rubber band from her bag, stretched it over the pages of music, and glanced up at Brad. She was struck by the soft expression on his face.

Could he sense the battle that was waging inside her? Should she tell him? She wanted to. She wanted to let it all out —to someone. Maybe if she spoke it out loud, it would quell the tsunami barreling through her. Could she confide that she was lost—that if she wasn't Jax Jensen's writer and wife, she really didn't know who she was? Could she tell him that all the constant fear and worry had decimated her confidence and she was completely blocked, not having written anything of substance in months . . . years, actually. No. Brad was a dear friend, Jax's college roommate until Jax dropped out and one of his best friends, but he was also Storyhill's manager and he needed her to help his clients.

All of a sudden, she was awash in a flash flood of anger and resentment, being pulled under by a lifetime of 'what ifs.' Jax had been so insistent she only work with him. She was offered opportunities to write with other artists. If she had accepted even one offer, where would she be now?

"What if I can't do it?" she asked, the words sneaking out before she could stop them.

"Do what?"

"This." She snapped the rubber band around the sheaf of

paper and tapped the stack. "What if I can't write without Jax? What if I don't have what it takes to do this on my own?"

"Nonsense. You've written songs without Jax—in that magic notebook of yours."

"Nothing that ever made the cut."

She tried to fire up the resentment again but couldn't do it. The songs not recorded by Jax Jensen weren't his style. They were deeper, more sentimental, the voice of her soul . . . and, frankly, less commercial.

Brad lowered himself into the chair next to her and placed his hand over hers. "I get that this situation is far from ideal, but you can do this, G. I never spoke to Jax where he didn't marvel at your talent."

"Sure. That's why he never let me write with anyone else— because he thought I was so good."

Brad squeezed her fingers. "That's exactly why. He understood the depth of your talent and yes, maybe selfishly, wanted all of you. But, look at what you accomplished. The two of you left an indelible mark on the music industry, creating a legacy that's going to be difficult to repeat."

Grace bit her bottom lip. "That's what I'm worried about, that'll I'll never be able to do it again."

Brad rose from his chair, offering a hand to her. "I said difficult, not impossible. And since you've already done it, you already have the road map. You're going to be fine, Grace. Ford threw this at you with hardly any notice. Anyone in the same situation would have some jitters. That's all this is. Okay?"

Grace sighed and nodded. She was pretty certain more than nerves were to blame, but it didn't matter, did it? There was only one way to determine her future and it didn't involve sitting in this conference room and wallowing in doubt. What was it that Yoda said? *Do or do not, there is no try.* She swept the giant stack of sheet music into her bag and sucked in a deep breath. "Okay."

"Good. Now, airport or drink?"

"Drink. Definitely a drink."

Andrew slipped his messenger bag over his head and dropped it with a thud onto the gray vinyl chair in the terminal waiting area and sat. The screen behind the counter told him boarding would commence in thirty minutes.

He massaged the back of his neck and circled his head, willing the tension away. The woman across the aisle kept staring at him, like she was trying to place him, so he fished his phone out of his bag and opened his email hoping she wouldn't figure it out and come over. Pasting on a fake smile right now was something he couldn't do. Nashville to New York and back again in twelve hours was too much. Scratch that. Nashville to Ford Marini and back again was the problem.

Well, Ford Marini *and* Grace O'Connor.

He swiped up, closing his email and tapped on his web browser. One beat, two beats, the curser flashed in the search bar. He slowly typed in 'Grace O'Connor' and pushed the blue 'go' button.

Stats from her Wikipedia page filled the right side of the screen. Age, spouse, education, job title—all the usual stuff. He clicked on the images tab. Pages and pages of photos popped up. Photos in the studio. Photos on the red carpet. Photos of her clutching a Grammy. Happy. Smiling. Beautiful. And always with Jax Jensen. He couldn't find a single picture of her alone.

What was Ford thinking? After two decades of writing for a single artist, no matter how successful they'd been, he was supposed to be thrilled she was brought in to 'save' him? *Hell, no*. He didn't need her, and he certainly didn't need saving.

It didn't matter though, did it? The decision had been made for him. He might not have a choice on whether or not he wrote with her, but it didn't mean he had to like it.

Andrew jolted as the gate agent announced pre-boarding. He pulled his bag's strap back across his chest as another image flashed before his eyes. Yes, Grace was a problem, but she was a problem for another day. In less than three hours, he'd be home and face-to-face with another difficult situation—how to tell his bandmates, the men that had become his brothers, that he'd done the one thing he swore he'd never let happen—he'd failed them.

The cab pulled away from the curb and Andrew took a couple of steps up the front walk and hesitated. Warm light flooded out of the century-old windows and cast shadows on the large wrap-around porch. He caught a glimpse of his best friend and band-mate, Joe, moving through the living room toward the kitchen.

Sheltered in the shadows, he could still cancel. Pretend he was never here. Sleep a few hours before having to admit to his best friend that he'd failed the band.

He fingered the phone resting in his hip pocket. One text and he could hide from the truth for twelve, or fifteen, hours. No. This was Joe. He had invited Andrew to dinner and asked for a debrief. It was time to own up to his inadequacy.

While contemplating how to break the news, Joe's wife, Julia, pushed open the front door carrying a tray full of glasses, napkins, and cutlery. She whistled a Storyhill song as she placed the items on the café table situated between four outdoor rockers.

"Hey," Andrew said, stepping out of the darkness. Julia

jumped and twisted toward him, nearly dropping the glass in her hand.

"You scared me! What are you doing lurking out there?"

Andrew smirked. "I'm sorry, isn't this the dinner Joe demanded I attend?"

"Demanded?" Julia cocked a single eyebrow. "You don't have to stay. Joe would be more than happy to eat your serving of fried chicken."

Andrew groaned. Jules made the best fried chicken in the tri-state area. He ascended the three wooden steps onto the porch and pulled her into a hug. "Run away with me," he whispered in her ear, "but first go inside and get the chicken recipe."

"Hey!" Joe said, coming out on the porch. "Get your own girl, Andy." Andrew dropped his arms and put his hands out in front of him, palms out, taking two dramatic steps back.

Julia rolled her eyes and motioned for Andrew to sit in one of the chairs. "It's such a nice night, I thought we'd eat outside." She pulled the foil wrapper from a bottle of Prosecco in one fluid motion and expertly popped the cork. After pouring two glasses she turned to Andrew, tipping the bottle his way.

"Bubbles aren't usually my thing, but after the day I've had, make mine a double."

"Uh oh." Joe dropped into the chair opposite Andrew. "Not good news from the label, then?"

Andrew shrugged and sunk deeper into his chair, trying to ignore the buzzing building between his ears. "Depends on how you look at it, I guess."

"Is it bad? Oh my god, did they drop us? Why didn't they call all of us into this meeting?"

Andrew studied his best friend. They'd met in first grade when Andrew stepped in between Joe and the school bully, cementing a nearly three-decade-long friendship. He'd been the one to convince Joe to join this group—to walk away from a more stable career. He couldn't be the one to screw it up for all of them. His father's words echoed in his head. *It's bad enough you're doing this, you had to go and drag Joe into it, too? He has a stable job. One* his *parents can be proud of.*

Letting out a slow, mirthless laugh, Andrew collected his hair in his hands and held it in a temporary ponytail, shifting his gaze skyward. "Because the issue is not the band. The issue is me."

"So, they didn't drop us?"

"No. Not yet, anyway." Andrew sucked in a breath, willing himself to rip the Band-Aid off as fast as possible. "They brought in another writer."

"What?" Joe's forehead crinkled in confusion, the drumstick he'd grabbed stopping mid-air, halfway to his mouth. "I thought you said you had the songs handled."

"I thought I did. Ford disagrees. I let everybody down. I put our contract in jeopardy. I failed you guys."

"C'mon dude, you haven't failed us," Joe said around a piece of chicken, pointing near-naked bones at Andrew. Joe swallowed and wiped the corners of his mouth. "Who'd Ford bring in?"

Andrew tilted his head back and emptied his wine glass in one shot. "Grace O'Connor."

Joe let out a long, deep whistle. "Shit, Andy, they're not fooling around. They wouldn't bring in someone like her if they didn't think we had a real shot."

"Or didn't agree that I'm a total fuck-up."

Joe rolled his eyes and picked up another piece of chicken. "I am a little confused, though. My understanding was that she quit the biz when her husband passed."

"Apparently not." Andrew scrubbed his hand over his face. "Though I did get the distinct impression she didn't want to be in the room any more than I wanted her there."

"Why does that name sound familiar?" Julia put two pieces of chicken on a plate and handed them to Andrew.

"She wrote for Jax Jensen. And also happened to be his wife."

Julia snapped her fingers and nodded. "Ahh, yes, famously gracing red carpets worldwide. She's beautiful, Andrew."

Stunning was the word he would choose. The vision of her standing in front of him, eyes flashing as his coffee soaked through her shirt, was seared into his memory.

Joe snorted. "Doubt that Andy would even notice if she was pretty or not."

Andrew's eyebrows came together in the center. "What is that supposed to mean?"

"Um, I think it's pretty obvious."

Andrew placed his glass on the table and leaned forward, resting his forearms on his thighs. "Enlighten me."

"Dude, when is the last time you had a date?"

Andrew opened his mouth and shut it. When was the last time? He couldn't remember. He shrugged and shook his head. "Doesn't matter. I'll have time to date once Storyhill is bankable. Music first, remember?"

Julia looked at him with soft eyes. "It doesn't have to be one or the other, Andrew."

Andrew rubbed his hand along his stubbled jaw and dropped his gaze to the patio floor. "It does for me."

"Doesn't really matter, she's a little too old for our boy, anyway," Joe said.

Julia refilled their glasses. "How old is she?"

Andrew studied the bubbles dancing up the side of his glass. "Forty-four." Two sets of eyes flashed to his face. "What?" He shrugged. "I Googled her on the flight home."

"So, nine years older than Andrew." Julia narrowed her eyes and turned toward her husband, folding her arms across her chest. "You're telling me that Adam Levine *and* Ryan Reynolds *and* Jay-Z can marry women a decade or more younger than them, but it's not okay the other way around? That Andrew can't date Grace because she's nine years older? No more chicken for you." She wrenched his third piece of chicken from his hand and sunk her teeth into it.

"Hey!"

Andrew cleared his throat. "Much as I'm all for gender equality, I think we've gotten ahead of ourselves. I'm not going to date this woman. I don't even want to work with her."

"So don't," Joe said, trying to sneak another piece of meat off the serving tray and getting his fingers slapped.

"Not an option. I wasn't presented with an offer. I was given an ultimatum."

"I don't get it," Julia said. "Why is it a bad thing to have the help of a Grammy-award winning songwriter?"

Andrew slumped in his chair, resting his wine glass on his chest. "Because I want to do it myself. Because I *have* to do it myself."

"Men." Julia picked up the remaining food and headed inside.

"Hey, I wanted more of that!" Joe called.

"Too bad," she called back from deep inside the dark house.

Joe sighed, eyeing the door before turning back to Andrew. "I know you want to do this on your own, but maybe Jules is right. You work on the songs, exchange a few emails, maybe have a couple of Skype calls. Doesn't seem so bad."

Andrew snorted. "Maybe not, if that was the case. Ford booked us a studio in Manhattan next week . . . and after the New York concerts she's coming on tour with us."

"On tour? With us?"

"Yep." Andrew drained the remaining drops from his glass.

. . .

After two slices of Julia's mind-blowing white chocolate lemon blueberry cake, Andrew wished his friends good night and walked the ten blocks to his apartment.

The residential neighborhood had gone to bed for the night, the only sound a buzzing streetlight, sputtering on and off. Andrew shoved his hands into his pockets. His mind was the exact opposite of this sleepy, placid scene. Dread stirred inside him as images of his father and Ford and Grace O'Connor bounced frenetically through his mind like an errant pinball ricocheting off bumpers and flippers.

Andrew missed a step as his phone vibrated in his pocket. A three-word text message flashed across the screen.

Grace O'Connor??? Shit.

Three words that perfectly framed his state of mind.

The coffee Julia insisted he have with his cake probably wasn't even cold before Joe started texting the other guys. Andrew bristled. It wasn't Joe's news to deliver.

Blake, Storyhill's tenor, had fired off the three-word message. His expletive would be from disbelief, not anger, because, despite his flaming red hair, he didn't have an ounce of the temper normally associated with it. His shirts might always be starched, but his attitude wasn't—the dude personified the word 'chill.'

He scrolled through his contacts and added all four men to a group text. He wasn't going to do this more than once. He raked his hand through his hair. What to say? Should he be apologetic? *Sorry, I couldn't get the job done.* Or funny? *Hey guys, I've decided to bring a date along on tour.*

Before he could decide, the phone buzzed again. This time it was Matt, the group's high tenor.

So, Grace O'Connor? Is she as hot in person as she looks in pics?

Mattie. The guy who'd spent the better part of his twenty-nine years trying to substantiate the platinum effect—that blonds do in fact have more fun. His concerns always ran deep. Not.

It only took seconds for the next text to arrive. Process of elimination told him it was Nick, their baritone and resident micromanager. No one would guess he was the worrier of the group. The six-four, two-hundred-and-thirty-pound, flannel-wearing, beard-sporting baritone looked like he moved through life all calm and casual, but nothing was further from the truth. What was it their fans called him? Oh yeah, lumbersexual. More like lumberworrisome. There was no way his text was only three words long.

Andrew sucked in a breath and tapped the screen to open it.

Dude. You okay? Do you need me to bring anything to New York since you're heading up early? Do we need to call Brad about booking an extra room for Grace? Do you think it'll actually work to write while on tour? Do you think Ford is regretting his decision to sign us?

Andrew laughed. Only five questions. About half what he expected.

He poked at the dialog box to get the cursor blinking and, deciding brief and upbeat was the way to go, thumbed in a response. This was his problem and he would solve it without bringing everyone else down.

Seems you got the basics from Joe (big mouth). I'm headed back to NYC Monday to start working with GOC. Brad is handling all of her travel stuff. Sorry if her coming on tour is a pain in anybody's ass. See y'all at next Friday's concert, ready to knock out those Xmas tunes.

He sat down on the bench just outside his apartment and reread the text. Not one hundred percent upbeat, but it covered the important stuff. He hit Send.

He waited, staring at his phone. Minutes passed, and when

he got no responses, he pulled his keys out of his pocket and walked toward the front door of his building. His phone vibrated as he slid the key into the lock.

You didn't say if she's hot or not.

He dropped his phone into his pocket, but quickly pulled it back out and thumbed, *Didn't notice.* Making him the world's biggest liar.

CHAPTER FOUR

G race traced a swirl in the baggage claim carpet with the toe of her decades-old Adidas and flinched when the horn sounded, and the baggage carousel began to rotate. A never-ending loop, empty and spinning. Just like her thoughts. No matter how many pep talks she gave herself, she kept reeling between craving this career and drowning in doubt—stuck oscillating between ambition and fear. There was a difference between a 'has been' and a 'once was,' right?

The first bags bounced off the delivery belt onto the silver oval and Grace said a silent prayer that her bags wouldn't be the last ones off. All she wanted was to get to the hotel, throw off her oversized sweats and Minnesota Vikings jersey, and go to bed.

"I'm looking for a world-class songwriter. Blonde hair. Beautiful. Serious addiction to designer shoes and handbags. Do you have any idea where I might find her?"

"Haven't seen anyone fitting that description," Grace muttered, pulling down the brim of Jax's well-worn Yankees hat.

Brad chuckled. "In the future, if you want the disguise to work, think about losing the Louis Vuitton Keepall."

"You know this bag is called a 'Keepall'?" Grace shimmied her shoulder to readjust the bag and turned, cocking an eyebrow at her friend. "And how did you know my arrival time?"

"One," Brad said, raising a single finger, "I pay attention when my wife talks. And, two," he continued, raising a second finger, "Annie."

Of course. Grace and Annie had squeezed in their standing Saturday morning coffee date between Grace's flights. After meeting with Ford, Grace needed the counsel and comfort of her best friend, her ever-present voice of reason. But instead of the commiseration Grace expected, Annie served up a heaping platter of tough love, reiterating that while Ford's tactics were appalling, it was time for Grace to quit doubting herself and get back in the game.

"I'm assuming that is your bag," Brad said, pointing at a Louis Vuitton roller bag.

"That's one of them."

Brad raised his eyebrows.

"Don't judge me, I'm here for a week and then off to an all-expenses-paid trip to London and Dublin."

Brad laughed. "You never miss a chance to throw my words back at me, do you?"

Grace smirked, feeling a little joy bubble up for the first time in days. Even with the tough love and teasing, she loved her friends. And, they loved her. That was one thing she never doubted. "You'd be disappointed if I didn't."

Brad nodded and stepped up to the carousel to pull off her bag, just as the second one bumped down the chute. "Car's waiting." He snapped up the handles and swiveled the bags toward the nearest exit.

"Snazzy ride." Grace handed her carry-on to the limo driver and climbed into the car, collapsing into the soft leather upholstery with a groan.

"I love spending Ford's money." Brad slid in beside her and rattled off the address of Grace's hotel to the driver.

Grace shifted in the seat, turning to face Brad. "Undisguised threats and a free-flowing expense account? Neither fit Ford's M.O. There's clearly some major shit going down with this group."

Brad snorted. "Fancy language there, G."

"What can I say, I'm good with words." Grace tapped her chin in mock thought. "Maybe that should be the title of Storyhill's first single"—Grace spread her hands in a high arch —"Major Shit Going Down."

"Um . . ."

"What? You don't think that will play in the country world? According to a certain bass, the one masquerading as a songwriter, I'm not a good judge and have no idea what I'm doing outside the pop landscape."

Brad's face shifted from amused to concerned in a flash. "Do you really think he doesn't have any songwriting chops?"

Grace sighed and dropped her head to her chest. "No. Much as it hurts to admit it, he's actually pretty good."

"But something is missing?"

Grace nodded. "There's just too much—too many songs and too much story. The songs need to be stripped down and . . ."

"And, what?"

Grace searched for the right words. "It's too much telling. He writes about love, family, and friendship and the words are there, but the feeling is missing. They all seem a little . . . hollow. Any idea why that might be?"

Brad shook his head. "I'm still getting to know them, but the good news is no one can reach inside a chest and squeeze a heart like Grace O'Connor—no one puts the love into a love song like you do, G."

Another compliment she wasn't sure she deserved.

"Now, as far as Ford goes, I think it's a dangerous mix of spending too much money and an unchecked ego."

"I've never known him to gamble. It's totally off brand for him."

"Agreed. I think that's why—" Brad's phone rang, and he pulled it out of his pocket. "You mind? I should take this."

"Of course, go ahead," Grace answered, waving her hand toward his phone. She settled back into the seat and watched the shorter buildings near the airport be overtaken by the skyscrapers of Manhattan. The city lights clung to the buildings like a dusty beige halo. The four lanes of traffic crisscrossed like an overactive ant farm as they passed through the metal lattice of the George Washington Bridge.

Brad's voice faded to static, replaced by a series of shadowy pictures, flashing by her eyes in rapid succession, until one clicked into place in vibrant Technicolor. Grace's chest constricted. She grabbed the armrest and tried to suck in a full breath. They'd been in a nearly identical limo . . .

"Ready to take a bite out of the Big Apple?" Jax asked as they reclined in the back seat of the limo.

It was well past sunset when the driver dropped them at their Midtown hotel. The Empire State Building glittered against the night sky and the lights of Times Square bounced off all the glass and metal lining the busy city streets.

Jax gazed skyward. "I love New York, but I miss the . . ."

"Stars," she said.

"How did you know?" Jax had asked, turning toward her and putting his arm around her shoulders.

"You might have mentioned it a time or two in the past," she said, amusement filling her voice.

"Pretty soon I'll be one of those stars. Promise me you'll look

into the night sky and remember me," he said, allowing himself a rare moment of melancholy. Her voice caught in her throat and she could only nod.

"Grace?" Brad called her name from somewhere far away. "You okay?"

She swallowed and rubbed her clammy palms down the legs of her pants. "Sorry. Memories." She shook the vision from her head. "I've done the therapy, attended the support groups, but damn if the grief doesn't sneak up when you least expect it and sucker punch you."

"I'm happy to stay with you for a while if you don't want to be alone," Brad said as the driver pulled under the hotel's portico.

She squeezed her friend's hand. "Thank you, but I'm good. They're hard, but I hope the memories never leave me." She only wished that they'd give her a little warning before sucking all the air from her lungs.

"Call me if you need me. Tomorrow, I'm in meetings most of the day, but I'll stop by the studio on Tuesday—you know, to watch a genius at work."

Grace snorted. He really needed to stop with the compliments. She knew he thought he was being supportive, but every flattering remark felt like another brick on her chest. Pretty soon, she wouldn't be able to breathe at all. There was so much on the line—not just her career, but Brad's investment in the group, the label's outlay, and Storyhill's dreams. Damn. She pushed a hand against her heart, trying to slow its throbbing beat and climbed out of the limo. The driver was already loading her bags onto the valet's brass cart.

"Text Annie and let her know you got here safe," Brad hollered from inside the car.

"And to let her know you did what she asked?"

Brad laughed, waggled his fingers at her and pulled the car door shut.

The limo signaled and slithered into the Manhattan traffic. The taillights grew smaller and smaller until they were no longer discernible from the rest of the other taxis and cars. Streets full of traffic. Sidewalks teeming with locals and tourists. She was surrounded by millions of people and yet felt utterly alone.

The alarm blared. Grace rolled toward it and slapped in its general direction. Opening her eyes to locate her phone seemed too much work. She had only slept in fits and bursts —again.

Throwing off the duvet, she rolled out of bed, padded over to the single-serve coffee maker, and squinted at the fuzzy labels on the assortment of pods. Where were her glasses? The last thing she needed was to accidentally select a decaf. Decaf was fine—for any day that didn't end in 'y.'

The coffeemaker burped its last splutter and Grace filled the hotel-issue white ceramic mug with a creamer single that she was pretty sure read 'caramel macchiato' and inhaled a large hot gulp. "Ready or not, today is the day you resurrect your career," she said to no one, her voice reverberating through the empty space. "Can't be late to the rest of your life," she mumbled on the way to the shower.

After trudging seven city blocks and three flights of stairs, Grace stood in front of an imposing oak door. She willed her hand to grab the cast iron doorknob, but it hung limply at her side. "It's only a door. You open and close them every day," she whispered, "just lift your arm and pull it open."

She expelled an unsteady breath that was high on nerves

and low on confidence, forced her shoulders back, grabbed the handle and pulled . . . and nearly fell on her ass.

"It's a push," a muffled voice called out from the other side of the door.

She couldn't help it. Laughter ripped through her. This whole situation was ridiculous. *She* was ridiculous.

She grabbed the handle and *pushed*.

"We really should put a sign on the . . . Grace O'Connor!" a voice squeaked from behind the reception desk. "Wow. I've followed your career forever."

Surprise colored Grace's cheeks. Songwriting was still somewhat the ugly stepsister of the business, far less visible than the artists who performed the words and music the writers created. Being recognized as Jax Jensen's wife was commonplace, but she was rarely acknowledged for her own career.

"But, you're not on my calendar," the receptionist said, furrowing her brow while rapidly clicking on her mouse.

"It's under Ford Marini, or maybe Storyhill?"

"Oh. Lucky you."

"I'm sorry?"

"You're working with Mr. Hayes." She sighed. "Fill up my bowl and throw me a spoon—that man is yummy."

She wasn't wrong. He was 'yummy'—until he opened his mouth. His bad attitude canceled out the sex appeal. At least that's what her brain told her. The butterflies in her stomach hadn't gotten the message. They fluttered their wings even now as she thought about how those emerald eyes had held hers as he apologized for the coffee incident.

She shook her head. Nope. No way. She'd been there, done that, got the t-shirt. She'd loved Jax with all her heart, but she didn't need to go there again. One musician per lifetime. She was sure that was a rule.

Focus on his bad attitude, Grace. The way he fills out of a pair of jeans is irrelevant. This is a job, not an episode of The Bachelor.

"I'm sorry, Ms. O'Connor. What did you say about musicians?"

Crap. Had she said that out loud?

Grace cleared her throat, in need of a quick recovery. "I said that you have to watch out for the yummy ones—especially when they're musicians."

The young woman narrowed her eyes and tilted her head to the side. "Huh. All the magazines said you had a love for the ages . . . with a musician."

"I did. But they're not all like that."

"Yeah, I guess I get that. My last boyfriend, Jeremy, was a total nightmare and he fancied himself a musician. Though I don't think getting together with your friends in your mom's basement on Saturday mornings makes you Keith Richards or Bruno Mars."

Grace laughed. "See? You need to watch out. Especially working here. Now, is Andrew, I mean, Mr. Hayes, here by himself?"

The receptionist shuddered and pulled a face. "Mr. Marini is here, too."

Grace found herself laughing for the second time in a matter of minutes. She nodded knowingly and winked at the receptionist. "Point me toward them."

Andrew surveyed the studio. Standard issue. Mixing board, speakers, a few microphone stands—he couldn't imagine they'd need much more than a laptop and the keyboard this week. He walked to the window that separated the control room from the recording booth. On the other side of the glass, a drum kit was perched atop a faded area rug, along with a baby grand piano.

He should be on that side of the glass recording Storyhill's future hits, not on this side still hammering out the music and lyrics.

He dropped into a chair that looked like it had been left for dead on the side of the road. It sunk so low under his weight that his knees nearly reached his chin. A situation he needed to remedy immediately. He was not going to be sitting on the floor like some toddler when the mighty Grace O'Connor strolled in. He tried to push himself up and felt the arms slide away from him. He only had two choices: stay put or roll out of this sorry excuse for a chair.

He slid out of the chair onto his butt and flipped over to all fours.

"You praying or groveling, Cowboy?"

Andrew froze. He'd only heard that voice a few times, but that deep, sexy rasp could only belong to one woman.

"Grace, nice of you to finally join us," Ford said from his position next to the mixing board. "Andrew and I . . . Andrew, what the hell are you doing on the floor?"

"Cushion . . . springs . . . arms," Andrew managed to croak out, pointing at the offending chair.

"Get up, Hayes."

Andrew raised himself to his full six feet two inches, shoved his hands into his pockets and leaned a shoulder against one of the many acoustic panels lining the walls. Grace walked by him, flashed a smirk, and reached down to flick a few carpet fibers off his knee. She dropped her bag into the non-offending chair on the opposite side of the room, pulled out a stack of papers, and dropped them on the coffee table.

Last week she'd been all buttoned-up in a jacket and pencil skirt. Not today. Today she was in jeans artfully distressed and torn in all the right places, black boots with the same red soles his sister favored, and a fringed gray cardigan covering a concert t-shirt. Her hair was pulled back in a messy braid and large silver rope earrings dangled from her ears. Half sophisticated woman, half rocker chick, and all drop-dead gorgeous.

He scowled. *See Joe, I notice women. No matter how big a pain in the ass they are.*

"Andrew," Ford said, snapping his fingers in front of Andrew's face. "Here's the deal. I need all twelve songs written and arranged by March first so that Storyhill can cut the album immediately after your West Coast tour dates."

Andrew pushed off the wall and folded his arms across his chest. "Are we recording in Nashville?"

"Absolutely not." Both men turned to Grace. "I only work with one arranger and sound engineer. You want me, you get him. Non-negotiable." Grace stared directly at Ford without blinking.

Ford returned her stare. "Chris at Unstrung Studios?"

Grace nodded. "I got verbal confirmation he's willing to take on an *a cappella* group, and is available to work with me on arrangements after we return from the U.K."

"Us," Andrew corrected.

"Excuse me?"

"He'll work with *us*." Andrew took a step closer to Grace. "No way I'm not having input on the final arrangements."

"That's fine, Andrew," Ford said, "as long as you realize that shortens the timeline."

"I don't care how good you think she is," Andrew said, motioning toward Grace, "this is my music and I'm seeing this album through until the end."

"Okay." Ford nodded. "Looks like you're going home with Grace after the tour."

"Home?" Andrew's eyes widened. "Where is home? Please tell me it's somewhere warm."

"Minneapolis," Grace and Ford said in unison.

"You own a parka, Cowboy?" Grace's usual smirk grew into a full-blown smile, and he felt like he'd been punched in the gut. He squeezed his eyes shut. He had one job here, and it wasn't to notice her smile.

Ford shot a warning glare at Grace, but she didn't even bother to look up at him. She stuffed a hand into that huge bag of hers and waved Ford off with the other.

"I've made myself clear?" the music executive asked.

She grumbled something under her breath and pulled out a laptop and another small hard-shell case. "For someone so keen on us working, you sure are spending a lot of time talking at us."

Andrew snorted, biting back a laugh. Damn, he didn't want to like this woman, but the backbone on her was impressive.

Ford stomped out and she opened the smaller case, removing a pair of blue glasses and sliding them on. "Before we go through my notes," she motioned at the stack of paper on the coffee table, covered in red pencil, "tell me about your process. Do you start with lyrics or do you hear the melody first? Where do you draw inspiration?"

She raised the lid on her laptop, punched the power button and tucked a stray curl back into her braid.

He watched every fluid, confident movement. She clearly was the type of woman who kicked ass and took names later— much later. If he didn't take control of this situation now, he probably wouldn't get a second chance. But how to do it? Time to go with his strengths. He might not remember his last date, but he hadn't forgotten how to flirt.

"Lyrics generally come first, though I start hearing a melody pretty early in the process. As far as inspiration, it can come from anywhere—a book I'm reading, a photograph, overhearing a conversation at a restaurant," he leaned in, flashed a smile, and winked at her, "or sitting across from a beautiful woman."

She cocked an eyebrow and gave a little snort. "I've been in this industry for over twenty years and I've seen and heard it all. Save your phony charm for the stage."

His smile faded. Fine, if she wanted to play hardball, he could do that too. "Your attitude stinks. Why are you even here? Don't you have enough mailbox money for the rest of your life?"

"My attitude stinks? *Mine?*" She pushed a finger into her chest. She slid her glasses off her face and pinched the bridge of her nose between her thumb and forefinger. "You can't possibly think I'm here for the residual checks."

"Why else?"

"Why are you so angry?"

"I'm not angry." He sucked in a breath and lowered his voice. "There's just no reason for you to be here. I don't need you."

"Really? That's why Ford forced me to upend my life to help you? Because you're doing so well on your own?"

His temper flared. "Your career? You mean the one that Jax Jensen built for you?"

Grace reared back and slapped her laptop shut. "Listen, you giant braying beast—"

"Are you calling me an ass?"

"If the horseshoe fits." She stood up, grabbed her coat and rammed her arms into it. "You *are* angry. I don't know why, and I don't care. But we need to find a way to make this work—not because either of us wants to—but because we don't have a choice. You want the label and the label wants me." She turned toward the door, reaching for the handle.

"Where are you going?"

"I'm going to get coffee."

"When are you coming back?"

"When I no longer want to push you out the window." She sighed, her shoulders dropping, and walked out, leaving a handprint in the middle of the glass door.

Andrew blew out a breath and let his head drop to the back of the sofa. She was right. He was an ass . . . and angry . . . and tired. So fucking tired. He'd given up any kind of personal life, devoting his entire life to making this band a success. He'd pissed off his father and let his bandmates down. He was so exhausted from trying to prove himself to everything and everyone.

He slipped farther into the sofa, laying his arm across his eyes. Much as he wanted someone to blame, Grace wasn't the enemy. She just was a representation of his failures—a mind-numbingly beautiful reminder of everything he couldn't get done.

He stood up and paced the room. He needed to pull himself together. He grabbed the stack of sheet music and slipped through the door into the recording booth. He lowered himself onto the bench in front of the baby grand and ran his fingers over the black and white keys, playing the scales he'd learned in his very first piano lessons.

Andrew stared at the red marks littered across the song on the top of the stack, a sigh reverberating in his ears. He hummed a few bars of the changes, moving his fingers over the keys in time with his voice.

He leaned forward, dropping his head into his hands, his elbows forcing discordant sounds from the keyboard. These changes, just suggestions at this point, made the songs better. He grimaced. He was going to have to grovel—one of his least favorite activities.

"Where's Grace?" A hand clamped down on his shoulder and he jumped. Damn soundproof studios. He whipped around and found Ford attached to the hand resting on his shoulder.

"I thought you left." Fumbling with the music, he sent up a silent prayer that Ford had not overheard their fight or worse, witnessed Grace storming out. No need to turn his already short leash into a choker.

Ford plunked his finger on the nearly silent B flat ebony key at the end of the keyboard. "I was almost to the lobby when I got confirmation on a favor I called in. I got you a headline gig at the Ryman Auditorium for your album release party. July of next year—eight months from now. I don't need to tell you what this means. And I certainly don't need to tell you how it's going to look if you don't get the album finished on time."

"The Ryman?" Andrew couldn't mask his astonishment. He'd been dreaming of stages like that for as long as he could remember. If they could fill the Ryman, the Opry was the next logical step. And if they could get to the Opry, everyone would have to admit they'd made it. *Everyone.*

Ford smacked his hand on top of the piano. "The place where bluegrass was born and where Johnny met June. It's country gold, my friend. Now, find Grace and get your asses in gear. Don't mess this up, Hayes."

Restless, Andrew glanced at his phone. He flipped over a couple more pieces of the sheet music, but his mind kept bouncing between the image of standing on stage at the Ryman and wondering how long Grace had been gone. It felt like hours.

"Ready to write some music?" Grace's voice shot through the intercom and echoed through the silent recording studio. She stood on the other side of the glass window holding two coffees. He picked up the music and joined her in the adjacent room.

She took a long drag from an insulated cup and pointed at an iced coffee in the middle of the small coffee table.

Andrew's eyes widened. "How did you know what I drink?"

"Once you've worn a man's coffee, it's hard to forget."

He laughed. "Listen, I owe you an apolo—."

She waved him off.

"This then." He reached for his coffee and sucked down half of it. "Truce?" He thrust out his hand. She gave a faint smile, the corners of her mouth pulling up, and placed her hand in his.

A current shot through him, starting with a faint buzz between his shoulder blades, gaining speed and strength as it hurtled down his spine, settling low. His eyes locked with hers. Ice blue with pupils surrounded by a snowflake pattern. They looked like winter, but they were anything but cold.

His gaze dropped to their intertwined hands and he could almost see the electricity arc between them. Or he would have if she hadn't ripped her hand away and then rubbed her palm down her leg like she was trying to remove any trace of him.

"There really isn't need to do that. I was checked for cooties last week. I'm clean."

An almost smirk played across her lips before they flattened into a straight line. "Drink your coffee, Cowboy, we've got work to do."

CHAPTER FIVE

Willing her heart into a rhythm that was more 'just finished meditating' and less 'grab the pads, nurse, the patient is in VFib,' Grace turned away from Andrew. What was happening? An hour ago, she wanted to push him out the window. Now her hormones were standing at attention and singing in four-part harmony. They clearly were not on the same page as her much smarter heart and head. Later she would give them a stern talking to, but until then she needed a distraction, and fast.

Her eyes swept the room and landed on the stack of music sitting in front of him. Music. Yes. Focus on the music. That was the reason they were here, after all. "Looks like you had time to check me out?"

Andrew smirked and one eyebrow slowly traveled up his forehead.

Shit. Shit. Must remember to install autocorrect on my mouth as soon as possible. "I mean, it looks like you had time to check out *my notes?*" She grabbed her coffee with more force than necessary and fumbled with the lid. Steam erupted from the uncapped drink and she blew ripples across the top. Anything not to look at him.

He chuckled, but, thankfully, didn't draw any further attention to her fumble. "I read through a few pages."

"And?"

"And, it's probably better if you take me through your thoughts."

"Overall, the bones are good."

"That's what I told Ford."

"And, as hard as it is for me to agree with Ford, they're not ready."

"All of them?" Andrew fisted his hand in his hair, sliding his fingers through it and rubbing the back of his neck.

"Um, no." Grace grimaced, tapping a hand against her thigh. "Two of the twelve songs are . . ."

"Ready to go?"

Unable to meet his gaze, she stared at the black and gray speaker mounted over his right shoulder. "Not worth our time."

His eyes pinched shut and a hiss slipped through his pursed lips.

"The others can be salvaged, but 'Whiskey Made' and 'Crossroads' have to go. Given our tight timeline, we have to concentrate on the ones we can save."

Andrew stood up and started pacing the small room. "Save? Salvage?" he spit out. "Pretty harsh words for someone who hasn't had a hit in how many years?"

Direct hit. Her already shaky confidence wobbled a few inches closer to the edge of the cliff. Shortest truce ever.

Grace gritted her teeth, digging deep for the scant remains of her confidence, and locked eyes with him. "You need to trust me. I know what works in this industry and what doesn't."

"You know what works in the industry or what works for Jax Jensen?"

Grace's spine stiffened. "Same thing. Jax understood that to make a song a hit, the artist needs to bare their soul. And, that, Cowboy, is what your songs are missing. Feeling. Depth. Heart. They're empty. You're lucky we only have to trash two of them."

Grace sucked in air like she'd run a marathon. She'd said too much, but he made her so mad. Her stomach did a series of acrobatic leaps. Being around Andrew Hayes was a manic roller-coaster ride—one minute her hand was wrapped in his long, strong fingers with shock waves traveling up her arm and the next they'd thrown off the gloves and were aiming sucker punches below the belt.

Andrew took a step closer and swiped the music off the table. "You about done?"

"I'm sorry."

"Save your apologies for someone who can appreciate the feeling. Us cold bastards aren't worth it."

"Andrew, I . . ." She stopped at the sight of his frozen expression.

He held her gaze for a single beat before stomping out the door.

Grace stared at the door, embarrassed by her outburst. Throw another worry on top of the anxiety pile. When Ford issued his ultimatum, she'd doubted her talent, her ability to write songs without Jax, never once stopping to consider this scenario—that she couldn't play nice with another writer. Was this why Jax hadn't wanted her to write with anyone else? Had he been able to see something she couldn't?

She dug through her bag and fished out her phone. She punched the green button with the white speech bubble and tapped Annie's name.

Got a minute?

The bubble with the three dots appeared immediately.

What's up?

Years from now historians will say, "It only took her a single day to destroy her future."

Melodramatic much?

What can I say, I'm an artiste.

Grace stared at the screen, no words, no three dots. In seconds, her phone lit up with an incoming FaceTime call. Grace hit Accept and waited for Annie's face to fill the screen.

Annie shoved her AirPods into her ears. "What happened, *mi amiga?*"

Grace stood, moving toward the mixing console. She pushed a slider up to its max and pulled it back down. "Verbal mud wrestling."

"You or him?"

"Yes. He makes me nuts. But we do have one thing in common."

"What's that?"

"We're both really good at storming out."

Annie cocked an eyebrow, tapped a manicured nail against her cheek and sent a penetrating look through the phone. "*La línea entre la ira y la pasión es muy delgada.*"

Grace pulled a face and stared up at the ceiling, avoiding Annie's truth stare. "You know I don't speak Spanish, Annie. Translation?"

"The line between passion and anger is very thin."

Grace's eyes flew back to her screen. "What are you talking about?"

Annie shrugged. "Fighting, foreplay, there's really not much difference."

"Um, excuse me? I know it's been a while for me, but I think I still know the difference between disdain and desire."

"You sure?"

Grace pulled the phone close to her face and pinned her bestie with a stern look. "Annie."

Annie sighed and shrugged. "Come home, then. You don't need the money."

The other stuff she was talking about was nonsense, but she had to give Annie this one, she was right, she didn't need the money. She needed something far more important . . . she needed a new purpose and an identity of her own. All the money in the world couldn't buy her that—but this job might. "I need to prove I can still do it," Grace said, barely above a whisper.

"About time you admitted it." Annie's lips curved into a smug smile. She'd done what she always did—helped Grace find her fight. "Okay, we've determined you want this job, so what's making it so hard?"

Him. Me. Everything. "His music has real potential, so that's not it. He's so arrogant—you know the type—young, good-looking, full of himself. Typical musician." Suddenly, Grace was looking at the ceiling in Annie's office and Grace heard the unmistakable sound of fingers on a keyboard. "Annie? Why did you set me down? What are you typing? Are you working in the middle of my meltdown?"

"I'm asking the interwebs for a picture of Mr. Hayes." More typing . . . and a sharp intake of breath. "Holy Macaroni."

Grace laughed. "That's some strong language, counselor."

"The six and ten-year-old I have at home require me to be mindful of my language."

Grace blinked as her phone screen suddenly blurred into a sea of color. When it stopped spinning, she was staring at Annie's desktop—and twenty different photos of Andrew. "I know what he looks like."

Annie gave a low whistle. "That man is not just good looking, G. He is 'get his own calendar' hot."

"Remind me again about your stance on objectifying people?"

"I'm not object*ifying* him; I'm object*ively* saying that if this man took his shirt off and held a puppy, he could raise a lot of money for shelter dogs everywhere. Calendars save lives, Grace. And, according to famousbirthdays.com, he's thirty-five. I don't think that qualifies as young."

"And your point is?"

"New plan," Annie said, waggling her eyebrows. "I think the best way to work out your frustrations is horizontally."

"Annie, this is not a romance novel."

Annie shrugged. "I'm a lawyer, what can I say? I need to see someone get their happily-ever-after on occasion."

Grace snorted. "You're an intellectual property attorney."

"Irrelevant. Why not channel all that energy into something more satisfying than verbal mud wrestling? Do some real wrestling."

"My husband just died."

The smile faded from Annie's lips and she paused, staring at Grace. "Almost two years ago, *cariño*," her voice softened, "it's okay to start enjoying yourself again. Jax would want that for you. Cut yourself some slack. You're allowed to have a fling."

"With a man nearly a decade younger than me? With a *musician* I have to work side-by-side with for the next three months? Who clearly despises me?" Grace stuttered to a stop. Two facts followed by a half-truth. Based on the electricity that flowed between them, his brain might despise her, but it was clear his body didn't.

"Yep. And, if you can't do it for yourself, you can always do it for me."

"For you?"

"I could live vicariously. I've been having sex with the same man for the last twenty-five years. That's a quarter of a century, for eff's sake."

"But who's counting?"

Annie laughed and laid her chin in her palm. "Who's counting indeed."

Grace's smile faded. "Even if I could find a way to pack away all my baggage, you're assuming he'd be interested in me."

"Look at you. Gorgeous, smart, wealthy. Heck, I'd do you if it wouldn't complicate our friendship."

"And if you were interested in women."

"Love's love, baby."

Grace laughed and nodded. "Thanks for listening."

Annie nodded. "Anytime. Talk to you soon. Stay strong, *chica*."

Stay strong. Annie had ended every conversation with those exact words since Jax's diagnosis. "Give my love to my two favorite girls—and that guy you've been having sex with for two and a half decades—tell them I miss them."

Annie blew Grace a kiss and her face faded to black.

Lost in thought, Grace tapped out a drumbeat on the table. Work out their issues horizontally? Annie was crazy. Plus, that would only be possible if Andrew returned to the studio. Dropping the pen that was vibrating faster and faster in her fingers, Grace shook the thought from her head. What was she thinking? It didn't matter if he was here or not, nothing horizontal would be happening. Not today. Not ever.

No. More. Musicians.

She needed to focus on the task at hand. Should she pack it in for the day or try and get some work done?

The studio was reserved for the remainder of the day and the baby grand in the adjoining room was calling to her. She scooped up her laptop, pushed through the soundproof door, and dropped onto the tufted, black leather bench. She double-clicked on the file of music she had scanned during her brief return to Minneapolis. A song filled the screen as her fingers contacted the keys.

You can do this, Grace. Depress the keys, one note, then another. It's nothing more than reading music at this point. Annie and Brad believe you can do it. It's time for you to believe, too.

She struck the first chord, the sound reverberating up her fingers, up her arms, familiar and foreign all at the same time. At the second chord, muscle memory took over and her fingers danced over the keys as if it had been two hours since she'd last played not two years. She heard someone singing along and realized it was her. Rusty, but still strong. Soon there was nothing but sound. No recording equipment, no walls, no arguments with a sexy singer, no hunger for anything more. She was lost to the music . . . and something else. What was it? It felt a lot like . . . relief.

One song led to another and three hours elapsed unnoticed. This was her home, the place she felt the most comfortable, the most alive. Why, then, had she waited so long to do this?

Grief. Doubt. Fear.

Her three constant companions. That's why.

"Ms. O'Connor?" The receptionist poked her head in the door. "I'm leaving. You can stay as long as you'd like, but the outer door will be locked, so don't go out unless you really mean it."

"Thanks . . ." Grace realized she'd never gotten the young woman's name.

"Becka," the receptionist helpfully filled in.

"Thank you, Becka, but I think I'll call it a day, too." Whatever magic bubble had kept her tethered to the piano for all those hours had popped and she knew getting it back was unlikely. "I'll walk out with you."

"You seemed to be working really hard. It was so nice of Mr. Hayes to come back and bring you a treat."

Grace's whirled toward the young woman. "Mr. Hayes was here this afternoon?"

Confusion crossed the young woman's face. "Um, yes . . . about two hours ago. He brought this," she said, picking up a bag of colorful candies tied with a rainbow ribbon and thrust it at Grace.

Grace took the bag. Sour gummy worms. Her favorite. A small card dangled from the ribbon. Grace pried it open. A short, simple message printed in black block lettering: *These start sour but end up sweet. Hoping the same for us.*

Andrew paced his hotel room, sat on the bed, and stood again. He couldn't get the image of Grace sitting at the piano out of his head. He'd only meant to drop off the candy and quickly slip out, but the reference monitors had been left on and the sound booth was filled with the sonorous chords of a single, perfectly tuned piano.

He'd immediately been captivated by the way her long, slim fingers skimmed across the piano keys, playing the songs he instantly recognized as his own. She'd taken her hair out of the braid and it flowed down around her face. He couldn't see her eyes, but he didn't need to. Her body spoke volumes. She leaned into the notes, her shoulders and torso swaying with the rhythm of the beat. It was like she was one with the instrument.

Is this what Ford meant when he said she was one of the best in the business? No one could watch her and not instantly recognize that this is what she was born to do.

He wanted nothing more than to stay and watch, but he hadn't been ready to talk to her yet and turned to leave, until she started singing. He went from captivated to absolutely spellbound. He'd never heard a voice quite like it. Low and raspy, it wrapped around him, riveting his feet to the floor.

He knew a lot of musicians. Some of them played music, others embodied it. Grace was definitely the latter.

And, that, Cowboy, is what your songs are missing. Feeling. Depth. Heart. They're empty. Her words reverberated through him and standing there, watching her, he knew she was right. Somewhere along the line, music had become a means to an end for him. But not for her. Everything about her, in that moment, had been raw, vulnerable, real.

If he lived to be a hundred, he'd never forget the sound of her voice.

And, he wanted more of it. He retrieved his phone from atop the bed, navigated to YouTube and typed her name in. If anybody looked at his browser history, he'd have some explaining to do. *Stalk much, dude?*

Surely, there would be videos of her singing.

But nothing.

Well, not nothing. A video from Billboard News reporting the "Six Things to Know About Jax Jensen's Wife, Grace O'Connor." And a couple of early Jax Jensen music videos featuring shots of him singing to her. But not a single hint that she'd ever appeared on stage. It felt strange . . . and wrong.

He dropped his head into his hands and jumped as a text alert vibrated his phone. He took one final glance at the still video images and swiped over to his texts.

How's it going, brother?

Joe. It wasn't a hard question. Why then did he have no idea how to answer it? His first inclination was to answer, 'moving along, making progress.' He'd become an expert at faking optimism, to never let 'em see you sweat. But if he'd learned anything by watching Grace earlier, it was how beautiful raw honesty could be.

Long day. Hoping for a better tomorrow.

What does that mean?

It means I'm tired and going to bed. Check in with you tomorrow.

Andrew switched off his phone without waiting for a response, threw it back on the bed pillows and headed to the shower. He really was hoping for a better tomorrow—and, much as he didn't understand it, looking forward to seeing a certain sexy, crazy talented, maddening songwriter.

Andrew stepped into the studio to find Grace already there. He stood in the open doorway for a couple of minutes watching her type with her right hand and tap out a beat with her left.

Before he could say anything, the tapping ceased and she raised a hand in the air, a gummy worm pinched between her thumb and forefinger. "Was this your way of *worming* your way back into my good graces?"

Andrew laughed. "That depends. Did it work?"

She turned to him. "At first I was certain you were trying to get rid of me via diabetic coma, but when I talked to Brad, he was pretty sure it was repentance, not retribution."

"And you believed him?"

"We've been friends for a long time. And, he may have mentioned that you called him inquiring about what kind of flowers I like."

"He steered me in a better direction."

"I'm glad he did—and I'm also sorry. It wasn't my intention to make an already difficult situation even harder."

"How about we try that truce thing again? I've heard the third time's the charm."

Grace closed her laptop with a snap, dropped it into her bag and stood, squaring her shoulders to him. "Well, I'd hate to be the one that finally disproved that idiom," she said, flashing him a grin. "How about I buy you an iced coffee at the shop across the street?"

"Deal. But I'm buying. And, how would you feel about working there for a while?" He reached for her bag, slid the sheet music into it before swinging it over his shoulder and holding her coat open for her.

She nodded while slipping her arms into her coat. "Works for me."

Coming to the end of the hallway Andrew turned to the receptionist. "If Mr. Marini comes looking for us, tell him we quit and went home."

"Will do," she said, her attention focused on her screen.

Grace gasped. "No, Becka. We're going across the street to get a cup of coffee."

The young receptionist smiled. "Not that Mr. Marini needs to know that . . ."

Andrew smirked. "I knew I liked you." Her eyes went wide and she turned tomato red.

They stepped out into the small vestibule and Grace punched the down button. When the elevator chimed, he pressed his hand against one of the open doors, motioning for Grace to step inside. "Why haven't you ever performed?"

Grace's eyes flashed to his, a quizzical look passing over them. "How do you know I haven't?"

"Mr. Google says you haven't."

The doors popped open at street level and Grace stepped out. "Far be it from me to question the accuracy of Mr. Google. I'm a behind-the-scenes girl. That's where I belong."

"You sure about that?" It didn't seem right. Someone with her voice—and her writing chops—should be standing center stage. "I heard you singing yesterday when I dropped off the gummy worms. Your voice is amazing."

"Thank you, but yes, I'm sure. The spotlight isn't meant for people like me."

He wanted to ask her why she believed that, but based on the expression on her face, now was not the time to ask.

"Want to risk it?" Andrew asked, motioning across the congested street, "or do you want to go down to the corner?"

She flashed him a mischievous smile, grabbed his hand and squeezed. "Can you run in those high heels, Cowboy?" She pointed down at his well-worn western boots. Before he could answer, she yanked his hand and stepped out onto the pavement, fearlessly weaving through the cars and cabs, flipping the bird at a taxi driver that laid on his horn as she nearly slid over his hood—without breaking stride . . . or dropping his hand.

"Impressive," he said, stepping up on to the curb. She let his hand fall and he immediately missed its warmth.

She chuckled. "Act confident and no one messes with you."

"Confident like the woman I saw playing piano and singing yesterday?"

She looked up at him and narrowed her gaze. "Listen, Fido, you know nothing about me. Probably best you drop that bone."

He shouldered the door open and she dipped under her his arm, walking into the coffeehouse. "Okay. Got it. Andrew is not allowed to compliment Grace's voice or ask any questions about why she's not using her amazing God-given talent."

"Exactly. We write. We tolerate each other. We put Story-hill on the map. That's it."

"And drink coffee? I'm hoping we're allowed to do that."

"Coffee is always acceptable."

"Then, what can I get you?"

"It's pretty technical, maybe I should order it."

"C'mon, give me a shot to prove that I'm not just another pretty face."

She raised an eyebrow and snorted. "Did you just call yourself 'pretty'?"

He shrugged and a smile broke across his face.

"Huh. So, you do know how to do it."

He winked. "I know how to do a lot of things. You'll have to be more specific."

"Smile," she answered, her cheeks turning the softest shade of pink. "You should do it more often. It looks good on you."

Andrew's brain froze. Was she flirting with him? He tried to come up with a snarky comeback, but nothing came. Probably better. He far preferred this softer, pinker version of Grace than the insult hurling one he'd met yesterday. He cleared his throat, trying to regain his mental footing. "Coffee order?" he numbly repeated.

"Fine, but if you get it wrong things will get ugly." She flashed her baby blues up at him and laughed. "Ug-*lier*."

She tugged the notebook from his fingers, tore out a piece of paper, and scribbled down her coffee order. There were at least ten words on the page. "I like it hot."

"Excuse me?" His fingers crushed the edges of the piece of paper. How could four little words shoot a lightning bolt straight to his groin?

"Hot. None of this iced crap, I want my coffee hot."

He grabbed her shoulders, turned her toward a table in the corner, gave her a gentle nudge and stepped into line. He fisted his fingers in his hair and willed the swirling thoughts in his head to settle the fuck down. He couldn't let her distract him from the job at hand. He'd made a promise to the guys. She was his writing partner. That was it.

The line moved and he forced his feet forward. So what if she was beautiful? And smart. And funny. He glanced over at her as she pulled glasses from her bag and slid them on. It was totally normal to be attracted to her. He was just a guy, like any other, reacting to a beautiful woman. Simple as that.

"Next, please," the barista called out as the man behind him poked him in the shoulder.

Minutes later he gathered the coffees and the dessert he'd ordered and wound himself through the mismatched tables toward Grace.

"One black, *iced*, coffee for me," he said, lowering himself into the chair opposite her, "and one high maintenance espresso drink for the lady."

"Cake?" she asked, pointing at the towering dessert he placed in front of them. "Isn't it a little early for that?"

"Says the woman who demolished a pack of gummy worms before 8:00 a.m."

"Touché." She reached over and ran her finger over a drop of lemon curd that had escaped onto the plate, popping it into her mouth and sucking it off her finger.

He drew in a shuddery breath. Partner, he reminded himself. Nothing more. His brain was on board. Too bad other parts of him had yet to get the message.

He cleared his throat and dropped his gaze. "How long have you worn glasses?"

"One of the joys of aging." She pulled them off and flipped in the bows, laying them on the table. "Just you wait."

"I matured young." He tapped his finger on top of her glasses case. "Got my first pair at twelve."

"Talented, mature, and"—she tipped her coffee toward him —"not just another pretty face."

Andrew's eyes darted over her face, settling low on her lips. He gripped the side of the plastic cup, willing the ice inside to smother the heat seeping down his spine.

"Excuse me, but aren't you one of the guys from Storyhill?"

Andrew blinked several times and forced his gaze away

from Grace, turning to the willowy blonde standing next to the table.

"I know you are, because I've watched, like, every YouTube video. Your voice is sooooo sexy." She twirled a lock of her hair around her finger and flipped it behind her shoulder.

Grace stiffened, looked down and started flipping through the sheet music.

"Will you sign this?" She pushed a napkin and pen in front of him without waiting for an answer.

He reached for the pen and napkin and signed his name. "Are you coming to one of the concerts this weekend?"

"Both," she said, bouncing on the balls of her feet. "I'm your biggest fan." Out of the corner of his eye he saw Grace squeeze her eyes shut and felt her knee start to jiggle under the table.

"If you come to the signing table after the show, I'll sign something better than that napkin." The woman's face lit up and she nodded vigorously before walking back to a second woman who sat at a nearby table with her mouth hanging open.

"Sorry about that. Part of the gig, I guess."

"Married to Jax Jensen, remember?" she said, pulsing a single finger against her chest. "That is nothing new. Couple of words of advice, though—you might want to be a little more specific as to what you'll sign, or you'll end up autographing her cleavage with a Sharpie."

Andrew tipped his head and laughed. "Wouldn't be the first time." His eyes found hers and his smile faded. "Was it hard?"

"What?"

"Being married to someone so famous?"

Grace twisted her lips and stared at the table, knocking a knuckle into the side of her coffee cup. "Yes and no. Eventually I got used to the press and all the people clamoring for his attention, but . . ." Her words drifted away and she got very interested in a knot on top of the wood table.

"But, what?"

She shook her head. "Never mind."

"Another thing Grace and Andrew don't discuss?"

"Yes," she whispered.

He reached for her hand, placing his fingers lightly on top of hers. Her eyes shot open, sadness shimmering behind them.

She pulled her fingers from his, blinked the unshed tears away, and pasted on a smile. "I'm going to make the dangerous suggestion, knowing that this is the part when the fighting usually starts, that we work on the songs. I can show you what I came up with yesterday—while you were out shopping for candy."

CHAPTER SIX

Hidden in the wings, Grace peered into the audience. Ghosts of performances past swirled around her, rushing across her skin, drawing heat away from her and threatening to pull her into their vortex. How many times had she stood on the sidelines, just like this, watching a concert happen, but not directly involved? Too many to count. For so long she'd yearned to step on stage, to grab the microphone and feel the audience lean into her music. But it wasn't long before she realized their relationship couldn't survive two stars. Jax had loved the spotlight and she let him have it.

She'd dissolved into the background. Willingly.

With every concert she'd become a little more 'Mrs. Jax Jensen' and a little less Grace O'Connor.

She shook her head, sloughing off the specters and refocused on the audience. One excited whisper added to another and an energetic buzz pulsed through the auditorium, building bit-by-bit as the start of Storyhill's first New York City concert loomed.

The seats of the sold-out show were filled with people of every shape, age, and gender: a gentleman in a three-piece suit sat next to a man sporting a faded concert t-shirt and cowboy hat; a grandmother hurried her granddaughter into a front-row seat—refuting every claim that country didn't play in the Big Apple.

"How's it looking?"

The hairs on her neck bristled and warmth shot from her ears to her toes. She forced herself to breathe. She wanted her life back, but there were parts of it she'd prefer to jettison. Like fans interrupting every meal and women who thought boundaries didn't pertain to celebrities. And, speaking of that fan in the coffee shop . . .

"I think the woman from the coffee shop is sitting in the front row. And"—Grace leaned forward and squinted—"what is she holding in her hand? Oh, I think it's a Sharpie." She turned and met Andrew's smile with one of her own. "What are you doing out here?"

"I came for you. The rest of the guys are in the greenroom and I want you to meet them." He offered her his hand and her eyebrows shinnied up her forehead. "What? It's dark back here. I don't want you to fall. I got a lot riding on you lady."

Grace rolled her eyes and slipped her hand into his. "How do I know you're not leading me to the exit?"

He chuckled and pulled her into the shadows. "Still don't trust me?"

"Not a chance, Cowboy. It was less than two weeks ago when you were begging Ford to send me home. I think you might have even offered to pack my bags."

Andrew snorted. "Only two weeks? Feels like I've been shackled to you for ten years."

"I need that chain to pull your dead weight around."

He laughed and ran his knuckles over the top of her head, ruffling her hair. "Sure. You just keep thinking that."

"Did you just give me a noogie?"

"Did you just use the word 'noogie?' Careful, Grace, your inner seventh-grade boy is showing."

Grace pulled a face and smoothed her hair down as Andrew elbowed open the greenroom door. Grace recoiled, her hands flying to shield her eyes from the burst of fluorescent light. She blindly followed the cacophony of voices as her eyelids fluttered, blinking to bring the bright room into focus.

"Why is this called the greenroom? I've always wondered," a Paul Bunyan doppelgänger yelled. He had massive shoulders and wore a plaid shirt rolled up to his elbows. A full beard secured his look-alike status. He only needed an ax and to swap his vintage Chuck Taylors for a pair of work boots to transplant Grace into the mythical world of American folklore.

"One of the first theaters in London painted a backstage room green," said a redhead sporting a perfectly tailored navy jacket over a three-button white Henley.

"Some people think it's a corruption of the words 'scene room'—the place where early actors and musicians were forced to wait and warm-up among the scenery storage," Grace interjected.

Silence fell over the room and five pairs of eyes snapped to her face. She shrunk back under their penetrating gazes. It hit her full force for the first time since landing in New York. She held these people's futures in her hands. They expected magic. They expected her to deliver Jax Jensen-level success. Even after a week back in the studio, she'd only proven she could rearrange a few notes and words. Editing was a different skill than writing. She still had no idea if she could compose another hit.

"Hi," Grace said, giving the group a weak wave. "I'm—"

"Grace O'Connor," a man clad in tight jeans and a black leather jacket finished. He rose and shook her hand. "Andy said you'd be here tonight. I didn't realize you'd be here-here." He pointed to the floor in the greenroom. "Nice to finally meet you. He hasn't been giving you too hard a time, has he?"

"It's been terrible," she said, biting back a smile. "But I'll survive."

Black-leather-jacket guy leaned in and whispered, "Want to know the secret to dealing with Andy?"

"Joe," Andrew warned in that deep bass voice that did funny things to Grace's insides. Andrew gave Joe's shoulder a shove and he tumbled into the sofa, landing next to a pretty brunette.

"That's Joe," Andrew said, turning to Grace. "Our beat boxer, Members Only jacket fanboy . . . and, unfortunately, my best friend."

Andrew turned his attention to a tall, blond man draped over a club chair, boots in the air. "Matt is our high tenor."

"And, resident ladies' man," Matt said, pushing a hand through his closely cropped hair and turning his ice-blue eyes on Grace.

"And humility expert," Grace teased, and laughter erupted.

"She'll fit in just fine," Paul Bunyan said, stepping up to her. She followed his chest up to his bearded chin. Clearly, being over six feet was a Storyhill requirement. "I'm Nick. I sing baritone."

"That leaves the tenor, right?" She turned to the man in the navy blazer. "You must be Blake?"

"Yes ma'am," he drawled, his voice dripping with southern charm. "Pleasure."

Andrew settled his hand in the small of Grace's back, awareness skittering down her spine and making some very specific spots tingle that had no business doing so. Traitorous body. No matter how many times she presented her argument that Andrew was a bad idea in every way, it wasn't listening.

His hand slid north and he leaned over her shoulder. "And

that beautiful woman," he said, pointing at the sole woman in the room, "is Julia, our marketing and social media manager."

"And my wife," Joe quickly added.

"Yes, and your wife. Though nobody understands what she sees in you."

Grace laughed. "Nice to meet all of you. I look forward to getting to know you better while on tour and, if anyone is interested in helping write the new songs, please let me know."

Andrew stiffened and his hand dropped from her back. "No!" All eyes swung from her to him. "Songwriting is *my* job. I started it and I'll finish it." There it was, that stubborn streak that kept rearing its ugly head. He fought her help and now he was fighting theirs. What was up with that?

She'd hit a nerve without intending to—something that, in a very short period, she'd become quite skilled at. Trying to bring a smile back to his face, she tugged on the edge of his jacket and softly said, "You afraid to share me?"

He lowered his gaze and grunted—no that wasn't quite it—it was more like a growl. And there went the tingles again.

"Was that a no or a yes?"

"Get your mic and IEM's," Brad hollered through the partially ajar door, pulling Andrew's attention away from her. "You're on in five."

Brad offered Grace his arm and they followed the guys into the wings. Minutes later, the sound engineer bellowed, "New York City, put your hands together for Storyhill!"

The lights went down, the applause exploded, and the men ran onto the stage. The auditorium fell silent and five blue spotlights flashed, showing each man in turn.

"How y'all doin' New York City?" Matt called to the audience after the first song. Grace instantly understood their fanatical following. When they stepped onto stage it was as if someone had turned on a giant switch—they were electric.

Andrew finished off the next song with one of his famous low notes, vibrating the house speakers. It was a bit of a party trick, but the audience loved it and erupted into a cacophony of applause, whoops and whistles. He grinned broadly, soaking up the attention, and moved to center stage. He flipped his hair back and powered up the charm.

Focusing on the audience, he shared funny stories about each of the guys in turn and he looked . . . what was it? Happy? Yes, that was it.

He stepped back to his place on the end of the line and locked eyes with Grace. He smiled and winked. It was quick, but unmistakable, and unequivocally directly at her.

"I got the impression the two of you didn't get along."

Grace spun to see Julia standing behind her, a Nikon with a large telephoto lens resting in her hand.

"That wink suggests something else entirely," she said, pulling the camera in front of her face and snapping a series of photos.

Grace grimaced. "It seems he lives to tease, taunt, or throw me off my game by any means necessary. All part of his master plan to wrestle control from me."

"Andrew's a lot of things—stubborn, bossy, a little moody, but he's not a player. He's a straight shooter. If he's winking at you from the stage, it's far less likely to be part of a nefarious plan and far more likely that he's interested."

"Interested in what?" Grace croaked out. But Julia was gone, moving down the stage steps, her focus back on the men as they seamlessly transitioned between a popular cover and a timeless song of the season.

Grace let out a puff of air and dropped her head to her chest. She was trying so hard to build a wall between them, but every time she turned around her body had kicked another brick off the top.

She forced her attention back to the stage and in, what felt like a blink, Matt sang the opening notes of a stylized version of *Jingle Bell Rock*, the last song on the setlist.

"This one is nearly in the books," Brad said, sidling up behind her. "Planning on joining us for a drink after the show?"

Saying no was the right answer, or at least the safer one, but . . .

"They give so much of themselves out there. I never thought about how an *a cappella* group performs the entire time, with no musical bridges to give them a breather. Won't they be tired?"

"You'd think, but no. It takes them a while to come down after a performance. They find an out-of-the-way bar to have a drink, decompress, and debrief before returning to their rooms. So, what do you say, Grace? You in?"

Grace glanced out to the stage, her eyes immediately finding Andrew. It was only one drink, right? It's not like they'd be alone. And, she reminded herself, having a casual drink with a big group of people in no way resembled following Jax Jensen to wherever he decided they'd go next. "Okay," she said, turning to Brad, "I'm game."

Andrew slid a finger through the condensation hugging the sides of his pint glass. Grace had surprised him by accepting their offer to join them at the bar. Matt was regaling her with stories from the road while Grace stifled a series of yawns. He glanced at the yellowed Budweiser clock over the back of the bar. The neon on the left side flickered, spitting out weird blue shadows onto the clock face. It had seen better days. This whole bar had. It wasn't uncommon for them to end up in a dive bar after a performance. Destinations were chosen less for their ambience and more for the place least likely to attract fans.

Grace hadn't complained when they'd arrived and the whole place smelled of spilled beer and cheap scotch. Nor did she complain when her expensive shoes stuck to the remnants of cocktails past on the worn pine floors. In fact, the only time she flinched at all was when he slid his arm over the back of her chair.

Matt finished his story and Grace leaned forward, swallowed the last dregs of her stout, and added the glass to the pile of empties littering the center of the table. "Hey all, thanks so much for inviting me along, but it's time for this old gal to get some beauty sleep."

"Don't get too much," Matt said, "my heart couldn't take it if you got any prettier." He patted his hand over his heart drawing groans from the group.

"Can I walk you back?" Andrew said, pulling her coat from the back of her chair and handing it to her.

"No, you stay," she said. "I'll grab a cab."

"Then I'll walk you out and wait until your cab arrives," Andrew said, his chair scraping on the floor as he pushed away from the table. "Don't anyone finish my drink while I'm away," he said, pointing his finger at the members of the group.

Winding through the thinning crowd, Andrew placed his hand on the small of her back and he felt her spine stiffen, but she didn't ask him to remove it.

They shimmied around the bouncer filling the tiny vestibule at the entrance and stepped outside. The crisp autumn air rushed into his lungs. "That's a temperature change," he said.

She stepped toward the curb, turning to face him. He pulled the lapels of her jacket across her chest. "You need to stay warm." His gaze traveled from her ice blue eyes southward, lingering on her lips, swaying into her before regaining his balance. He released her jacket and slid his hands down her arms. He wanted to kiss her. Or parts of him did. His brain was ineffectively yelling, *Abort! Abort! This is a bad idea.*

She was right. Two weeks ago, he wanted nothing to do with her. Now, though? She wasn't only one hell of a lyricist, but also funny and strong. She didn't take any of his crap—and gave as good as she got.

"Thanks for walking me out," she said, stepping away from his grasp and breaking their connection. "And for letting me watch the concert from the wings."

"Glad you liked it. There's nothing better than performing live. I love the energy from the audience, plus after all the years of county fairs and tiny little venues, it's cool to pack an auditorium."

Grace tilted her head toward the bar. "Will you stay much longer?"

"Maybe an hour at the longest."

Grace leaned out, searching the street. "I can't believe there are no cabs, there's usually three on every corner."

"What time should we meet at the studio tomorrow?" he asked, pleased a taxi hadn't immediately come and swept her away.

Grace nodded, still searching the street. "It'll have to be late morning—I have an early appointment."

"What kind of meeting happens that early on a Saturday?"

Grace shrugged. "It's a 'must-do' every time I come to New York, and it only works early in the morning."

"Now I'm intrigued."

"Want to come with me?" Her eyes grew wide and her cheeks flushed pink. "Never mind," she said shaking her head. "I'm sure you like to sleep in after a concert."

"No, wait, you put an invitation out there. You can't immediately take it back." He smiled. He should let her off the hook, but it was fun to see this normally cool and calm woman squirm a little. Plus, the idea of spending more time with her didn't stink.

"It's really, really early," she said, scrutinizing the sidewalk and pushing a tiny piece of trash with her toe.

"How early?" He stuck one finger under her chin and pushed upward, forcing her gaze to his.

"6:30."

"Whoa. That is early."

"There's a cab," Grace said, motioning to the taxi that swerved up to the curb. Andrew reached out to open the door as Grace's hand covered the handle. She wobbled in her heels as she pulled her hand away and stepped into the cab.

"If you want to go, meet me in the lobby at 6:30," she whispered, suddenly very interested in his knees. She slipped inside the cab and he closed the door behind her.

The taxi disappeared into a blur of traffic. Tonight sealed the deal. She'd officially moved from co-worker to major distraction. He'd almost kissed her. Earlier, he sought out the chair nearest her, winked at her from the stage, and last night she'd had a starring role in his dreams, her legs wrapped around his waist, whispering his name.

He was in so much trouble.

"Get a grip, Andrew." Now he was talking to himself? He scanned the people weaving around him. No one seemed to notice. This was New York, after all. The neon signs hanging inside the bar's grimy panes of glass flashed blue and red, creating an eerie pattern on his black jacket. Should he go back in? Should he take the next cab back to the hotel? Shit, now he couldn't even make up his own mind. She was making him crazy.

He shoved his hands deep into his pockets and stepped toward the door.

"Hey Andy," Joe said, stepping out of the bar and nearly

plowing into him. "We're calling it a night. Don't worry, I finished your drink for you—because that's what friends do."

"What would I do without you?"

Joe shrugged and slapped Andrew on the back as the others turned in the direction of the hotel. "You were gone so long I was beginning to think you went home with the pretty songwriter," Joe said, lowering his voice and leaning into Andrew.

"She has a name," Andrew growled. "And, *Grace* is my writing partner, nothing more."

"If that's the truth, then you better find a way to dial down the sexual tension," Joe said.

"What does that mean?"

"It means that in the couple of hours I've seen the two of you together, you can cut it with a knife."

CHAPTER SEVEN

G race lay in bed, an arm across her face. Did every hotel chain purchase their radiators from the same company? The one that promised it would thud every time the heat kicked on and then proceed to hiss like a hundred-pound python for the next twenty minutes?

It didn't matter. She couldn't sleep anyway. She kept thinking about her big mouth. Why had she invited him along? Simple. His gaze had zeroed in on her lips like he wanted to kiss her, and she couldn't let that happen. She'd blurted out the first thing that came to mind.

Lucky for her, he wasn't a morning person. She'd seen the evidence over the past week. He'd never get up this early.

On a giant exhale, she rolled over and righted herself. The red numbers on the standard-issue alarm clock read 5:12 a.m. She pushed off the bed, padded to the bathroom, and was blinded by the harsh fluorescent lights bouncing off the white subway tile. *Ugh, maybe I'm not a morning person either.* Blinking to bring her reflection into focus, she ran her fingers through her hair and swept it from her face, braiding the front from one side to the other, across the top, twisting the ends in a messy bun at the nape of her neck.

Now, to deal with the shadows under her eyes. Sleep. She'd heard it was all the rage. She should really try it sometime. After a little make-up, she pulled on a navy-blue maxi dress, careful not to disturb her up-do, and studied herself in the mirror. She smoothed her hand down the front of the dress and swiveled in the mirror. Would Andrew like this dress?

Stop, stop, stop. He was making her feel and think things she didn't want to think or feel. And instead of distancing herself from him—which clearly was the right thing to do—she was pulling him closer. Letting him into her private world.

Inviting him to breakfast was one thing, but introducing him to one of the most significant people in her life? That was something else entirely. If he showed, in less than ninety minutes he'd be face-to-face with Chef Curtis.

She could count on one hand the people she let close. Annie. Will. And Curtis. None of them blood, yet each one a member of her family.

A shiver trickled down her spine. She was about to introduce Andrew to her *family*.

She stared into the mirror. "Okay Universe, I need a solid. Something simple, like making sure his alarm clock doesn't go off." She looked up at the ceiling. "Deal?"

She swiped a final coat of gloss across her lips and flicked the bathroom light off. She grabbed her trench coat from the closet and draped it around her shoulders. Grabbing her handbag, she headed for the elevator and punched the down button.

I'm on my way, she texted Curtis on her ride to the lobby, reminding herself that this morning was about Curtis, not Andrew. Today was the only day they'd both be in the city and she was beyond excited to see her oldest friend.

The elevator wobbled to a stop and Grace nearly tripped

over the threshold. There sitting on the opposite side of the lobby was Andrew. Head reclined, eyelashes resting on his cheeks, and with his large frame draped across the tiny lobby sofa, he looked even more imposing.

He'd actually shown up. So much for her deal with the Universe.

"You getting off, lady?" a man dressed in a hotel uniform and pushing an industrial vacuum asked, irritation lacing his voice.

No, uh-uh, no way. "Yes. Sorry." She threw her shoulders back and commanded her feet forward. Making sure to step wide over the vacuum's dangling cord, she crossed the lobby and stopped in front of Andrew.

"Come here often, Cowboy?"

"That sounds like a pick-up line, lady, and it's far too early for that. Plus, I'm waiting for someone," Andrew said, without opening his eyes.

"She must be a good friend if you're willing to get up this early."

"Naw, but I'm thinking I'll need a favor someday and this should score me a big one." He sat forward on the sofa and gave her a slow perusal, unleashing that damn colony butterflies that seemed to have taken up permanent residence in her belly. *Down girls*, Grace commanded. *You've spent your entire adult life around charismatic, beautiful men, he's not any different.*

"Now," he said, pulling her from her thoughts, "where are we going at this ungodly hour? You never did tell me."

He unfolded his frame and rose to full height in front of her. Grace peeked up at him through her eyelashes. How tall was he? Six-two? Six-three? Tall enough to hoist her up and carry her to bed and . . . she jiggled the image from her mind. She reminded herself that this wasn't attraction, it was just a little arousal, purely chemical. Nothing to worry about. Basic, natural, and totally out of her control. She was human, that's all.

She drew in a steadying breath. "I didn't think you'd actually show up."

Andrew smirked. "I like to keep the ladies guessing." He grabbed a saddle brown suede jacket from the sofa and strung his arms through it. "Am I dressed okay?"

How could those jeans ever be wrong? And that jacket? It pulled tight across his broad shoulders, draping down his well-defined chest. "You'll do," she said, swallowing hard.

Andrew yawned. "Will there be coffee where we're going?"

"It's New York City, everything's available for a price."

"Everything?" he said, the corners of his mouth turning up.

"Let's go," she said, rolling her eyes.

"Wait," he said, grabbing her arm. Her eyes flashed to where his fingers encircled her wrist. The unexpected touch both intimate and challenging. "Tell me where we're going."

"I'll tell you in the cab."

The bellman hailed them a taxi and minutes later they were whizzing past high rises and skyscrapers in all colors and sizes. The driver cut in and out of traffic, heavy even at this time of day. The lights of the Brooklyn Bridge appeared in the distance, and Grace's excitement kicked up a notch.

"Okay, lady, where are we going?"

Grace bounced in her seat. "My best friend from high school is a chef, and he creates these fabulous breakfasts for me when I come to town. I've been looking forward to it all week. Just the thought of it helped me survive all your drama."

Andrew didn't take the bait. He cocked his head and a smile built around the corners of his mouth, spreading slowly across his face. "Huh."

Grace's brow furrowed. "Huh, what?"

"I have a theory."

"Just one? I'm disappointed, you're usually so full of opinions."

"I don't think you hate me anymore."

"No?"

"Nope. I think you might even like me."

Grace snorted. "You're arrogant, way too good looking, and too used to getting your way."

"You think I'm handsome?" He stroked his fingers over his two-day stubble.

"Of course, that's what you heard out of all that."

He poked her arm. "Come on. Admit it, you like me. Why else would you have begged me to come with you this morning?"

"Begged? Please. I only mentioned it because I was worried a simple, country boy like you might be afraid to venture out of the hotel into the mean streets of Manhattan. I thought you should get out, so that you'll be ready for the even meaner streets of London."

Andrew chuckled. "So, you felt sorry for me?"

"Exactly."

"Grace, show some restraint, you're embarrassing yourself. You really have to stop throwing yourself at me."

"Hmph. If I was throwing myself at you, you'd know it." Andrew cocked one dark eyebrow and Grace's face flooded with color. "Not that I would," she mumbled, turning back to the window.

The cab driver slowed and pulled up to a small, nondescript brownstone. "We're here!" she announced, causing the cab driver to jump in his seat. Andrew laughed at her exuberance and grabbed for the door handle.

"Um, Andrew," Grace said, giving his sleeve a tug and pulling his hand from the door, "before we go in, there's something I need to tell you."

"I got it earlier. You think I'm handsome. I understand it's a lot to handle this early in the morning. I'll try to dial it down a notch, but I can't make any promises."

"There's hardly room for me and your head in this cab." Her smirk flattened to a straight line. "My friends don't know you are coming. It might be a bit awkward."

He turned to her, eyes narrowing. "Why awkward?"

Grace grimaced and shrugged her shoulders. "They might think you're a . . . like a . . ." She sheepishly flipped a finger back and forth between them.

Understanding dawned and his face exploded into a smile. "They might assume I'm your newest boy toy?"

Grace crinkled her nose and smacked him on the arm. "No, I just don't want anyone getting the wrong idea."

"We wouldn't want that. That would be truly terrible."

"If they think this some kind of date, there's bound to be a mountain of questions. Best to keep things straightforward . . . and simple."

She could feel his scrutiny as she turned and swiped her credit card through the reader attached to the front seat. She lifted her head and met his stare. Amusement ran through his beautiful emerald eyes. This close she could see they weren't a solid green like she thought but flecked with tiny nuggets of gold. She needed to amend her previous statement. He wasn't good looking. He was beautiful.

"I'm going to need to start the meter again if you're not getting out," the cabbie brusquely said, strumming his fingers on the steering wheel.

"Right, right," Grace said, poking Andrew in the thigh . . . the solid, muscly, ungiving thigh. She was overcome with the desire to place her hand on top of that leg and squeeze. *Bad Grace*. She curled her fingers into a fist and followed him out of the cab.

Andrew turned toward the building. The only identifying feature was a name stenciled in the bottom right corner of the plate glass window. He pointed at the lettering. "Your friend is Curtis Owens?"

"You've heard of him?"

"My sister is going to wet her pants when I tell her."

"Sorry?"

"My sister. She's a major foodie. She's tried to get a booking for years. She said getting reservations here is a full-on blood-sport."

Grace laughed. "Don't tell Curtis, his ego doesn't need any more padding. Wait until your sister hears that you got a special seating on the rooftop terrace . . . she'll probably lose her mind."

"I take it this is a very exclusive reservation?"

Grace nodded quietly. "As far as I know I'm the only one who's ever gotten it. Well, me and Jax . . . and now you."

"Well then, we shouldn't keep him waiting." Andrew stepped toward the heavy silver door.

Grace knocked and it opened revealing a statuesque beauty. Auburn curls cascaded down her shoulders framing her high cheekbones and dimpled chin.

Her stoic expression broke into a wide smile. "Grace. Aren't you a sight for sore eyes," she said in a thick Irish accent.

"Megan," Grace said, holding her arms open for a hug.

"Curtis has the rooftop all set up for you," Megan said, releasing her hold on Grace and turning her attention to the man standing behind her. She elbowed Grace aside and stuck out her hand while raking her jade eyes over him. "Megan Dunne," she said, stepping closer, "and you are?"

"This is Andrew Hayes," Grace answered, shifting uncomfortably from right to left.

"A good Irish name, at least," she said, covering her surprise with another of her mega-watt smiles. "You're looking a bit wrecked, sweetie. Cup of coffee for ya?"

"Uh, yes, please," Andrew stuttered, all of the charm he showed on stage last night completely absent. "Big night last night," he added, raking his fingers through his hair.

Megan arched her eyebrow and turned her gaze back to Grace. "Oh, I see."

Grace flushed pink and stammered, "No, Megan, *no*. He had a concert."

Megan turned, but not before raising her eyebrows at Grace and mouthing, "wow." Grace shook her head and Megan rolled her eyes.

Watching her walk away, Andrew turned to Grace letting out a low whistle. "I am tired, but I'm pretty certain that is not Curtis Owens." A sharp pang erupted in her stomach that felt a lot like jealousy. Couldn't be. She didn't do jealousy. You couldn't be married to one of the most recognized musicians in the world and do jealousy—the green-eyed monster would eat you alive.

"Megan is Curtis' business partner," Grace said, forcing a calmness she didn't feel. "He runs the kitchen and she does everything else—except don't tell Curtis I said that," she added with a wink.

"Two cups of coffee." Megan handed the first one to Grace and turned her full attention on Andrew. "I apologize for my surprise," she said, giving him his steaming mug, "it's just that we were only expecting Grace. How is that you find yourself here this morning?"

Andrew opened his mouth and then closed it, turning to Grace. She inhaled a steadying breath and silently willed away the flush creeping up her neck. "Andrew is a member of Story-hill. I think I mentioned them in my email. We've been writing together this week."

"That explains who he is, but not why he's here. Or why he's the only one here. Didn't you say there were five men in the band?" Megan said, without taking her eyes off him. Andrew squirmed under her gaze.

"Grace!" Curtis yelled from the back of the restaurant, interrupting Megan's interrogation. He wound through the white linen-covered tables, slipped the coffee mug from her hand, handing it back to Megan, and wrapped her up in a bear hug, lifting her feet off the ground.

"When are you going to move to New York so I can see your beautiful face every day?" She had seriously considered it after Jax died, but Minneapolis was home. He twirled her around—and abruptly set her down.

"Curtis Owens," he said as he stuck out his hand to Andrew. "Megan, did you know our friend was bringing a plus one?"

Megan smirked at Grace. "I did not. This gorgeous man is Andrew Hayes. He's Grace's *friend*," she lilted, punctuating the last word.

"Co-worker," Grace squeaked, placing a single hand on Curtis' arm.

Andrew smirked. "Yes, colleagues, collaborators, workmates, certainly not her date."

Grace shot a glare at Andrew as Curtis looked between them. "Okay. I've got everything ready to go. I'll rustle up another place setting."

"I asked Tyler to take a setting up when I fetched the coffee," Megan interjected.

Curtis examined Andrew from head-to-toe and back up again. He narrowed his gaze and turned his eyes on Grace, giving her the same once-over. "Well, then, I guess we're all set. You know the way, Grace. I'll see you up there in a few minutes with the first course."

"Will you be joining us, Megan?" Grace asked, silently willing Megan to agree.

"Oh no, I think you have all the company you need."

Warning bells pealed in Grace's head. This is precisely what she'd been afraid of, Curtis and Megan clearly thought this was a date. She needed to get him up on the roof before Megan asked any more questions. Questions she had no answers to.

"Andrew, let's head upstairs." Grace pointed to a narrow set of steps hidden behind the vintage bar.

"Do you need a refill on your coffee before you go, darlin'?" Megan asked and Grace shoved him toward the stairwell.

Reaching the top of the stairs, Andrew placed a hand in the small of her back and reached around her to push the door open. He really needed to stop doing that . . . every touch poked another hole in her armor.

They stepped out into Curtis' rooftop garden. Things had changed since her last visit. Now covered in weather-hardy decking, the garden had expanded from a couple of containers of herbs to dozens of brimming boxes, only the sturdiest vegetables hanging on in the November chill. In the center, sat the old iron table she'd dined at so many times before. Grace ran her hands over the last of the lavender and brought her fingers to her nose. Something, anything, to calm her jangling nerves.

Andrew dropped into one of the chairs alongside the table. "I don't think your friend likes me."

"Nonsense," she said, joining him at the table. "He doesn't even know you. It's been my experience that someone has to have a conversation with you to truly dislike you."

"There you go again, flirting with me."

Grace snorted and stood, walking to the brick half-wall bordering the edge of the building. She wrapped her hand around her steaming mug, sipping slowly, waiting for the pulse of caffeine to hit her veins.

Heat spiraled up her back and she looked down to see the worn tips of size twelve boots on either side of her feet. He had followed her. "Why are we here so early?" he whispered against her ear. His soft breath blowing a stray piece of hair against her cheek, sending a shiver through her.

"Cold?" He rubbed his hands up and down her arms.

"No." *Not especially when you do that.*

"It seems the great Curtis Owens could make you breakfast at nine or ten versus this crazy hour."

"It's not the food that brings me here so early."

"Then what?"

"Patience. You'll see soon enough." Andrew opened his mouth to speak, but Grace placed one finger over his lips and shook her head.

"Hold that thought. I need to excuse myself to the ladies' room."

Andrew folded forward onto his elbows, leaning his weight against the cool bricks and rubbed a finger over his bottom lip, still tingling from her touch. His eyes traced the shadowy outline of the Brooklyn Bridge and the tall towers of Manhattan and wondered the same things as Megan. Why had Grace invited him? And, why had he willingly gotten out of bed at this hour with no idea where they were going? It wasn't like him. And it clearly wasn't the actions of a man who had spent a lifetime keeping a considerable distance between his personal and professional lives.

It had been so long since a woman had registered on his radar. He figured he's simply lost interest in dating. He'd had plenty of offers over the years, but no one made him even consider suspending his career-only pledge. But Grace? She made him wonder if it wasn't a lack of interest that made him 'all work and no play,' but rather that he hadn't met the right woman.

Except Grace was the wrong woman for so many reasons—hell, for every reason. It felt like he was playing with fire. A fire that could burn down everything he was working to build. Yet . . .

Footsteps sounded behind him. He turned, a smile pulling up the corners of his mouth, expecting to see the very woman dominating his thoughts. It wasn't Grace, but Curtis. He set two plates down on the tiny table in the center of the patio and pinned Andrew with his gaze.

"Don't hurt her," Curtis said.

"I'm sorry?" Andrew said.

"You're a musician."

Andrew narrowed his eyes. "Yes. And?"

"And, if you're just playing around, walk away. She's been through enough."

"It's not like that, we're simply two people writing a few songs together." Was he trying to convince Curtis or himself?

Curtis stared at Andrew, sizing him up. "I'm not sure she thinks you're just colleagues. She's never brought anyone here—except Jax." He stepped closer to Andrew.

"O - kay," Andrew said, annoyance crawling up his spine.

"I stood by and watched as she lost herself in another musician's world and as her friend—her best friend—I won't let it happen again."

"Your regrets have nothing to do with me," Andrew said frostily, not breaking Curtis' stare. "We're just friends, not that it's any of your business."

"She's my family. That makes it my business. She seems strong on the outside, but her heart is easily broken."

Andrew rubbed his temple with his thumb and flashed to her standing up to Ford—and him. "I assure you, she can hold her own."

"I mean it," Curtis said, "you hurt her, you answer to me."

Where did this guy get off, going all caveman on him? If he needed a reminder of why he avoided dating, he was getting it. Relationships were distractions filled with drama.

"Hey, guys," Grace called, reappearing at the top of the stairs, interrupting the standoff. "Look to the east, you can see the first rays of sunshine." The icy blue November sky gave way to brilliant pinks and purples as the giant orange orb climbed its way over the shadowed buildings of Brooklyn. She walked up to Andrew's side and grabbed his arm, causing both men to follow her fingers with a surprised gaze. Her touch was cold, but her cheeks flushed warm with excitement.

"If you turn to the northeast you can see the sun reflecting off the East River and watch as it slowly bounces off all the glass in Manhattan." She pulled Andrew closer. "Lean toward me and, right through there, you can see the Empire State Building. It's almost as if the sun is lighting the building one window at a time.

"I've seen this so many times, but it never gets old." She peered up at Andrew. "This is why I come here so early. Sunrise over New York City. Isn't it breathtaking?"

Andrew turned his gaze to Grace and smiled at the almost child-like anticipation on her face. The sunrise wasn't the only breathtaking thing. One smile neutralized every thought about her being a bad idea and a dangerous distraction. Was the success he craved so deeply worth walking away from a woman like her? Was shutting people out just another way of letting his father win?

Curtis cleared his throat, interrupting his thoughts. "I've left the first course on the table. You should eat it before it gets cold," he said, directing his comments to Grace.

"Shall we?" Grace asked Andrew, motioning to the table. She seemed oblivious to the tension between the two men. Watching Curtis make his way down the stairs, Grace caught his puzzled expression. "He cooks, I eat. He never joins me until after dessert." Andrew nodded and pulled out Grace's chair.

Grace cracked open the perfectly poached egg topping her plate and smoothed the napkin in her lap, keeping her focus on it. "When we arrived, you said we were co-workers, but just now you just told Curtis that we're friends. Which one is it?"

"You were eavesdropping?"

Grace ignored his question. "Is it true? Are we becoming friends?"

"I'm not sure that's what I'd call it . . ."

He waited for her to ask for an explanation, but instead she threw the napkin from her lap and ran to the edge of the rooftop. Leaning over the century-old brick wall she exhaled, "Andrew, isn't it glorious?" The sun had summited the buildings, a small sliver peeking over the top of the skyscrapers, beams of light shooting straight into the sky.

He got up and walked to her side, setting his hands on her shoulders, feeling her still under his touch. "You're right, it's amazing. Almost worth getting up so blasted early—almost."

Andrew couldn't take his eyes off her. There was something about the way the morning light struck her, adding a golden glow to her already beautiful features. The expression on her face so different than anything he'd seen previously. Was it happiness? No, it was more than that. It was peace. The walls this snarky, smart, private, grieving woman had meticulously built were dissolving right in front of him. And it was stunning. She was stunning.

"Grace," he said, touching his hand to the base of her neck, "why did you bring me here? From what Curtis said, you never bring anyone here."

She nibbled a fingernail and dropped her gaze to her feet. "I don't know."

Andrew slid an arm around her waist. She let out a small gasp as he pulled her into his body. With a single finger he turned her face back toward him and traced down her cheek. She leaned into his hand and her eyes dropped shut.

"What are we going to do about this, Gracie?" he whispered, leaning in.

"About what?" she said, not opening her eyes.

"This crazy chemistry between us."

Her eyes flew open. For the briefest moment, fire flashed, but it was gone as fast as it had appeared, replaced with something cooler. "I think you're confusing chemistry and irritation."

Andrew tucked a stray curl behind her ear. "You sure?"

"Ready for dessert?" Curtis called, breaking the moment.

Grace cleared her throat, spinning to face Curtis. "What magnificent concoction have you made for us today?"

"Panettone bread pudding." He held out two small ramekins and set them next to their half-eaten entrees. Grace hastily moved toward the table, dropped into her seat, and got very interested in the dessert.

"Friends, my ass," Curtis muttered as he slipped past Andrew on his way back to the kitchen.

CHAPTER EIGHT

A ndrew slid into his chair and watched as Grace fiddled with the napkin in her lap. If Curtis hadn't interrupted, he would have kissed her. And he was pretty sure she would have let him. In that moment, he wanted nothing more than to taste her cherry red lips, to feel every inch of her pressed up against him. To get lost in the feeling.

But now? His niggling conscience warned that his career rested on their partnership and mixing business and pleasure was never a good idea. After all, it was only days ago that they'd been at each other's throats. Could his feelings really change that quickly? While the angel on one shoulder told him to keep his distance, the devil on the other encouraged him to abandon his promise of nothing but work, if only for a little while.

Women are exhausting.

Who was he kidding? It wasn't Grace who was tiring, it was all his rules.

"Cowboy?" Grace poked her fork lightly into the top of his hand.

Andrew blinked and forced himself to focus on the beautiful woman across from him. His eyes washed over the table and up her body to meet her gaze. "Sorry. Lost in thought. Did you say something?"

She poked him again with her fork, a little harder this time.

"Ow. I'm paying attention now. No need to wield weapons."

A tremor of a smile played at the corners of her lips. "I asked if you were planning on eating your dessert. If not, I'm happy to take it off your hands." She pulled the small ceramic crock a few inches closer to herself.

He pulled it back and twirled his fork in his hand. "Hey now, you're not the only one who knows how to use one of these. Hands off the good stuff, lady."

"It is good," she said, lifting her napkin to her lips and brushing them off. "I'm guessing Curtis made this. He's one of those rare chefs that's equally good with savory and sweet. He still makes a lot of the desserts." She dropped his gaze and scraped the sides of the dish with her fork. "I wonder if he'd give me the recipe. Would you like the recipe, too?"

She was rambling. Nice to know he wasn't the only one thrown by the almost-kiss.

"I don't want the recipe. But there is something else I want."

"What's that?" she said barely over a whisper, still very interested in the remains of her bread pudding.

"Did you and Curtis ever date?"

Grace's head snapped up in surprise. "What?"

"Did you and Mr. Fancy-Pants-Chef date?"

"Date? That's what you've been thinking about over there?"

No. Not even close. But he'd be keeping his other thoughts to himself. He shrugged, trying to make his expression unreadable. "Inquiring minds and all that."

Her eyes narrowed, but she answered. "No, we've never dated. He's never been interested in me like that."

"You're sure about that?"

"Yes. Absolutely certain. Why would you even ask that?"

"Well, there's the fact that he's still single. Why is that? And, then there's how crazy protective he is of you."

"You and the Storyhill guys seem pretty tight. I'm sure they're protective of you, too. Do any of them want to date you?"

Andrew snorted. "We do have each other's back, but this seems different."

"If I didn't know better, I'd think you were jealous."

He arched a single eyebrow and pinned her with a speculative look. "And if I am?"

Her eyes grew wide and a pink flush raced up her neck, dotting her cheeks. She pushed back from the table, the iron chair legs screeching against the decking. "We should go—we have a lot of writing to do."

Andrew reached for her hand. "Grace . . ."

"Everything okay, Grace?" Curtis said, walking up to the table and causing them both to jump.

Her eyes flicked to Andrew's before turning to Curtis. She flashed a smile at the chef that Andrew now recognized as the smile she pasted on when she got uncomfortable. "Fine. Great. Everything was great. As always."

"Will you be back for dinner?" Curtis asked.

"Do you have space for me?"

"I reserved a table the minute I got your email."

"I can't turn down the hottest reservation in NYC, can I? Andrew," she said, turning back toward him, but not fully meeting his gaze, "what was it that your sister said about getting a reservation here?"

"That it's a blood sport," Andrew grumbled.

Curtis laughed. "Blood sport. Hah. Might have to use that in my marketing. Can I steal that?" he asked Andrew.

"Have at it."

Grace linked her arm with Curtis' and started walking toward the staircase. Andrew had no choice but to follow behind like a lost puppy. "Will you and Megan be able to join me? I always prefer company to eating alone."

"Alone?" Curtis asked, raising an eyebrow and glancing back at Andrew.

"He has a concert tonight."

Curtis nodded. "Megan will join you, and I'll pop out of the kitchen as I can."

"All the other guests will be so jealous, what with the famous chef paying special attention to me."

"Jealousy seems to be running rampant this morning," Andrew grumbled under his breath. If Curtis or Grace heard him, neither gave any indication.

"I don't suppose you called us a cab?" she asked, descending the stairs.

"That's why I came upstairs. It's waiting outside. Now go, and I'll see you tonight. Got the best table in the house for my best girl," Curtis said, wrapping Grace in a hug as they reached the front door. "I miss you. I wish you'd visit more often."

"Planes go both ways, you know." She pulled out of the hug and patted him good-naturedly on the face. "It'd be good for you to come home once in a while."

"This *is* home. There's nothing for me in Minneapolis."

"Excuse me?" Grace said, pointing at herself.

"You know what I mean."

Grace sighed and Andrew watched as a look of melancholy passed over her beautiful face. Awareness slammed into his gut and instantly he knew he'd do whatever it took to keep sadness from her face. So much for keeping a professional distance.

Curtis held the door open and they slipped into the waiting cab. Grace waved and blew kisses at her so-called friend. Yep. No denying it. He was definitely jealous. He turned away from her and gave the driver the address of the studio. Resting his arm on the cab door, he looked outside the car window, trying to focus on something, anything, other than Grace.

Nope. Not happening. He turned back to face her. "You're not coming to the concert tonight?"

She looked up from her phone and gave him a playful grin. "Isn't it the same as last night?"

"Yes."

"I'm flattered you want me there."

"It's not that."

"Then what is it?"

His mouth dried up and he licked his lips. This was not the time for honesty. He couldn't very well tell her that if she was at the concert, he didn't need to worry about her being with Curtis. Even he wasn't that much of a prick. Was he?

"Cowboy, what is it?" She was yanking his chain and she knew it.

"Well, it's . . ."

Her phone vibrated and she looked down, her face crinkling up like she'd just taken a big bite of a lemon. She swiveled the phone to show him the caller ID. It might be the very first time he'd been happy to see the name 'Ford Marini' flash in front of him.

Saved by the bell. Literally.

Grace punched Accept and before Ford uttered a single word, she said, "Andrew is here with me. I'm putting you on speaker."

"It's good to know you're working."

Grace bit back a laugh and looked at Andrew. "What do you need, Ford?"

"I've been talking with Publicity, and we've agreed that Storyhill needs to release a new single before the album launches."

Grace nodded her head. "That's pretty standard. How about I email you my idea for the title track?"

"No." Ford's dismissive response echoed out of the phone's speaker and hung in the air. "It's got to be bigger than that. I want a single that is not on the album—a bonus track, of sorts. And, I want it at least two months before the album drops. Got it?"

Andrew moved to speak, but Grace waved him off. "A thirteenth song? Not possible. They leave for tour tomorrow morning and then they're off for the holidays."

There was that backbone he found so sexy. Go get him, girl.

"I don't care if you have to record something while they're on tour. You've got contacts all over the world, Grace. Get it done or I'll make good on my threat."

Grace squeezed her eyes shut and pressed her fingers into Andrew's thigh. In any other situation he'd welcome her touch, hell, he'd encourage it, but this touch was all frustration, nothing more.

"Fine," she gritted out while simultaneously ending the call.

The cab pulled up to the curb and Andrew jumped out, his long legs reaching the building's glass and metal door in three steps. "You coming?" he asked briskly, turning his head in her direction.

"Go ahead," Grace said, "I need a minute."

He walked back to her, placing a gentle hand on her shoulder. "What's Ford got on you? I know the stakes for Storyhill, but for you? What is he threatening you with?"

Slipping her phone into her bag, she remained silent.

"Grace?"

She flipped her hair behind her back, sucked in a breath and locked eyes with him, unblinking. "He's made it perfectly clear that if I don't write these songs—and make them hits—he'll blackball me in the industry."

Andrew resisted the urge to pull her into his chest and assure her that everything would be okay. "Christ, Grace. You're not doing this because you want to, you're doing it because you have to?" He shook his head. "Do you really think Ford can take down someone of your stature?"

"I don't know, but I'm not willing to find out. If I stand up to the label and they blackball me, I'll lose everything. Again."

He watched as a torrent of emotions flashed lightning-fast behind her eyes. Fear. Anger. Sadness. She took a step back from him, she closed her eyes, sucked in a breath and shook out her shoulders. When she opened them, only a single fiery sentiment remained: resolve.

"Honestly, this is probably a good thing," she said.

"A good thing?"

"We've gotten distracted from the mission. This was a timely reminder."

"Grace, c'mon . . ."

"No. You go. I left the music and my notes on the table yesterday. You get started and I'll join you shortly."

He grunted and walked into the lobby. He fisted his fingers in his hair. Was it really only 9:00 a.m.?

"Good morning, Mr. Hayes." Andrew's head snapped up and he blinked, bringing the receptionist into focus. Somehow, he'd gotten on the elevator and to the studio without realizing it.

"Is Ms. O'Connor not joining you today?"

"She'll be here in a minute. I hope."

He shoved the door to the studio open with more force than necessary, slamming it against the wall and slumped into a chair, laying his head on the table.

He needed to stop imagining the taste of her full lips and get his head back in the game. They only had a few hours to write before he needed to be at the venue for tonight's call. And, with the label's new demand, they'd have to pull a rabbit out of a hat. He needed a miracle—and sooner rather than later.

Andrew grabbed the edge of the table and rolled himself over so that he was in front of the fanned-out pages of notes and lyrics. The leather-bound journal Grace had been scribbling in all week laid open to the right of the music.

He'd be lying if he didn't admit he was curious. Her notes from their sessions were nearly at the end of the book. What else did the pages hold? The secrets to Jax Jensen's number-one hits? Maybe the answer to the label's new demand? He glanced up at the door and with no sign of her, he grabbed the journal.

Thumbing through the pages, he let the journal drop open to a page about a third of the way through. He scanned the page, and the next, and the next. These were not Jax Jensen songs. He knew, not because he'd heard every one of Jax's songs, but because they had an entirely different vibe.

Resting his head in his palm, he flipped another page, unable to stop himself. These were more than scrawled ideas, they were nearly complete songs . . . and they were amazing.

In a flash, he understood. This is what she meant when she'd said his songs lacked emotion.

"What. Are. You. Doing?" Grace flew through the doorway and yanked the journal from his hand. "Is going through people's private things another one of your bad habits, Cowboy?"

Andrew raised his hands, palms out. "It was open on the table."

"That doesn't mean you have any right to look through it." She shoved the journal into her bag and snapped it close.

"You're right. But, Christ, Grace, those are some of the best lyrics I've ever read. Storyhill would record any of them in a heartbeat. Any one of those songs could be the answer to the bomb Ford just dropped."

He could see her pulse beating at the base of her throat. Her eyes flashing with anger. "You dig through my stuff, uninvited, and then have the audacity to ask for one of the songs?"

"Think about it, Grace," he said, standing and placing his hands on her arms. "The one about having faith in your dreams would be perfect for Storyhill. I can already hear the harmonies with Mattie floating the melody over the top. We arrange this one and get Ford off our back. Problem solved."

She shrugged out of his hold. "No."

"But, Grace —"

"I think I made myself clear. Don't ask again."

Could this get any worse? The woman who was supposed to 'save' him was distracting as hell and now she was refusing to part with any one of a whole notebook of songs? He was screwed in every way but the good way.

CHAPTER NINE

G race leaned back in her chair and laughed quietly as Megan did a spot-on impression of Curtis barking out orders in the kitchen. Her words faded out and Grace ran her hands over the white linen tablecloth, smoothing down the tiny wrinkles that had appeared during dinner and brushed away the stray crumbs.

"Earth to Grace." Megan fluttered her hand in front of Grace's face. "Where are you tonight? That was some of my best material and you hardly laughed."

Grace sighed. "I'm sorry. I guess I'm a bit distracted with everything going on."

Megan waggled her eyebrows. "Yes, well, a man like that could distract the strongest among us."

"What? No, it's not him, at least not in the way you're insinuating."

"Tell me then."

Grace leaned onto her elbows and steepled her fingers, tapping them to her lips. "Where do I even start? Put simply, I got strong-armed into writing again and just when I thought maybe I had a handle on things, the label threw another curveball. After we left this morning, we got a call from the music exec asking for another song on an even tighter timeline." Grace exhaled a long, shuddering sigh. "Let's just say that when I imagined coming back to the industry, it looked nothing like this."

Megan reached for her hand, catching it in her own. "And it's all complicated by a heavenly musician who got up before sunrise for you?"

"Meaning?"

"Meaning it's not just business anymore, is it? From where I stood, it seemed he might be interested in more than just your eighth notes." Megan bit back a smile. "But the bigger question is, are you interested in checking out how good his whole notes are?" Megan used her thumb and pointer finger to make a giant O.

"Depends on which part of my body you ask." Grace groaned and Megan chuckled. "Why couldn't I have met a nice accountant or actuary? Someone simple—and not part of the business. Why? And, why does he have to be so good looking? I look at him and my brain turns to mush—it's like every glance is a shot of tequila. He's killing my brain cells, and I'm too old to be losing brain cells. And, speaking of age, he's nearly a decade younger than me." Grace grimaced and squeezed her eyes shut.

"All the more reason to take him for a test drive." Grace's eyes grew wide and her cheeks burned scarlet. "What? Men have been dating younger women since the beginning of time. It's about our turn, don't you think?"

"Ms. Dunne," the host interrupted, "I've pulled receipts and end of day reports. Do you want them, or should I put them in your office?"

"I'll take them," Megan said, reaching for the stack of paper. "Sorry, Grace, duty calls. My advice? Don't overthink this."

Grace snorted and shook her head. Over-thinking and overcomplicating were her specialties. If a situation could be made more difficult, she seemed hell-bent on making it so. Exhibit A, bringing Andrew to breakfast this morning.

"Want me to tell Curtis you're waiting?"

"No, I'll go find him. Thanks for dinner."

Megan nodded. "Any time. Text me what you learn about the whole notes."

"How is it that you make everything sound dirty?"

Megan rose from the table and laughed. "The sole benefit of growing up with three older brothers."

Left alone, Grace surveyed the impressive dining room. The restaurant was officially closed, and the staff was busy cleaning up and setting tables for tomorrow's service. Grace wandered toward the kitchen, pushed open the swinging door, and poked her head inside. It always felt a bit too familiar to enter the kitchen without permission, but then again, she had known Curtis since they were fourteen.

"I missed you tonight," Grace said, catching the chef's attention. "Do you have time to join me for a cocktail?"

Curtis sighed and rubbed his hands on his nearly immaculate apron. "Let me wrap up a couple of things here and I'll meet you at the bar. Order what you'd like before the bartender leaves—and ask him to pour my usual."

When the door to the kitchen swung open and Curtis strode through it, Grace couldn't find a trace of the awkward, insecure, neglected kid she'd met so many years ago. In his forties now, he was confident, muscular, and one could argue, handsome. Faint lines framed his piercing hazel eyes and silver strands had started to appear at his temples, twining their way into the thin dark braids coiling over his scalp.

Placing a hand on Grace's shoulder, he slid onto the barstool and surveyed his staff.

"Tough night?" Grace asked, following his gaze across the room.

"Just long. Sorry I didn't get out to your table."

"You're here now and that's better. This way I don't have to fake paying attention to you when all I'm really interested in is the food."

"I've always thought you only liked me for my food." He waggled his finger at her. "Now I know for sure." He looked back out across the restaurant and slowly shook his head. "Late at night, like this, I wander out here and often wonder where I'd be without you and Megan."

"Me?" Grace asked with a hint of astonishment.

"You're the two people in my life who've always believed in me. Always lifting me up when times get tough."

"A little nostalgic tonight, my friend?"

"Times are changing," he looked directly into her eyes, the mask he wore for everyone else immediately dissolving, "you with a new guy . . . me opening a new restaurant in LA . . ."

"What?! You're opening a new restaurant in LA? And, I'm just hearing about it now?" Grace squealed and slapped his thigh.

"I noticed how you skipped right over the 'new guy' part."

"Because there's nothing to tell. Anyway, he's convinced you have a giant crush on me."

Curtis chuckled and pushed back into his chair. "As if I could ever be that smart." He cocked his head to the side and studied her. "Do you ever wonder about it?"

"About us being a couple?" Grace asked and Curtis nodded. "We're too close to the same person—we'd spend too much time trying to out Type A the other person. It would not end well."

Curtis laughed. "You mean only one of us would survive?"

"Pretty much." Grace wanted to ask about Megan, they would make such a great couple, but she had learned to leave the subject alone. "Enough of this," she said, "tell me about this new venture."

"I didn't tell you because I just closed on the property two days ago—that's where I was this week. I wanted to surprise you with the news in person. I planned on telling you this morning and then . . ." he trailed off, waving his hands in the direction of the rooftop patio.

She'd shown up with Andrew. "Is Megan going with you?"

"Way to change the subject," he said, a smile tugging at the corners of his lips.

"Well, is she?" Grace said, undeterred.

He narrowed his eyes. "She's going with me to interview architects and contractors and begin the design process. Then she'll come back here for a while."

"And what then, chef?"

"Tell me about Mr. Tall, Dark and Deep Voice."

They sat and stared at each other in silence, neither willing to give up their secrets, until a voice behind them said, "I'm sorry to interrupt, Chef, but mise en place is complete for tomorrow. Is there anything else you need before I go?"

Curtis turned to his sous chef and Grace released a breath she didn't realize she was holding. "Did you move the beef stock from the freezer to the walk-in?'"

"Yes, Chef."

"Did you give Megan the specials for tomorrow?"

"She was already gone, so I laid them on her desk."

Curtis nodded. "I think you're good to go."

The young man nodded at Curtis and turned to Grace, running his eyes over her from head to toe. Clearly, another person thought he had finally caught a glimpse into Curtis' very private personal life. There'd be talk during food prep tomorrow, she was certain.

"Is he new?" Grace asked, as the sous chef retreated into the kitchen. "I don't remember him."

"New and highly talented. He's one of the main reasons I was able to think about expanding to the West Coast."

Grace nodded and tried, unsuccessfully, to stifle a yawn. Today had started early and been an emotional rollercoaster. "It's getting late Chef, and I have an early morning flight across the pond. I'm going to have to call it a night."

Curtis shook his head. "You're going back on tour. I thought that part of your life was over."

"Me, too."

"You're completely sure about this . . ."

"Not at all. But the decision has been made."

He rose from his barstool and offered her his hand. "Can I drive you back to your hotel?"

"I would love that." She slid off her stool and collected her handbag. They continued to chat about the restaurant and his hopes for the new venture as they walked to his car and drove through the ebony streets—still alive in a way that only New York City could muster.

When they reached the hotel, Grace grabbed him and pulled him into a hug. "I'm sorry this was such a short visit. I promise it will be longer next time."

"I hope so," he said, his eyes growing a little misty. "You're right, maybe I am a little nostalgic tonight. Must be age," he finished with a chuckle.

"Don't worry, your secret is safe with me. Nobody needs to know what a softie you really are."

"Can't let a single night ruin the reputation I've spent the last twenty years cultivating."

"Nope, can't have that," Grace said softly. "Talk soon?"

"Of course. And, Grace, about this guy. I saw the way he looked at you and . . ."

"Curtis," she said, warning tingeing the edge of her voice.

"I'm so happy to see you writing again, but I don't want you to get hurt. Another musician? Please be careful."

Grace let his words sink in. One friend encouraging her to take more risks, the other telling her to do just the opposite. Just like her body and her mind. "I appreciate your concern, I do, but I'm really just here to prove the critics wrong."

"The critics?"

"All the people who think I lost my muse . . . and buried my talent with him." *Including me.*

"Grace, I know his death broke you into pieces, but the talent? Honey, you had that long before Jax Jensen. I knew it and he knew it. It's still in you."

Curtis, no matter how infrequent they saw each other, had always been able to see into her soul and say exactly what she needed to hear. "I love you, Chef. I'll Skype from London, okay?"

"I love you, too. You're my family. I'll never stop worrying about you."

Grace nodded and slipped out of the car. She gave one quick wave before he signaled out into traffic.

Grace dropped her bag in the London hotel room with a thud. She rolled her neck one way, then the other, kneading the tight muscles. She could think of nothing but a hot shower and a soft bed—well, almost nothing else. She'd napped on the flight over, but dreams featuring none other than Andrew Hayes punctuated her sleep. What he had done to her in those dreams might not be legal in all fifty states. Parts of her tingled just thinking about it. God, she hoped she hadn't talked in her sleep—Nick and Blake had been in the row directly in front of her.

Unzipping her suitcase, she pulled out her shampoo and

pajamas and walked into the bathroom. She studied her face in the mirror. Should she stop fighting her attraction to Andrew? Give in and have the fling Annie suggested? Would it truly complicate everything?

She stepped into the shower and let the hot water wash away all thoughts of Andrew. Tomorrow was a new day; she'd deal with her feelings then. Or not.

Toweling off, she pulled an old sweatshirt over her head and wrapped her arms around her middle. It felt like a much-needed hug. She pulled back the crisp, white sheets of the king-sized bed just as her phone buzzed.

Are you there yet?

Grace counted back on her fingers. 5:00 p.m. at home. Annie would be wrapping up her workday.

In my room. Exhausted. Going to bed.

2 tired 2 talk?

Yes. Sorry. Looking forward to Skyping with you over Thanksgiving weekend.

Grace set her alarm and fell back into the pillows. Sleep couldn't come soon enough.

The alarm blared at 7:00 a.m. and Grace groaned, her body screaming it was the middle of the night in the States. Jet lag got harder and harder the older she got.

After dressing, she checked the time on her phone. Almost two hours before Andrew was due to arrive for their arranged work time. Plenty of time for breakfast and coffee. Lots and lots of coffee.

"Good morning," an elderly gentleman said to Grace as she boarded the elevator. "Lobby?"

Grace nodded and managed a garbled "Thank you" before breaking into a yawn.

"Come across the pond yesterday?" he asked, in a crisp British accent.

"Is it that obvious?"

"If the yawn didn't give you away, the accent did," he said, his eyes twinkling. The lift arrived at the main floor and the man held the door open for Grace. "Enjoy your stay."

"I'm going to give it my best shot."

"Interesting answer."

"Interesting trip," Grace said. At the concierge desk, she asked for directions to the nearest restaurant serving breakfast—and coffee.

"Are you with Storyhill?" he asked.

"Yes," Grace responded, surprised. "How did you know?"

"Couple of American blokes came down earlier, introduced themselves, and sounded just as desperate for a cuppa as you."

Grace laughed.

"I sent them to the cafe around the corner, perhaps you'd like to join them?"

"That would be lovely," she responded, hoping that Andrew would not be up this early. She'd be ready to face him—and all the strange feelings he'd been stirring up—after her coffee. The concierge gave her directions and encouraged her to enjoy the day—a rare November day in London—fifty degrees and sunny.

The buzz of early morning commuters filled the air as Grace stepped outside the hotel. She melded into the flow of people headed to work, most navigating the throng while looking down at their phones. She turned left at the corner and spotted the orange and yellow awning the concierge described.

Pushing open the door, smells of freshly baked bread and pastries washed over her. With walls painted in a sunny yellow and the chairs covered in cheerful chintz, the interior was a pleasing juxtaposition to the brick, stone, and cement of the city streets. The small brass bell announcing her arrival took the cafe from cute to charming. As amazing as the cakes, croissants, and crullers looked, she needed something a bit more substantial.

"Menu?" a tiny gray-haired woman asked from behind the counter, as if reading her mind.

"The waffle is quite good," a vaguely familiar voice called.

Grace turned her head toward the sound and, there in the corner, sat Joe, Blake, and Julia, all waving at her.

She placed her order at the counter and walked over to them. "Can I join you?"

"Of course," Joe answered, pulling out the chair on his right. "You're one of us now—whether you want to be or not. You're always welcome."

"It is so cute in here," Grace said to the group. "Is the food good—outside of the waffle, of course?" she asked, gesturing to their near-empty plates. They all nodded. "Coffee not so good?" she asked, pointing to an abandoned cup.

"That's mine," came a deep voice from behind her. The hair on the back of her neck stood up and her nipples tightened. Her traitorous body registered who it was before her brain caught up. She fought the urge to suck in a giant breath and inhale the delicious scent that could only be Andrew Hayes.

Andrew slid around the corner of the table and lowered himself into the empty chair directly across from her.

"Up two days in a row for breakfast. That must be some kind of record for you," she said, unable to look directly at him.

Joe cocked an eyebrow and shot a look at Andrew. "We lured him with the promise of black coffee and bacon."

"Despite those washboard abs, Andrew's never met a plate of bacon he didn't like," Blake added, elbowing Andrew in the ribs.

Her gaze fell to Andrew's chest and her fingers tingled. She could still feel the way his muscles twitched under her hands as he'd pulled her close on Curtis' rooftop. Grace ducked her head to hide the heat creeping into her cheeks. When she glanced back up, Andrew was staring at her over the top of his coffee cup.

She was in so much trouble.

Joe swiveled his eyes between them, a flash of a smile darting across his lips. "You two writing today?"

"Just as soon as Grace finishes her coffee. Don't make me tell you how much of a nightmare she is before she's caffeinated."

"Charming," Grace said, leaning back in her chair as the server delivered her breakfast.

"It's the way he flirts," Blake said with a laugh.

"And yet, the ladies love him. Apparently 'coarse and grumpy' is a type," Julia said, biting back a smile. "Be careful Grace, I've been told he's irresistible."

"By him?" Grace said, and laughter filled the corner booth.

Grace paced the length of her suite, flopped into the wingback chair in the corner, crossed her legs, uncrossed them and hopped up to straighten the pencils and paper on the coffee table—again.

She'd quickly eaten her breakfast and excused herself from the restaurant, telling Andrew she'd meet him back here. Where was he? And why was her pulse racing?

"Why?" she asked the empty room.

The empty room had nothing to say.

She yanked her gray-cabled cardigan off the arm of the sofa, slinging her arms into it. She leaned down to zip up her boots and nearly hit her head on the coffee table as three loud raps sounded through the steel door.

She pulled her hair out from underneath the collar of her sweater, gave it a fluff and took a few shaky steps toward the door. Her hand stilled on the handle as she drew in a deep breath and pulled it open.

Andrew was standing across the hall, leaning up against the wall. There were only three words to describe this man—Sexy As Hell or maybe, Trouble In Pants, either worked.

"Nice shirt. I didn't notice it this morning. I find bacon highly distracting," he said.

She looked down at the tee peeking out from under her sweater and chuckled. It was last year's Christmas present from Curtis and Megan. White script popped off the black cotton announcing one of the more salient points of her personality: *'Classy, but I cuss a little.'*

"A gift," she said, pulling at the hem of the shirt, "from friends that know me a little too well."

"Let me guess. Curtis?" Andrew stared at her for a long beat before pushing himself off the wall and walking past her into the suite. Her eyes dropped to his butt. She tried not to stare but failed miserably.

"See something you like?" he asked, without turning around.

How did he do that?

"My ass is one of my better features."

"I'm sorry, did you just say you're acting like an ass?"

Andrew snorted and made his way over to the spot where Grace had laid out the pencils and pulled several pieces of folded paper out of his back pocket, dropping them on the table. "I'm ready," he said, sliding into the sofa, "are you?" He looked up into her eyes and they shared a long look.

"Almost."

He cocked an eyebrow at her.

Grace flushed. He'd asked her a loaded question, and she'd answered with the truth. "I'm going to make a quick call to

Room Service and order some coffee and then we can get started."

Resting the phone back in the receiver, she chose the chair opposite him—no need to tempt fate. Grace opened the Garage-Band app and they plunked away for hours, agreeing on changes to the melodies, effortlessly smoothing out the rough spots. Somewhere in the process, she had moved from the chair to the couch, their thighs touching as they leaned over the computer.

"Can I use your restroom?" he asked, stretching his arms over his head, giving Grace a small peek of the rippled abs below his t-shirt.

"Through the French doors." She straightened the sheet music in front of her, trying to avert her eyes, but damn, if she couldn't stop herself from looking up and watching him leave—and return. He was saying something to her, but she was too distracted to know what. She lifted her gaze to his face with an expression of confusion.

"You with me, Grace?" The corners of his mouth lifted upward.

"Could you repeat what you just said?"

"You seem distracted." A full smile played on his lips.

"How am I supposed to concentrate with you in those jeans?" Shit. She really needed to get more sleep or a new filter for her mouth—probably both.

"You want me to get rid of them?"

"Yes."

Andrew flashed a wicked smile and popped open the button on his pants.

"No! We're working."

He slowed for a moment and pushed his glasses back into his hair. "Are you saying that if we weren't working . . ." He played with the pull on his zipper, flicking it up and down.

"No. I am not saying that." She dropped her head into her hands and leaned forward, bracing her forearms on her legs.

He laughed and stepped up in front of her. "How about this instead? We've worked really hard this morning, how about we go out and explore London this afternoon?"

She peered through her fingers, making sure she saw denim and not skin. "Okay."

"C'mon, Grace, everyone else has already left and you need to get out . . . wait, did you just say 'yes'?"

"Yes," she said, a laugh bubbling out of her.

"But I had this whole argument planned. And, a warning."

"A warning?"

"Yep, I want to do all the cheesy tourist stuff—Big Ben, Buckingham Palace, 10 Downing Street, the London Eye. I even have the appropriate clothing." He pulled his hoodie over his head revealing a t-shirt emblazoned with the Union Jack.

"Classy," she said. "When did you have time to get that? Is that why you were late getting back here this morning?"

Andrew smirked and winked. "Maybe. You ready to go?"

"On two conditions."

Andrew cocked an eyebrow.

"No fighting and you must take off that ridiculous shirt."

"You want me to take my shirt off right here?" he said, inching the hem of the t-shirt over the waistband of his jeans.

"First the pants, now the shirt? You having a hard time keeping your clothes on, Cowboy?"

Heat blazed in his eyes. "On or off, Grace?"

"On. Do not take anything off. I couldn't handle all that sexiness so close to me." It was out of her mouth before she could stop it.

"You think I'm sexy?" he asked, his voice settling into its low rasp.

"Please, you have women telling you you're sexy all the

time. How long after puberty did it take for you to realize the power of that voice?"

He smiled and shrugged his shoulders. "Didn't realize it right away. Might have taken a day or two." Grace snorted and rolled her eyes. "Took me from a shy, scrawny kid with enormous ears to middle school stud in the time it took me to say, 'Looking good, ladies.'"

"Humble."

"You didn't answer my question," he said, his smile softening.

"Yes, Andrew, I think you're sexy. I'm old, not dead. There, are you happy?"

"Very," he said, pushing his hair back from his face, mimicking a supermodel.

"Let's not push it," she said, putting her hands on her hips. "Now, are you going to change or not?"

"I'll be back in ten minutes. And Grace," he said, as he turned toward the door, "for the record, you're sexy, too—and not old."

CHAPTER TEN

"First stop, lunch?" Andrew asked as they cleared the hotel's revolving door. The sun pierced the clouds creating shadows across the pavement and casting Grace in a warm, golden glow. Every moment he spent with her had him craving more. He wanted to know everything about her. What she liked, what scared her, what was still on her bucket list, and how she managed to pour her soul into the songs written in that pretty blue journal.

"You up for a little walk?" she asked, pulling him from his thoughts.

"What'd you have in mind?"

"Some friends suggested a pub, but it's about a twenty-minute hike."

"I'm game." Hell, he'd have gone to Scotland with her, if that's what she wanted. "You going to be warm enough in that jacket?" He ran his hands over her shoulders. He couldn't possibly be the only one who felt the shock of electricity that surged between them the moment they touched. Could he? *Look at me, Grace*, he willed, *let me see your eyes. Show me I'm not the only one feeling this way.*

"Andrew!" Grace yelled, grabbing his hand and pulling him toward her. His head snapped around and he jumped toward her to avoid an on-coming bicycle.

"Thanks," he said, wrapping his arm around her waist. "That will get the heart pumping." Though he suspected his racing pulse had more to do with the woman in his arms than the wayward bicycle.

She spun out of his grasp and stepped to the side. "New plan. I'll watch the map and you watch for bikes."

"Sounds good."

"I think the pub is this way." She consulted her phone and pointed to the left. She expertly navigated them through a sidewalk full of wandering tourists and businesspeople scurrying back to work, hands full of takeaway bags.

"Have you been here before?"

She sighed. "I've been everywhere."

"You say that like it's a bad thing."

"I don't mean to sound ungrateful. It's just after decades of 'world tours'"—she flexed her fingers into air quotes—"the cities and countries started to blur together. And, so many times we only saw the world's great sites from the window of a hotel room." She waved her hand in front of her. "Ignore me. I sound like a spoiled brat."

"I guess not everything is as glamorous as it appears."

"Meaning?"

"Meaning, the press makes it seem that celebrities have these perfect lives. But, I'm guessing, the truth is a lot more complicated."

"Please don't misunderstand. I loved my life . . ."

"But?"

"But, much of the time, it was like running a never-ending marathon. More than once, I asked him to walk away—we certainly had enough money—but he fed off the music and fame. When we got his diagnosis . . ." She sucked in a deep breath. "I can't believe I'm admitting this, it makes me sound like a horrible person. A tiny little part of me was grateful for the disease. For eleven months, it was just me and him—no red carpets, no bright lights, no demands. I was so certain that he'd beat it that I greedily took the time. When I started to under-stand it was taking him, I felt so guilty. I'm a terrible person, aren't I? I'd give up all that time for the outcome to be different."

"You are not a terrible person. None of us know how we'll react in a situation like that," he said, pulling her into a hug, resting his head on hers. "I'm sorry for your loss. I don't think I've ever told you that."

She nodded into his chest, unwound herself from his arms, and started down the sidewalk. Andrew ached for the warmth of her body tucked against his. That was the second time in the last few minutes she had pulled away from him. "Does it bother you when I touch you?"

A smirk pulled at the corners of her mouth. "Not used to women being able to resist you?"

"Do you deflect all questions you don't want to answer with a joke?"

"Yep," she said, popping the 'p' and turning her attention back to her phone.

"Grace, do you not like it?" he asked, undeterred.

"Just the opposite actually," she said to her phone, barely over a whisper. "I'm scared of how much I like it." Her honest admission shot straight through him. How could a few words excite him so much?

"New subject," she said, without raising her head. "Why a career in music? Performing is not an easy choice, for so many reasons."

"Singing was just something I did. I never thought about making it a career until college. People—well, not people, just my father—convinced me that going to college was the right thing to do, that the odds of making it in this business were a zillion to one. He had a series of arguments on repeat. His favorite was, 'You're a Hayes and Hayes men do not fritter away their lives on flights of fancy'." Andrew screwed up his face and mimed straightening a tie. "And insults disguised as compliments, like, 'Andrew, you're too smart to throw it all away on music'."

"Really? Too smart?" she teased, elbowing him in the ribs.

"You don't have to sound so surprised," he retorted with a wide grin. "I enrolled at Vanderbilt to major in biomedical or chemical engineering, but after three semesters, my heart wasn't in it.

"Instead of studying, I'd find myself at a bar singing karaoke or sneaking off to clubs to hear new acts. I realized that I'd chosen Vanderbilt because it was in Nashville, rather than what it offered academically."

She nodded and silently directed them left at the corner.

"So, I quit. I couldn't justify paying tuition if I wasn't giving one hundred percent." When was the last time he'd talked with someone like this? Likely never. He'd never told anyone why he chose Vanderbilt, not even Joe.

"We're here," Grace said, pointing up to a white stucco building covered in the remnants of summer flowers.

"The Mayflower," Andrew said, reading the gold letters popping off the black trim perched atop the large windows.

"This is where the Mayflower and her crew set sail for Plymouth, or so I'm told. Apparently, it's the oldest pub on the Thames and has a great view of London Bridge—which, I believe, is on your list of cheesy tourist attractions."

"That's right," he said, looking down at her. She'd remembered. He opened the door for her, and they took in the nautical-themed decor and the taxidermy covering the walls. "Joe would love this place," he said, his gaze darting from one ship model to the next.

"Because he's a fan of drunken sailors?"

Andrew laughed from his belly. "Not exactly what I was going to say, but let's go with that."

Grace marveled at the small, dark pub, taking in the rich colored walls, all but buried under framed artwork of all shapes and sizes. Above the central fireplace, a deer head topped with a sequined Santa hat served as a simple reminder that the holidays were fast approaching. Nailed below the festive taxidermy was a battered piece of wood stenciled with the words, 'A warm hearth and fine wine soothes the soul and passes time.'

They slid into a small table near the diamond-patterned leaded glass windows facing the river and Grace snuck a look at Andrew. If she was honest with herself, as much as this man pushed every last one of her buttons and sent her hormones from still water to roiling boil in 60-seconds flat, he also, oddly, soothed her soul.

"Are you ready to order?" the server asked. The young woman flashed a bright smile at Andrew, ignoring Grace.

"I'm going full-on American tourist and ordering the fish and chips," Andrew said, running his finger down the plastic-coated menu.

"I'm sure they're delicious, but I will mock you."

He chuckled. "I'd expect nothing less."

Grace smiled and stared into his green eyes. It was surreal to be back in London and looking across the table at a man who wasn't Jax. Who was she kidding? She and Jax would never have been able to sit in the middle of a restaurant, especially one that attracted tourists, without being mobbed. She peered at

Andrew. He'd invited her to lunch, not her *and* Jax. It was time to pack away the Specters of Tours Past and focus on the here and now. He deserved her full attention.

"I might need to share your fish and chips," Grace said, watching the waitress walk back to the kitchen. "I'm not sure she heard me over all the giggling and hair flipping."

"Jealous?" he said, cocking an eyebrow.

"Yes, I never really did master the hair flip."

"There you go again, ignoring my questions."

"A girl's gotta go with her strengths. So, did your parents eventually support your decision?"

"What?" Andrew asked, crinkling his brow.

Grace laughed. "That was an abrupt subject change. You were saying your parents weren't happy when you decided to quit college and sing for your supper."

"Oh," he said, nodding, the corners of his mouth pulling down, "my mother eventually came around, but my father, not so much. He blew a gasket when I quit, and we ended up saying some things that we can never take back—and neither of us has apologized."

"I'm sorry." She placed her hand over the top of his and watched sadness fill his eyes. She suddenly understood his writing. Understood why he held back, never diving too deep into his feelings. His relationship with his father kept him guarded—and it affected his songs. Did anyone else notice? She'd become an expert at faking happiness, and she guessed he had too. The pain in his eyes hurt her soul.

"I think I should talk to your father."

Andrew cocked a single eyebrow. "Because?"

"Because giving you a hard time is my job, and it's a responsibility I don't care to share with anyone."

He laughed and the sadness was replaced with a smile. A

real smile. One that met his eyes and melted Grace's heart just a little more.

Heat darted through her body, but this time it wasn't lust. It was something far more frightening. It was a sense of comfort and a feeling of safety and . . . hope.

Hope. A feeling so foreign, she almost didn't recognize it. Lust could be dealt with—even without his help. Hope was something else entirely. Hope could crush a fragile heart in an instant. Fear's icy fingers wrapped around her torso, squeezing the air from her lungs. She eyed the door.

No, she'd look like a lunatic if she got up now, before the food even came, insisting she needed to get back to the hotel. What had they been talking about?

"Is that when you formed the group? When you left college?" She grabbed the edge of the table and pushed until her spine met the back of the booth. Maybe she should have ordered a beer with lunch.

"No, I started performing on my own, just me and a guitar. I sang anywhere someone would let me and a few places that didn't. One night, at this seedy little bar, I met Nick and Blake. They were toying with the idea of putting together an *a cappella* group and needed a bass. They approached me after I finished my set and, long story short, I agreed to give it a try if they would give country a try."

"Didn't want to spend your life singing pop covers?"

"Country harmonies are my first love, but it was really a marketing decision. No one in the country world was doing the *a cappella* thing, not seriously anyway, and I thought the road to success would be easier."

"I'm afraid I may have underestimated you again, Mr. Hayes. There *is* more to you than simply being incredibly sexy."

Andrew snorted and Grace got very interested in the cocktail menu propped on the edge of the table. He didn't say anything, and she looked up to find his smile widening as red crept up her neck and onto her cheeks.

"You're really hung up on my sexiness."

"No more than you are," she said, chin jutting out.

"Your fish and chips, sir," the waitress said. With her back to Grace, she gave Andrew a million-watt smile. "Can I get you anything else? And by anything," she leaned in close, sliding his plate toward him, "I mean *an-y-thing.*"

"How about getting my date's meal?" he said, motioning to Grace. The server turned toward Grace, acting surprised to still see her sitting there. She gave him a slight eye roll and slumped off toward the kitchen.

"I didn't realize this was a date," Grace said after the waitress moved out of earshot.

"Not a date, just two people having lunch—who agree that I'm extremely sexy."

The waitress returned and dropped Grace's entree in front of her while winking at Andrew. Subtle.

"Are Joe and Matt original members of Storyhill, as well?"

"So, we're done talking about my sexiness then?"

"Well, I am, but the waitress seems more than willing to continue that conversation with you."

"I'm not interested in chatting up anyone but you, darlin'."

Grace rolled her eyes. "Joe and Matt?"

"Joe and I met in the first grade and have been friends ever since."

That explained why he called him Andy.

"He was always messing around with beat boxing, and I convinced him to see what he could really do with it."

"Obviously, that was a good hunch. That man can do amazing things with his mouth." Andrew raised one eyebrow at her. Grace flushed. "That came out wrong. You know what I mean."

Andrew laughed and continued. "Mattie's not an original member. Our first high tenor sang with us for about three years before leaving."

"Went solo?"

"Got married and had twins. Decided the time away from home was too much. We knew, at that point, we needed to replace him with someone who dripped country sound—to really solidify our position—and we found Mattie on YouTube, believe it or not."

"Rounding out your own little band of Village People."

"I'm sorry?"

"You know, the group from the '70s? The Village People? YMCA," Grace said, miming the letters.

"I know who the Village People are, but I'm not sure how they pertain to us."

"You don't see it?" Grace asked.

Andrew squinted and tipped his head. "Enlighten me."

"Well, there's Matt, the Rhinestone Cowboy, with his tight jeans, giant belt buckle, cowboy boots, and all that bling. And, Nick, with his whole lumber-sexual thing—beard, plaid shirt, stoic expression—he only needs a giant ax thrown over one shoulder to complete the character."

Andrew chuckled. "What about Joe and Blake? Who are they in this scenario?"

Grace pursed her lips and thought for a moment. "Can't you picture Blake in a corner office, legs propped up on a big desk, with his bespoke jackets, Italian loafers and perfectly styled auburn hair? Let's call him 'Bull Market Blake.' And, Joe, he's your classic bad boy—black leather jacket, white t-shirt, aviators . . . crazy post-sex hair."

Andrew choked and looked over the top of his glass at Grace, shaking his head. "You've really given this some thought." Grace shrugged her shoulders. "Wait until I tell Joe you think he's good with his mouth *and* he's got perma-post-coital hair."

"Don't you dare!" Grace said, swatting his hand with her napkin and shoving two more chips into her mouth. "Are you always this difficult?"

"Pretty much."

"Okay, then tell me this. Has it all been worth it?"

"Being difficult?"

Grace shot him a look. "No, quitting college? Traveling all the time? Getting ultimatums from everyone's favorite music executive?"

He twisted his lips and rubbed the back of his neck. "It's not been easy, but in my gut, I know this is what I'm meant to do. Though, fewer emails from Ford and a few less job listing texts from my father would make things a whole lot better." He dropped his gaze to his plate and pushed around the last of his chips with his knife. "Thank you for helping Storyhill. I don't think I could do it without you."

Her eyes popped wide and her mouth dropped open.

He laid the knife down and smiled at her. "Stunned silence from Grace O'Connor? Wonders never cease."

"That sounded suspiciously like a compliment."

"It is."

"So, I'm not all washed up?"

He winced. "I'm sorry about that comment. I was just so frustrated"—he looked up, meeting her eyes—"and, honestly, scared out of my mind. I may never be able to apologize to my father, but I can say I'm sorry to you. Can you forgive me?"

Grace gasped and clutched her chest. "Did that hurt?"

He frowned, concern creeping into his gaze. "Did what hurt?"

Her eyes danced mischievously. "Complimenting me and apologizing at the same time? Though I can't help but wonder if this is your latest attempt to get rid of me. You know, killing me with kindness?"

He leaned across the table, his face inches from hers. "Is it working?"

"I think it might be. You're kind of freaking me out."

Andrew threw his head back and laughed. "Wish I knew in the beginning that compliments, rather than insults, were your undoing." His smile softened and he ran a single finger over her knuckles. "I wouldn't have waited this long to tell you that you took away my ability to think straight the instant I spilled my coffee on you."

"At least you're finally admitting it was *you* that spilled on *me*."

"Ignoring the last compliment?"

"Yep. In self-preservation mode right now."

"Fine," he said, clearly enjoying watching her squirm. "What's next?"

"How about the London Eye and Big Ben? Though it's a little too far to walk from here. What if we try and find one of those red double-decker buses? Seems like something that should be on your 'cheesy tourist' list."

"Only if we can sit on the top deck."

"It'll be cold."

"I'll keep you warm," he said, letting his gaze wash over her.

With looks like that, you already do. "Okay," she croaked.

He drained the last of his pint. "London Eye, here we come."

The delicious warmth drained from Grace's body as Andrew raised the arm encircling the back of her seat and pointed at the transit map. "If we get off there, we can check out the Globe

Theater and then walk along the river to the Eye. You up for that? It's about a mile."

"That's part of the Queen's Walk," Grace said, nodding. "Great idea."

He let his arm fall back behind her. "Now it's your turn."

"For what?"

"I've told you all about me. What's Grace O'Connor's life story?"

How much should she tell him? Having lived in the public eye for so long people thought they knew everything about her, her life, her marriage. The truth was hardly as interesting as the things people imagined. She turned her head toward him and shrugged her shoulders. "You already know the basics. Songwriter. Married to Jax Jensen. Yada, yada, yada."

"I'd like to know more than the basics. Did you go to college for songwriting?"

"Mostly. USC Thornton School of Music for Vocal Performance and Composition."

"Vocal Performance, huh?"

"You trying to pick a fight, Cowboy?"

He tipped his head back and laughed a deep belly laugh. "Just trying to get to know you better."

"Ask something else."

"Okay, how did you get started in the business?"

Grace flipped through the tourist information brochure she'd picked up in the lobby of the Mayflower, causing the hair on her forehead to flutter. She tapped the back of it and sighed. "The great Jax Jensen discovered me."

"You submitted a song?"

"You'd think, but no. Long story short, a friend majoring in visual art asked me to write poetry to accompany his senior show paintings. He was a childhood friend of Jax's. Jax was at the show, introduced himself, said the poetry read like song lyrics and would I like to work with him on a couple of pieces." Grace shrugged. "The rest is history."

"That's a great story."

"Yeah, amazing," she deadpanned.

His brow furrowed and concern tinged his normally bright eyes. "It's not amazing?"

She used to think so. Now she spent far too much time wondering where she would be without that chance encounter. Could she have made it on her own? She'd never know. Unshed tears burned behind her eyes. Dammit, she was not going to cry. "This is our stop, Cowboy."

They disembarked and Andrew turned to her. "I didn't mean to upset you."

"It's not you." When he gave her a suspicious look, she added, "Really."

"Okay," he said, uncertainty running through the single word. He gave her one final look before reaching down and taking her hand. "This okay?" He gave their hands a shake.

"If it makes you feel better about not getting lost on the mean streets of London, I guess I can handle it."

"My protector," he said, placing his free hand over his heart.

"I do what I can."

Andrew laughed and guided her through the people strolling along the cobblestone walkway, sidestepping the sea of artists painting and selling their pieces. He ran his hand along the iron railing skirting the river, dropping it to his side each time they passed the ornate lampposts that rose toward the sky. The lamps flanked the right side of the sidewalk and bare trees strung with twinkle lights flanked the left.

"It's beautiful at night," Grace said, reading his thoughts. "The sun sets at about 4:00 this time of year. We should come back before returning to the hotel."

"I'm scared of the dark," he said, a slight grin playing at the corners of his mouth.

"So, I'll have to hold your hand again?"

"Exactly."

She laughed, marveling at how much she was enjoying this time with him. His touch was natural, comfortable, and she found herself craving more. What if they did explore their chemistry? *You're allowed to have a fling, Grace.* Annie's voice played in her head.

"There's the Eye." Andrew pointed to the giant structure.

She pulled her attention back to the present and focused on what looked like a Ferris wheel on steroids. "Did you know it had to be built on its side and lifted into place?"

They walked up to the long line snaking through the ticket area and slipped into the queue. "What other little-known facts do you have up your sleeve?"

She tapped her chin. "It's the fourth tallest structure in London."

"Remind me to make sure you're on my team on trivia night."

Grace laughed and nodded. "I think we'd make a good team."

"We already do," he said, scanning her face, lingering on her lips a little too long. He ran a finger along her temple, tracing her hairline. She shivered and her eyes fluttered closed. A warmth pooled in her belly and settled low.

"Next," the ticket seller called, causing them both to jump.

"That's us," Andrew said, placing his hand on the small of her back and guiding her toward the ticket booth.

"Do you have any tickets left for today?" Grace asked the man behind the glass.

"It's your lucky day, even with the sunshine, not as many people want to ride on the cold days."

Thirty minutes later, they stepped into a pod with a group of about twenty people. On their right stood an elderly couple from Germany with cameras strapped around their necks and too many questions about American politics. A young French couple on their honeymoon stood on the left.

"How long have you been married?" the young man asked.

"Oh, no, we're not married," Grace answered hastily. "We're colleagues on a business trip."

"Oh, pity," the woman said, "you should be a couple, you're both *tres jolie . . .* so beau . . . *quel est le mot Anglais?*" she asked, turning to her husband.

"Beautiful," he said, grabbing her hand and placing a delicate kiss on her cheek. She wrapped her arms around his middle and they turned away from Andrew and Grace, moving closer to the glass.

"At least she didn't say 'sexy'," Andrew whispered into Grace's ear.

Grace snorted. "Just watch out the window."

The rare, sunny day delivered unparalleled views—down the Thames nearly to Windsor Castle. As Buckingham Palace and Big Ben came into view, Andrew stepped up behind her. Her back was flush with the hard planes of his chest. The smell of him filled her nostrils and hunger exploded through her.

He brushed her hair aside and whispered in her ear. "Check two more things off the cheesy tourist list."

Everyone else in the pod faded away, along with the last remnants of her resolve. She shuddered and squeezed her eyes shut when he wrapped his arms around her waist and placed a single, soft kiss atop her head. She'd forgotten how much she loved to be enveloped in someone's arms. How was it possible to feel completely protected and totally aroused at the same time?

"What is happening?" Grace whispered, to herself or him, she didn't know.

"Hell if I know. I only know that I can't stop it. No matter how hard I try. What if we just gave in to it, Grace? What if we explored this thing happening between us?"

She turned into him and placed a hand on the center of his chest. His words perfectly echoing her earlier thoughts. "Andrew . . ."

"Hey, are you Andrew Hayes?"

Grace jerked her head toward the intruding voice. She'd forgotten they were still in public. She took a step back and sucked in a steadying breath.

"You are. You're Andrew Hayes," said a thin man with a beard that hovered just above his chest. "I'm taking my wife to your concert on Saturday. Think I could get a selfie? She'd go nuts."

"Um," Andrew said, glancing at Grace. "Is it okay, Gracie?"

"Of course," she said unnaturally bright. What was one more moment of cameras, selfies, and fans in a lifetime filled with them?

CHAPTER ELEVEN

Andrew's fingers tightened around Grace's as they squeezed between the wings of the hotel's revolving door. The risk of her circling through the entrance and exiting out the other side felt all too possible. Every small step she took toward him was quickly followed by a giant leap back.

Not that either of them were short on reasons for why their relationship should stay strictly professional. But today, while standing in the Eye with his arms wrapped around her, he'd officially run out of excuses.

He couldn't deny it any longer. He wanted her—no matter the cost.

He wanted to write with her, and more than that, he wanted her in his bed, under him, hearing her cry out his name. But how to figure out if that's what she wanted to?

"I'm hungry, but too tired to go back out," he said, once they were in the elevator. "Want to order room service with me?"

"In your room?" Grace squeaked.

Andrew tucked a lock of hair behind her ear and he let his gaze fall to her mouth. His heart thumped once, twice, against his ribs and he rubbed the heel of his hand against his chest to soothe the unfamiliar feeling. "That is generally how it works."

She leaned back and gripped the metal bar at the back of the elevator, knuckles whitening from the pressure. The heat swirled between them in the small space. Her gaze bounced from floor to wall to wall before finally landing on him. "Thank you, Andrew. But I'm tired. How about a rain check?"

He sighed. Cue the giant leap backward. "Okay but come with me so we can sort out our souvenirs." He exited the lift and turned toward his room. He held out a hand to her. "I think I have a few of your things in my bags."

She didn't take his hand, but she nodded and followed him down the hall. He slid his key card through the reader, opened the door, and ushered her in. Setting the plastic bags on the bed, he rummaged through them, pulling out a Big Ben teapot and a box of shortbread cookies with the Buckingham Palace coat of arms emblazoned on the front.

"Any of these yours?" he asked, holding up a die-cast replica of a K2 telephone box.

Her furrowed brow was replaced with a smile tugging up the corners of her lips. "Um, no. What are you going to do with all of those, um, super classy souvenirs?"

"Are you judging me?"

"Without a doubt."

"I suppose these very posh Vera Wang napkin rings and this eco-friendly Stella McCartney bag are yours?"

Grace opened her bag for him to drop the items in. "Are you judging me?" she asked, biting back the smile that was quickly becoming one of his favorite things.

If he lived to be a hundred, he'd never get over the way her smile settled in his chest, all warm and gooey, filling all the cracks and crevices that years of loneliness had left in its wake.

"Yes, you're going to be sorry when you get home and you

don't have one of these very special, not-limited-edition, Sherlock Holmes pub signs."

She laughed and reached out to touch the sign, but he caught her hand and pulled her into his chest. Screw being tentative. It wasn't his style. When he wanted something, he made it happen. "I had a good time today."

"Me, too," she breathed out.

Reaching his hand up to her face, he ran his finger down her cheek and across her chin. Her skin felt like silk under his touch. He dipped his head and felt her breath hitch. He pressed his lips to the tender area directly below her ear. She shuddered and her eyes drifted shut and flew open when a knock sounded at the door.

"You should probably see who that is," she said, pulling back slightly but not breaking his stare.

He ran his finger over the pulse point at the base of her neck, feeling its rapid beat. "Ignore it," he said, pushing his fingers into her hair.

"Andy, I know you're in there," a familiar voice yelled from the opposite side of the door. "I saw you get on the elevator."

Joe. For a beat boxer, he sure had a screwed-up sense of timing.

"Afraid you're busted." She pushed him back with a single finger to the chest.

He caught it and nipped it lightly. "We're not done here," he said, placing his thumb on her chin and giving it a little squeeze, "not even close."

Andrew moved toward the door, pulling at his jeans, trying to shake out the evidence of how much she excited him. Thankfully, Joe didn't usually spend a lot of time looking at his crotch.

"Yes?" Andrew said, opening the door a few inches.

Joe pushed the door open the rest of the way and ambled into the room. "There's a surprise arriving for you shortly. It's coming up in the elevator as we speak, and I don't —" He stopped short when he saw Grace leaning against the media console. "Oh hey, Grace," Joe said. "Didn't expect to see you here." In less than a heartbeat, his eyes went wide and he swiveled his head between the two of them. "I'd like to say I'm sorry for interrupting, but I'm not. Sorry, that is."

"You're not interrupting," Grace said.

"Yes, he is," Andrew said, shooting a glare at Joe. He wanted to push Joe out of the room—forcefully—and haul her back into his arms and finish what they started until they were both naked and sated, but she was already gathering her things and moving toward the door.

Grace gave him a long look before turning to Joe. "I was just leaving. See you both tomorrow—for Thanksgiving, all London-style."

He wrapped his fingers around her elbow. "Grace, I didn't think we were done . . . sorting out souvenirs."

She gave him a single, silent stare. One he'd quickly learned meant, 'Don't play your games with me.'

He sighed. "Fine, let me get the door for you." He crossed the room in two long strides, opened the door, and stepped directly in front of her. She bumped up against his back causing him to lurch forward, nearly tumbling into the two women standing on the other side of the threshold.

A familiar bubble of apprehension burst in his belly, sending a shot of acid into his throat. "Mom? Bridget?"

The older of the two women arched an eyebrow at Andrew, a look she'd been perfecting since his childhood, and stepped around him into the room.

"What are you doing here?"

His mother opened her mouth and then closed it, catching sight of Grace. She slowly held her hand out to her. "I'm Sylvia Hayes, Andrew's mother. You must be Grace O'Connor."

Grace shot him a furtive glance before placing her hand in his mother's. "Yes. Nice to meet you?"

Andrew stepped up behind Grace, placing a protective hand on her shoulder. He heard the question in her voice and echoed the sentiment.

How in the hell did his mother know about Grace?

Bridget.

He launched a glare in her direction, and she had the nerve to simply shrug her shoulders in a what-can-you-do manner. Bridget cleared her throat.

"That is my little sister, Bridget. Now tell me, what are you doing here? And how did you get my room number?"

Sylvia glanced, almost imperceptibly, toward Joe. Great, now he'd have to deal with both Bridget and Joe.

"We came to see your concert, of course," his mother replied with a wave of her hand.

"Mom." Andrew cocked an eyebrow. "What are you really doing here?" He could feel Grace's gaze bouncing from him to his mother and back again.

"Fine. I have a conference that starts tomorrow, and Bridget is here on a scouting trip. But we do have tickets for Saturday's concert."

"You have a conference that starts on Thanksgiving Day?"

"It's not Thanksgiving here, Andy," Bridget said, pushing past her mother and wrapping Andrew in a hug. "It's almost like you aren't happy to see us." She gave Andrew a conspiratorial wink, away from their mother's gaze.

"Bridget and I are going to freshen up and then we're taking you to dinner," his mother announced.

Andrew narrowed his eyes. "Why?"

"For god's sake, Andy, lighten up. It's just dinner," Bridget said, shaking her head, "there's no ulterior motive. We left Dad at home."

"Thirty minutes, Andrew. We'll meet you in the lobby. Joey, feel free to come if you want," Sylvia said over her shoulder, moving back out of the room.

"Thank you, Mrs. Hayes, but Julia and I have a quiet evening planned."

"And, Grace," Sylvia said, "nice to finally meet you." She tucked her handbag closer to her body and turned out of the room.

"Now aren't you glad I interrupted?" Joe said after the women left.

Andrew fisted his hand in his hair and dropped to the edge of the bed. He didn't want to have dinner with his mother and sister. He wanted to have dinner with Grace. Alone.

Wait. *Grace.* Yes.

"Gracie," he said, rising from the bed, taking her hands in his. "Come with me to dinner. Please."

Grace laughed. "You need me to protect you from your own mother and sister?"

"Yes. Unequivocally, yes. Say you'll do it. Please."

"I wasn't invited."

"I'm inviting you."

"Christ, Grace, how can you say no to that sad, pathetic puppy dog face?" Joe said, his lips twitching.

"Fine, I'll go. But you owe me. Big."

"Anything. You want my Big Ben teapot?" he asked, picking it up from the bed.

"It's going to take a lot more than that, Cowboy."

He pulled her in close and whispered, "I can think of all kinds of ways to show my appreciation."

"Gah," Joe said, screwing up his face. "I'd say 'get a room,' but it appears you already have one. I'm outta here."

. . .

Twenty-seven minutes later, the most beautiful woman in the world walked down the hallway toward him giving him an impish grin. People often wonder how they will die, Andrew was pretty sure his death certificate would read, 'death by dress.' It was emerald green, cut low, and the fabric flirted over the edges of the creamy swell of her breasts. A high slit up one leg made his mouth go dry. A skinny sash holding the dress closed was tied into a bow over her right hip. It would only take a single tug . . .

He followed the dress up her body and—busted. She cocked an eyebrow.

"You look incredible," he said. He wanted to kiss her until neither of them could breathe properly, but his mother waited. Likely she was already pacing the lobby.

"You clean up pretty good, too. Who knew you even owned a proper jacket? If I hadn't recognized the boots, I'd have walked right past you."

He smirked and offered her his arm, turning them toward the elevator. "Thanks again for doing this."

She curtsied, bending at the knee, one foot in front of the other. "One human shield at your service. I do have one question, though."

"Shoot."

"How did your mother know who I was? I got the impression you don't talk to your family."

"I rarely talk to my parents, but I talk to Bridget regularly. She must have told my mom."

The corners of Grace's lips tugged up. "Told her what? That you were saddled with a maddening woman who kept trying to change your songs?"

"Baby"—he picked up her hand, flipped it over and placed a kiss in the center of her palm—"you are maddening, but it has nothing to do with your need to control my music." She shivered under his touch.

The elevator doors slid open as he winked at her and stepped into the lobby. He turned, caught sight of his mother and sister, and stiffened. "Let's get this over with."

Bridget strode over to them as Grace stepped out from behind him. She stopped short and her mouth dropped open. "Grace. Are you coming along to dinner?"

Grace nodded. "I hope that's okay."

"Of course." She opened her mouth and let it fall shut again, her brow wrinkling.

"What is it, Bridge? Spit it out before mom walks over here."

She turned to Grace. "I was about to say that Andy usually keeps his personal life separate from the family and then I realized Andy doesn't have a personal life. Do you, big brother?"

Andrew snorted and gave his sister's sleek ponytail a hard tug. "I keep things separate because I have a nosy sister who runs to mommy and tells her everything."

Bridget's smile fell. "She worries about you."

Andrew rolled his eyes. "Sure, she does."

"Children," called the statuesque woman across the lobby while snapping her fingers. "Taxi is waiting, let's not be late for our reservation." She eyed Grace. "We're already going to have to bother them for another chair."

"I told you I wasn't invited," Grace hissed at him out of the corner of her mouth while still managing to keep a smile on her face.

"It'll be fine. She just doesn't like it when she's not one hundred percent in control of everything."

Grace smirked. "Sounds like someone else I know."

Bridget laughed and strung her arm through Grace's. "It's not entirely his fault. Control issues and stubbornness are baked into his DNA—from both sides of the family." Bridget looked over her shoulder and gave him a wink. "I'm told if you can get past that, there's a decent person underneath. I mean, I've never seen it, but I'm told it's there."

Andrew sighed and grabbed the elbows of his two favorite women and steered them toward the matriarch.

Dinner plates were cleared, and dessert menus placed in front of each of them. Andrew had to admit he was surprised. They were two courses and two cocktails in, and his mother hadn't asked any nosy questions and had only given him one or two disapproving looks. New record.

"Your father sends his greetings."

Damn. Spoke too soon.

Andrew twisted the napkin in his lap and scowled at his mother. "I think we both know that's not true."

"Andy . . ." Bridget patted his arm and peered at Grace out of the corner of her eye.

"No, Bridge, there's no reason to sugarcoat the truth. I doubt that Dad even knows you're here—or more likely, he has no idea Storyhill is in London. Isn't that right, Mom?"

His mother's lips puckered like she'd gotten a mouthful of fresh lemon. "You are both so stubborn."

Andrew persisted, slapping his napkin on top of the table, leaning toward his mother. "Does he know you're attending my concert?"

She deflated like a helium balloon taken out into sub-zero temperatures. "No."

He slammed his hands down on the table and pushed back, causing his chair to send a screech reverberating through the restaurant. "That's what I thought."

"Hey Cowboy," Grace said softly, wrapping her fingers

around his and squeezing. "I have some gummy worms in my purse. Do you need one?"

He couldn't help himself. He laughed. Loud. And every ounce of anger seeped out of him. He caught his mom's and Bridget's expression out of the corner of his eye, they were clearly bracing for one of his less-than-attractive explosions.

But not Grace. How did she know just what to say to diffuse the situation? To make him laugh despite all the anger and disappointment coursing through his veins?

He took her face in his hands and crushed his mouth on top of hers. From somewhere near he heard a female gasp. Was it his mom or Bridget or Grace? All three? Didn't matter.

In Ford's conference room, he'd told himself he didn't need saving. He'd been wrong. So wrong. This woman was literally his saving Grace. He chuckled at the pun. From his music to his family, she made everything easier. He pulled back, rested his forehead against hers and watched her open her eyes.

"Did you just slip me tongue in front of your mother?" she said, barely audible.

He smirked at her stunned expression. "I think I did. Did you just enjoy it in front of my mother? Because I'm pretty sure that moan I heard didn't come from her."

He chuckled as Grace's face flooded with color. "Now, do you want dessert or are you ready to head back?"

"I'm good to go back," she croaked out. "Though shock may have welded me to my chair."

"Shock and awe?"

She rolled her eyes and shook her head. "Shock and embarrassment."

Andrew stood and offered his hand to Grace, helping her up. He turned to his mother and sister. "Mom, Bridge, I'm sorry. I let my temper get the better of me. I'll see you after the concert on Saturday."

Both women stared wordlessly at him, mouths agape.

"Thanks for dinner," Grace warbled, clearly not fully recovered.

He placed his hand at the small of her back and turned her toward the door as he heard Bridget mumble, "And the show."

~

Grace collected her jacket from coat check and stepped outside into the crisp November evening. The change in temperature helped cool her burning cheeks. She ran a finger over her bottom lip. That kiss. Holy macaroni, as Annie would say.

Her initial gasp of shock had given way to the mind-blowing sensation of his soft lips moving over hers. She could still feel his palms cupping her face and the warmth of his breath against her cheek.

"Should we get a taxi?" he asked, pulling her from her thoughts.

"It's a nice night, let's walk back." She needed fresh air and some space, not to be pushed up against Andrew in the backseat of a cab.

"I know forty degrees is tropical for you Minnesotans, but my body is set to Nashville."

She dragged her gaze over him from head to toe and patted his cheek. "My delicate flower."

"And we've already established that I'm afraid of the dark."

"You, sir, are incredibly high maintenance. But don't you worry, I have one hell of a roundhouse kick and will protect you from muggers and make sure we never stray too far from the streetlights. Will that work for you?"

He chuckled. "I can probably work with that." He wrapped his arm around her shoulders and pulled her tight to his side.

"You trying to steal my heat, Cowboy?"

"Absolutely."

"In that case . . ." She twisted out from underneath his arm, but he caught her bicep and reeled her back in.

"Not so fast, missy."

"You know my name is Grace, not Missy, right? I'm sure it's hard to keep all your women straight."

"Naw, if I forget, honey, darling, or sweetheart, always seems to work."

She punched him lightly in the stomach. "You're terrible."

"So, it's Grace, is it?" he whispered, blowing a warm breath across the shell of her ear. She shivered and a tiny moan escaped. "Seems like that's a name I'll remember. You are pretty unforgettable."

"Whew," Grace said, stepping into the hotel lobby and uttering the first words she'd managed in nine city blocks. The lights were glaringly bright after the dark, cloudy skies. "One delicate nyctophobic flower safely delivered." She dramatically wiped the back of her hand across her forehead and flashed him a bright smile.

"Well, almost."

"Almost?" she asked, spreading her arms wide, palms up, gesturing to the lobby.

"I won't be completely out of harm's way until I'm safely inside my room."

She punched the up button on the elevator panel and inhaled a steadying breath. She nibbled her bottom lip and looked directly into his eyes. "If you're that worried, maybe you'd feel safer in my room."

His eyebrows shot up and his eyes widened into saucers.

And he said nothing.

Had he understood her meaning? It had been a long time

since she'd flirted, much less propositioned someone. Maybe she was doing it wrong?

The elevator chimed and the doors slid open.

She looked at her shoes and summoned her courage. In for a penny, in for a pound—or whatever it was that her grandad used to say. She reached for him, wrapping her fingers around his wrist.

His gaze followed the motion, but he remained quiet.

When they reached her door, she fumbled with her key card. After three failed attempts, he closed the gap between them, pressing his front to her back, suctioning them together from chest to knees. When he leaned in and moved a muscly thigh between hers, she nearly orgasmed on the spot.

He slipped the card from her fingers and got the green to flash on his first swipe.

Clearly, she was more worked up than he was.

He held the door open for her and she forced her feet forward. This was her idea, after all. It was time to make her move . . . in case she'd not been clear enough in the elevator. When the door dropped shut, she reached for him—and pushed him up against it. Hard.

He smirked and broke his silence. "And here I thought I was coming here for safety."

"Is this not a good idea?"

He slowly traced the shell of her ear with a finger. "Just the opposite. It's likely one of the best you've ever had."

He caught her chin and dipped his head to meet her mouth. When a moan fell from her lips, he buried his fingers in her hair and tugged, exposing her neck. He nibbled the skin, biting just hard enough to send a bolt of pain and pleasure down her spine. When she gasped, he soothed the spot with his tongue.

"I gotta say, Cowboy," she slurred as he kissed along her

jawline, "this is so much better without your mother and sister watching." She stiffened and winced. "That sounded bad."

He laughed against her neck, his warm breath leaving a trail of goosebumps. "And here I thought I did my best work with an audience."

"Maybe we limit this performance to one adoring fan?" Wait, that didn't sound right, either. "I mean, me. I'm the adoring fan. I'm the audience of one. Oh my god, I'm babbling, please stop me."

"That I can do." He smiled a slow, wicked smile before his hot mouth covered hers.

Need rocketed through her and settled low, making her keenly aware of the parts that had been ignored for so long. And then he was gone. Well, not gone, but she could fit a hand in between them and she missed the heat. "Andrew?"

He cupped her face in his hands and ran a finger over her swollen lips. "You seem nervous." His thumb glided over the spot on her cheek that tingled from the scrape of his stubble. "We don't have to do this tonight."

"It's just been a long time for me." She forced her lips into a smile and tried for an exaggerated wink. "Maybe sex has changed?"

He grabbed her hand, bringing it to his mouth, running his lips over her knuckles. "You haven't been with anyone since Jax?"

"Well," she said, "I've had some pretty serious three-ways with Ben and Jerry."

He shook his head, amusement playing in those beautiful gold-green eyes. "Always with the jokes. But, seriously, Grace, you're sure about this?"

The way her nipples were straining against her bra made it clear her body was one hundred percent on board. But the rest of her? She thought talking about Jax would have ruined the mood, but strangely, it had the opposite effect. That Andrew cared about her history made him even more attractive—if that was even possible.

She wanted him. All of him. She tipped her face up and nodded.

"I'm going to need the words, Gracie."

"Yes, Andrew, I'm sure."

Andrew's lips curled into a smile. "I know you're serious when you use my name."

She rose up on her toes and placed a delicate kiss on his lips. "Would you have preferred something like, 'I'm ready to get this rodeo started, Cowboy'?"

He laughed softly and pulled her against his chest, resting his head atop hers. "You are one amazing woman, Grace O'Connor. Beautiful, smart, funny, and so fucking talented."

Her lashes fluttered shut. His words a more powerful aphrodisiac than any kiss or touch. "You forgot rich."

She felt the laughter rumble in his chest and any last reservations leaked out of her.

"In that case, you're buying breakfast." His hands slid from her waist, up her torso, following the curves of her waist and breasts.

A breathless laugh escaped her. "Should I plan on meeting you in the lobby in the morning?"

Andrew grabbed a butt cheek in each hand, sliding her up his body until she had no choice but to wrap her legs around his waist. "Silly woman. Once I get you in that bed, I'm not leaving until the sun is shining. It'll take at least that long to do all the things I've been imagining."

"In that case, we might need provisions. I shoved a bottle of wine in the mini-fridge." She tipped her head toward the console facing the bed. "Why don't you open it?"

"Wine? I knew it. You planned this whole seduction scene.

Adding the nervousness in was a nice touch. Made it more believable."

She playfully slapped his chest. "No, I've been keeping a bottle on hand as a fortifying agent for the days you're particularly irritating."

The sound she loved more than anything tumbled out of him. She doubted she'd ever tire of making him laugh.

"Wine it is," he said, releasing his hold on her bottom and letting her slowly slide down every hard inch of him—some very hard, very impressive inches.

"Corkscrew is by the coffeemaker. I'll be back in a couple of minutes."

Grace slipped into the bathroom and placed her hands on the counter, meeting her gaze in the mirror. She searched her reflection for doubt, for hesitation, for feelings of betrayal, but found nothing. She was ready.

She gave the sash on her dress a quick tug and it puddled to the floor. She flipped it up with her foot and exchanged it for the robe hanging on the back of the door, letting the ties hang at her side. She stepped back into the room as Andrew slid the cork out of the bottle with a pop.

"Andrew," Grace said softly.

He turned toward her, his mouth slowly falling open. "Holy shit."

Grace lifted a shoulder, feeling all kinds of sexy. "I kind of have a thing for lingerie."

His eyes darkened with lust and he prowled toward her. "Add that to the list of things we have in common." Placing his free hand behind her head, he tipped it back and dipped his head to meet her lips. He kissed her raw and rough, sucking her bottom lip between his teeth—and she jumped.

"Too much?" he said, pulling back, his chest rising and falling.

"Wine bottle," she stuttered. "It's a little cold."

He looked down and laughed. The bottle was pressed up against her bare thigh. "Sorry."

"It wouldn't be a problem if you weren't so hot," she said with a small wink.

Andrew snorted and deposited the bottle next to the TV. "That's a terrible line."

She took a step back and unbuttoned his shirt, sliding the oxford off his shoulders and running her hands down his defined chest. "Then maybe we should do something other than talk."

"Like what?" he said.

She picked up his hand and dragged his fingers over the lacy edge of her bra, guiding them down over her nipples. "Grace," he uttered hoarsely as they hardened under his touch.

He was letting her lead, his eyes fixed on hers. She popped the button on his pants and slid them to his ankles. She crouched before him and slowly pulled one foot out, then the other. She stood, dragging her fingers up his thighs before pressing her lips to the hollow below his Adam's apple.

He moaned and, in one fluid movement, snaked his arm around her waist and flipped her onto the bed. She squealed and opened her eyes to find him kneeling between her legs. Oh no, he was not going to change the power position that easily.

"You praying or groveling, Cowboy?" she said, repeating the same question she'd asked him that first day in the studio.

He skimmed a callous finger up the outside of her leg and slowly slid it under the lace above her thigh, working his way toward her warm center. "I wouldn't get too cocky, lady. Before the night is over, you'll be doing both."

"Is that so?"

He slid a hand under her ribs and deftly unhooked her bra. Her breasts spilled free and he gathered them in his hands and sucked a nipple into his mouth. "Guaranteed," he muttered around her, his warm breath rushing across her skin.

She twisted, arching up into him. "Oh god, yes."

He chuckled. "See you're praying already. That was quick. I'm even more impressive than I thought."

"Wow. The ego on you." She tried to say it playfully, but her voice came out breathy and rough.

"It seems like you need a little more convincing." He dropped his mouth lower, leaving whisper-soft kisses across her belly. When he reached her panties, he hooked a thumb under each side and slowly pulled them down.

He kissed up the inside of one thigh, stopping right before he reached the place that was aching for his touch. He turned his attention to the other thigh. It was pure torture. Delicious torture, but torture, nonetheless.

"Andrew, please," she moaned, running her fingers through his hair.

"And there's the groveling," he said, rasping his stubble against her delicate skin.

She rummaged through her lust-addled mind for a quippy retort, but the only word that formed was 'more.'

"I can do that," he said.

Apparently, she'd said it out loud.

He sucked her into his mouth, circling his tongue and pushing a single finger inside. She arched off the bed and he added a second finger, curling it, bringing sublime pressure to that elusive spot.

She wanted to hang on, but the last threads of her restraint were unraveling.

He moved his fingers faster, matching the pace of his tongue and the final string broke. Shudders wracked her body as a rainbow of color pulsed in front of her eyes. She fell back to the bed with a deep, husky moan.

"Wow. Good. You. Turn," she nonsensically muttered, poking a finger into his chest.

He let out a low laugh and slid down his boxer briefs. How did she not realize he wasn't naked?

He lifted her farther up onto the bed and lay down between her legs. He reached for a condom, tearing it open with his teeth.

She sucked in a breath. Why was that so sexy?

He eased his body down onto hers, filling her bit-by-bit.

She gasped, arched her back to meet him and wrapped her legs around his waist.

He moved slowly at first, steadily deepening his thrusts.

The pressure built between her legs and she grabbed his hips and urged him on. He groaned and her body surrendered, convulsing as she flew apart a second time.

He stayed with her, moving inside her until she stilled. With a final plunge, he let out a growl and dropped his head to her shoulder as he came. He held her until their breathing returned to normal and ran a finger down the side of her face. "Thank you."

"I don't know why you're thanking me. You did most of the work."

He leaned down and kissed the tip of her nose. "I'm happy to reverse roles. Whenever you're ready."

"I might need a little time."

"Sure. Sure," he said, flipping onto his back and pulling her tight against him. "I can wait. Five, ten, maybe even fifteen minutes."

She laughed and patted his chest. "I guess a guy can dream."

"I don't need to dream, Gracie." He tipped her chin up and brushed her hair away from her face. "You're already here with me."

. . .

Grace glanced at the clock. 3:00 a.m. Tangled in the sheets beside her was a large, warm male form. Muscled and masculine, with long lashes nearly reaching his cheekbones and dark hair spread over the pillow.

When he'd finally eased inside her and stroked her to a second orgasm, it felt like a giant pressure valve releasing. All the pain, all the longing, all the loneliness that had been dammed up inside for so long rushed out, the floodgates opening all at once.

Frightening and freeing all at the same time.

Grace wriggled free of his arm. He stirred but didn't wake. She reached for her robe, discarded in a heap at the end of the bed. Pulling it around her, she padded silently across the room to the wing chair in the corner. She watched his chest rise and lower—slowly, methodically.

"Grace?" Andrew patted the empty space beside him.

"Over here."

"I thought you might have snuck out on me." He rolled over and propped himself up on an elbow.

"It's my room," Grace said, unable to hide her smile.

"As long as we're both awake, I think you should come back to bed."

"You sure you have another round in you, Cowboy?"

"I guess I'll just have to prove it to you." He threw back the covers and jumped up. The moonlight seeped through the crack in the curtains and cut across his chest, glinting off the hair that dusted his pecs and snaked down his belly, leading all the way to . . . whoa, he was clearly ready to go again.

He chuckled softly. "My eyes are up here, lady."

"I'm not really interested in your eyes right now."

He chuckled and reached down, effortlessly scooping her from the chair. "You're not going to be needing this," he said, as he pulled the knot out of the ties holding her robe closed.

CHAPTER TWELVE

The sun was shining through the curtains when Andrew opened his eyes. Where was he? The woman snuggled up to his side was an instant reminder. He dragged a finger over her bare shoulder. "Grace." He pulled her in a little closer and settled his hand under her bare breast. "Grace, it's time to wake up."

Grace stirred and opened one eye. "Am I correct that the same naughty man who kept me up half the night now wants me to get out of bed?"

"Guilty as charged. Though if I remember correctly, you were a *very* willing participant."

"Details, details," she said, rolling over, waving a hand in the air. "I'm pleading temporary insanity or I'm taking the fifth or something like that."

"That's right, your best friend is an attorney."

"Yes, and she can get me off on any charge."

"I thought I did a pretty good job getting you off all on my own."

Grace snorted. "Is it time for breakfast?"

"It'll have to be brunch, it's nearly ten."

"Yikes. When is our reservation?" Grace said, sitting straight up in bed, the sheet sliding down to her waist. His gaze dropped to her chest, and he instantly went hard. It took all his willpower not to cover her breasts with his hands and lay her back into the pillows, but it was late and someone was bound to be looking for one or both of them soon.

"Much as I'm enjoying the view," he said hoarsely, "how about I run to my room, shower, and meet you in the lobby in thirty minutes? We have plenty of time for a snack before we need to meet the others for Thanksgiving."

"And coffee. Don't forget the coffee."

"Anything you want, Gracie. Anything."

She smiled slowly, leaned back into the bed and pulled the sheet up to her neck.

He threw his jeans over his shoulder. "Where are my boxers?"

Grace picked them up from beside the bed, gave them a little shake and stuffed them under the covers. "Come and get them."

Andrew groaned. "You. Are. Killing. Me."

Grace shrugged. "It's a great way to go."

Andrew stepped into his jeans and zipped them up, sliding into his shirt and buttoning the bottom buttons. "Wicked woman. I need some food, but I will be back for those boxers."

"Promises, promises."

Andrew pulled the door shut behind him and kneaded a spot over his heart. He turned and stared at the door. She was changing him. With every decision, from walking away from school, to convincing Joe to join the band, to committing to writing the music for this album, the knot in his chest had pulled tighter and tighter. Until she'd come into his life. Okay, she'd yanked the rope taut when they first met, but now? Now, she eased the tension.

They'd moved from adversaries, to colleagues, to friends, and now lovers. The realization of how much he wanted her, and not just in his bed, swamped him. He rubbed the back of his neck and stiffened. A single thought formed. It landed with the subtlety of a cannonball to the gut. Not only had his fears of mixing business and pleasure dissipated, but he knew that if forced to choose between a chance with Grace and a chance at putting Storyhill on the map, he'd choose Grace.

Every time.

An icy awareness dripped down his spine—would she choose him? Did she want a man who'd yet to prove himself? Whose success consisted of nothing more than a few million YouTube views? He certainly was no Jax Jensen.

She'd invited him into her bed, not the other way around. That meant something. Didn't it?

He bounced a fist against his thigh and strode toward his room. Maybe instead of trying to prove his father wrong, he should channel his energy into showing Grace he was the kind of man she could rely on.

Grace waited for the snick of the door latch before flopping back onto the bed and staring at the ceiling. Thanksgiving Day. Before Andrew had woken her, she'd been buried in a dream. Jax stood on one side of a table, Andrew on the other, and they were pulling with all their might on the two ends of a wishbone. But it wouldn't snap. They just keep pulling.

What do you suppose that meant? Likely a warning about pressing your luck or tempting fate, or something like that. Is that what last night was? An exercise in tempting fate? She'd been so certain, but now, in the light of day? Her decision seemed to float somewhere between a little careless and a whole lot dangerous.

She punched the pillow next to her and buried her face in it to stifle a scream of pure frustration. Sitting up, she launched the pillow across the room, hearing a satisfying thud as it hit the wall. She grabbed her phone to check the time and it rang out at her touch. She jumped and gulped in a couple of giant breaths, reached for the t-shirt she'd discarded before dinner last night, and hit Accept.

"Happy Thanksgiving!" she said to the two faces smiling at her.

"Happy Thanksgiving!" Megan replied, while Curtis narrowed his eyes and asked, "Are you still in bed? Are you sick?"

Grace tried to stop her blush before it exploded on her cheeks at the same time Megan punched him in the arm and raised her eyebrows. Curtis' eyebrows followed suit.

"It's a national holiday. Do I not deserve to have a little sleep in on a day off?" Grace answered, trying to deflect Megan's clear insinuation.

"Sweetie, that may explain why you're still in bed, but it does not explain the current state of your hair," Megan said, smiling wide and winking.

Grace instinctively reached for her hair and groaned inwardly. She didn't need a mirror to know it was sticking out in all directions. But. She was not about to discuss the state of her hair—or anything else—with these two, especially when she could hardly explain last night to herself. She cleared her throat. "It's barely five a.m. in New York City. What are you doing up so early?"

"We did some early morning prep so we can take the rest of the day off," Megan said, gratefully taking the hint.

"Are you celebrating today?" Curtis asked gently,. "I wish we could be there with you."

"I'll be good. Brad made reservations at Balthazar in Covent Garden. Apparently, the ex-pat crowd has successfully convinced Londoners to celebrate our holiday in style."

"What are they serving?"

Grace laughed. "Ever the chef. Straight to the menu. It will be turkey with all the traditional trimmings, complete with pumpkin and pecan pie."

"Food aside, how's it going? Anybody I need to take care of for you?" Curtis said, pulling a face.

"Take care of?" Grace said, giggling. "Did you join the mob?"

"I just want you to know I've always got your back."

"And that is why I love you." Grace asked a few more questions about the restaurant, what their plans were for the holiday and thanked them for calling.

"You're really sure you're okay?" Curtis said.

"Megan . . ." Grace said imploringly.

"I know, I know," she said, shaking her mane of red hair. "Say goodbye, Curtis."

"Goodbye, Grace. Happy Thanksgiving," he said as their picture faded to black. Grace stared at the blank screen. Before she could even think about how much she missed them, a text popped up on her phone. It was a photo of Annie's husband, Will, and the girls lifting an enormous bird onto a grocery store conveyor belt, captioned with eight words.

Can you find the turkey in this picture?

Grace quickly texted back. *I see two.*

Exactly.

Why are you up? It's so early there.

I'm trying to finish a couple of things, so I don't have to go in on Friday. Can you Skype?

She smoothed down her hair. She was not making that mistake again. Megan may have let it go, but Annie most certainly would not.

Give me a couple of hours. I need to go find some coffee. That work for you?

Yes. Looking forward to it. Annie signed off with a turkey emoji.

Grace smiled. Her friends hadn't forgotten her. They might not be blood, but they were family, nonetheless. She laughed as she pictured it. A crazy intense chef, a Celtic beauty, a lawyer, a financial wizard, and two happy, bubbly little girls. Slightly dysfunctional, but all hers, and she wouldn't have it any other way.

"Why, Grace O'Connor, fancy meeting you here," Andrew said, his boots clicking on the marble foyer floor. "I was just about to go get some coffee. Join me?"

Grace dropped the magazine that she'd been staring at, but not reading. Her gaze followed the line of his leg, up his torso, connecting with an amazing set of green eyes that vibrated with mischievousness. Her core clenched and resoundingly yelled, 'Yes! Yes! More, please!' while the rest of her wondered if going back for seconds was really a good idea. Too much of a good thing, and all that.

Andrew leaned down, getting even with her eyes. "How about we don't over-analyze last night right now? No good thoughts come out of you before coffee, remember?" He reached out his hand to her.

She laughed and placed her hand in his, allowing him to pull her up. "You reading my mind again, Cowboy?"

"Just getting really good at decoding the lines on your fore-head." He ran a finger over the space between her eyebrows, smoothing the skin. "Two lines means you're thinking really hard. Three lines means you're overthinking."

"I didn't know I was so transparent."

"You're not, but I've been paying attention."

Grace exhaled a tremulous laugh. She waffled between feelings of freedom and fright—again. Having someone fully see her was amazing, but vulnerability and openness had never been her strong suits. "Is 'paying attention' a less stalkerish way of saying 'I've been watching you'?"

"And humor is your number one defense mechanism. So, coffee? Or should I continue detailing your quirks and traits?"

No. That was more than enough of that. "Coffee," she said, nodding her head. Coffee was one of the few things that still made sense in her world.

When they stepped into the café around the corner Andrew touched her arm and cocked his head toward the far corner. Joe sat alone in a booth, headphones in his ears, tapping out a beat with his pencil while studying the paper in front of him.

Grace bit her bottom lip and curled and uncurled her fingers. Clearly, even getting coffee was a dangerous experience now. "He's going to wonder what we're doing here together. Last night has to be our secret."

Andrew laughed. "I don't make it a habit to discuss my sex life with other people, but a warning, Joe might notice my post-coital glow."

Grace groaned. "Be serious."

"If I keep it quiet, you'll have to keep your hands off all this." He ran his hands down his chest. "And I'm not sure you're up for the challenge."

She rolled her eyes. "I'll manage. You're not completely irresistible."

"Ouch. You wound me, O'Connor."

"One beautiful woman at the signing table after the next

concert breathlessly asking you to sign her t-shirt, or her *cleavage*, and you'll forget all about me."

"Doubtful." He kissed her palm. "Not after what you did to me last night."

Grace blushed a deep red. "Seriously. What's our story?"

"That we were writing and now we're taking a coffee break? Something far-fetched like that?"

Grace slapped him in the chest. "Fine. Be reasonable if you must."

"It appears the mind-blowing sex actually blew your mind."

"Someone is a little full of himself this morning. Order me the cream cheese Danish and a cappuccino. I'm going over to talk to him."

"Wait. We're next in line."

"Afraid you'll miss me?"

Andrew snorted. "Your orders are so high-maintenance, I don't want to get it wrong."

"Sure. That's it."

They stepped up to the counter and Grace placed her order and his. "He'll have an iced black coffee, two eggs over medium, and two sides of bacon. And, don't worry your pretty little head, Cowboy, I'll pay." She pulled out a credit card and grabbed their order number.

"That was our deal," he said, placing a soft kiss on her temple.

Grace's eyes went wide and flashed to where Joe was sitting. Andrew shrugged. "He hasn't even noticed we're here."

Grace grabbed her coffee and pastry from the counter, and they wandered through the café tables until reaching Joe's booth. She tapped her fingers on the edge of the table, and he jumped, jerking his earbuds out.

"Shit, you shouldn't sneak up on a guy like that."

Grace pointed at the pieces of paper in front of Joe. "Are

ANNMARIE BOYLE

those our songs?"

"Yep. Andy gave me a few and asked me to pencil in some possible percussion lines for the arranger."

"I'd love to see what you've come up with."

"Do you need to order something first?" he asked, pointing at the counter.

"Already done." Grace cleared her throat and shimmied into the booth, unable to meet Joe's eyes. "We were writing this morning and Andrew needed a bacon hit."

Joe laughed, handed Grace the music, and excused himself to refill his coffee. Andrew slid in beside her and ran a finger down the length of Grace's thigh, giving her a quick wink. "You're a terrible liar."

"Making it even more imperative that you stop looking at me like that. You're practically broadcasting that you had sex last night." She flicked his hand off her leg.

"I told you. Afterglow."

"And, stop saying things like 'post-coital' and 'afterglow'," she hissed as Joe approached the table and slid into the green vinyl booth.

She sent Andrew a final warning look and turned to Joe. "I like what you've done here, really helps me feel the momentum of the song—rhythm really is its own standalone language, isn't it?"

A smile blossomed across his face and he nodded vigorously. "Finally, someone who gets me."

"Are you flirting, married man?" Andrew said the words casually, but a clear warning sounded under his words.

"You worried I'm going to steal your woman away?"

Grace snorted and pointed to the server standing at the edge of the booth. "I hate to interrupt all this useless posturing, but your bacon is here."

"So, the songs?" Andrew asked as he consumed his first slice of bacon in two bites.

"You sure you can think about music while eating bacon?" Grace asked.

"I am a man of many talents." He gave her a wide grin and an exaggerated wink.

She felt her cheeks go pink—again—and turned her attention to Joe. Thankfully, he seemed oblivious. A little voice asked her why she cared. She was a grown—single—woman who could sleep with anyone she wanted, whenever she wanted. Except, Andrew wasn't just anyone. He was her co-worker and more than that, a musician.

And, maybe more importantly, if Joe figured it out, it made the whole thing real. Not just something that happened once between two people who succumbed to forced proximity.

Andrew reached over and smoothed the space between her eyebrows again. He narrowed his eyes at her but didn't say anything, instead turning to Joe.

"What do you think?" he asked his bandmate again.

Joe launched into his thoughts on the two songs and Grace sunk back into the booth, hearing only about half the words he said. Andrew was right, overthinking wasn't productive, but it seemed she couldn't help it.

Grace clicked on Annie's name and listened as the familiar buzz and bubbles flowed out of her computer as the video screen popped up in front of her. The link connected and Grace heard scraping, shuffling, and young voices before the picture became clear. Finally, Ellie appeared on the screen. "Me first!" the child yelled, and Grace stifled a laugh. "Tía! I lost another tooth!" the child said, her face just inches from the webcam. She opened her mouth and got very close to the screen.

Grace couldn't see anything but tongue and tonsils. "How

exciting! Which one is it?"

"Vis won," she said, her mouth agape. She closed her mouth and announced, "Mom said the tooth fairy would probably come tonight if it wasn't against labor union laws to work on Thanksgiving." Grace nodded solemnly, biting back a smile.

"Now me," Abbie said, pushing in front of her younger sister, "Tía G, did you see my new website yet?"

"I checked it out before I left New York and I made a donation."

"You did? Thanks! I only need twelve more dollars before I can buy a dog bed for the shelter. Though Mami says I have to be careful or I will have to set up a C3 . . . Mom! What was that thing you said I'd have to do?"

"Apply to be a 501(c)(3)," Annie said, smiling, sliding into the frame, lifting Ellie into her lap.

"Legal eagle strikes again," Grace said, laughing. "Those girls won't have to go to law school once you're done with them."

"Saving them decades of student loans. Happy Thanksgiving."

"Happy Thanksgiving to you. I miss spending the day with you."

"We miss you, too. How are things going across the pond?"

How was she supposed to answer that? OMG, I forgot how amazing orgasms are. Or, WTF, I slept with a musician even after I promised myself I wouldn't. Probably better to leave Andrew out of the conversation. Once she opened that box, getting it closed again would be near impossible.

"Good. Got to see Curtis while I was in New York. The flight over was smooth. Songs are, mostly, getting written and yesterday I spent the afternoon seeing the sights of London. Tomorrow's the first concert here." *None of that was a lie. It just wasn't the whole truth.*

Abbie appeared in the lower corner of the screen, causing

Grace to startle. "Do they have turkeys in England? Are you gonna eat pumpkin pie today? Did you see those guards who never smile?"

"Yes, Abbie, they have turkey in England, though it's more of a Christmas thing for them. There are pumpkin and pecan pies on the menu, and yes, I went to Buckingham Palace, but not until I first saw it from the air," Grace explained, trying to recall all of Abbie's questions.

"From the air?" Abbie asked, pressing her face into the frame, eyes wide.

"Yep. Search 'London Eye' on YouTube. I'm sure there are tons of videos of it."

Ellie turned in Annie's lap and sat up on her knees to get eye-to-eye with her mother. She placed her hands on Annie's cheeks and asked, "Mom, can we go to London to visit Tía G? I miss her."

Annie laughed. "Tía G will be home in a few days. I'm sure she'll come over as soon as she gets here. Isn't that right, Tía?" she asked, spinning Ellie to face the computer.

Grace nodded. "You're my first stop."

Ellie leaned in toward the screen. "Are you bringing me a present?"

Annie rolled her eyes and mouthed 'Sorry' over Ellie's head. "Why don't the two of you find Papá and ask him to help you find that video while I finish talking to Tía Grace." The girls hopped down and retreated in the direction of Will's office.

"How was it sightseeing alone?" Annie asked after the girls were gone. "Kind of sad, I imagine?"

"Well, um, I wasn't exactly alone. You know, I'm traveling with a pretty big group of people," Grace said, fiddling with the pens on her hotel room desk.

"Cool. Did you all stick together?"

"Not everybody. It was a smaller group." Grace slid a file

folder closer to her, flipping through the papers inside.

Annie's eyes narrowed. "How small?"

"Um, two."

"Three total, then?"

"No, just two." Grace dropped the file folder, gathered her hair in her hands, dropping it down her back and looking directly into her web cam. "So, how's work?"

"Grace Elizabeth O'Connor! Did you spend the day with Mr. Sexy Pants?"

And all night.

"He has a name." Grace sighed. "Though I do have to admit, he does fill out a pair of jeans in all the right ways."

Annie glanced back over her shoulder, confirming the coast was clear. "I need details!"

She really hated lying to Annie, even if it was a lie of omission, but she wasn't ready to tell anyone about what had transpired. Not yet. "Not a big deal, really. We wrote in the morning. When we finished, everyone else had already left for the day so it made sense to see the sights together." Her stomach flipped over thinking about the day and how natural it had felt to walk hand-in-hand through the streets of London. And how safe she'd felt wrapped in his arms all night. She should tell her. "But Annie . . ." Her voice cracked on the final syllable.

Will appeared behind Annie and Grace blew out the breath she'd been holding. With the interruption, she dropped her admission back into the vault.

Will dipped his head to the screen and gave a quick wave. "Hey, Grace. I hate to interrupt"—he placed his hand on Annie's shoulder—"but we promised my mom we'd be at her place in fifteen minutes."

"Shoot! That's right. Can you get the girls ready while I wrap up with Grace?" He gave her a single nod and she turned back to face Grace. "But what, *chica?*"

Grace sucked in her bottom lip, releasing it with a pop, and aimed for an even tone. "I think he's starting to like me." *That was sort of the truth, right?*

Annie rolled her eyes. "Everyone likes you, Grace. It was only a matter of time before he stopped acting like a jerk."

Grace grimaced and slowly moved her head side-to-side, squeezing her eyes shut. "No, like, likes me, likes me."

"Hot single guy likes equally hot single woman. I'm not sure I see the problem here, Grace."

"Because I might like him, too," Grace whispered, inching closer to the truth.

A smile slowly enveloped Annie's face. "Well, Grace, now that you're getting older, I feel like you're responsible enough to learn some things about the adult world and some new feelings you may be experiencing."

"Are you giving me the birds and the bees talk?" *You're too late Annie, I took the refresher course last night.*

Annie snickered and continued. "Just know that the sexual feelings you're having are perfectly normal. There's no need to feel embarrassed. It happens to everyone eventually. Let's start by talking about what you're feeling, and later we'll talk about the importance of consent and protection."

Grace bent at the waist and a burst of staccato giggles flowed from her—not unlike the first time she'd been given the 'Big Talk'. "I'm impressed. It sounds like you've been practicing."

Annie smirked and shrugged her shoulders. "Yes, and I have to admit it wasn't nearly hard as I expected it to be."

"Annie!" Will called in the background.

"I'm coming. I'm coming." She turned back to the screen and rolled her eyes. "I've gotta go. The mother-in-law has decided to do a mini-pumpkin hunt, ala an Easter egg hunt, before the big meal for all the grandkids. Apparently, they're each getting a cornucopia, that she sewed and hand-quilted herself, to put the pumpkins in." She shook her head, a look of distaste flashing across her face. "Give me a courtroom any day."

Grace smiled, picturing Annie standing in the middle of her mother-in-law's large lawn with screaming kids running around her. "Have fun. Looking forward to seeing you in a few days."

"You too," she said, turning to her family assembling behind her. "Everybody say goodbye to Tía."

The girls yelled their goodbyes and Annie leaned in close to the computer and whispered, "About your 'problem,'"—she flexed her fingers in air quotes—"trust your heart—or your gut—or your ovaries. My guess is that they're all telling you the same thing, or you wouldn't be so scared."

"So that's where the little voice I'm hearing is coming from? My ovaries?"

"I'll text you a couple of links that will help explain things. Though my advice to you would be to ignore all the 'don'ts' and go straight to the 'do's'."

"Is that the advice I should remember when your girls start asking questions?"

Annie pulled a stern face and stabbed a single finger at her, then cracked a smile, blew her a kiss and faded into blackness.

Grace stared at the dark screen, trying to shake off the guilt niggling at the back of her neck. It's not like she had to tell Annie *everything* about her life. And she didn't blatantly lie to her, she merely skipped a few minor details. *Minor details, hah. Whatever you need to tell yourself, Grace.*

Maybe she simply wanted to keep it to herself for a while, to hold it close to her heart. Or maybe, she wasn't ready for her best friend to call out her 'no more musicians' hypocrisy.

She sighed, closed the lid on her laptop and grabbed her handbag. It was time for turkey and pumpkin pie.

CHAPTER THIRTEEN

"I thought it would be fun to take the Tube rather than rent a bus," Brad announced as Grace joined the Storyhill group in the lobby. He handed out Visitor Oyster cards to everyone. "If we get separated, you want to be on the Piccadilly Line and get off at James Street." They exited the hotel, still animatedly talking to each other. Julia linked arms with Grace as they navigated the busy city streets.

"Might be Thanksgiving for us," Julia said, leaning closer to Grace, "but it's just another workday here. Feels weird, doesn't it?" Grace thought of Andrew's mother at her conference. Weird, indeed. Before she could respond, Andrew linked his arm through Grace's free one. She looked up at him, brows coming together.

"What?" he said, shrugging his shoulders, "I thought this was what we were doing." He pointed at Grace and Julia's intertwined arms.

Julia laughed and let her arm fall away, giving Grace's elbow a little squeeze. "I'll leave you in his capable hands." Grace started to protest, but Julia waved her off and dropped back, lacing her hand into Joe's. Grace peered at Andrew's muscular arm woven through hers and glanced back at the others. She began to move away, but he placed a firm hand on top of her arm and reeled her back in.

"I don't want to get left behind," he said.

"And, you think I'm the one to get you there safely?"

"You've been here before," he said, his green eyes dancing.

"Now's probably the time to tell you that my last trip on the Tube to Covent Garden didn't go so well."

"I trust you." His simple words heavy with meaning.

They descended the steps to the Tube and pressed onto a waiting train seconds before the doors closed behind them. "You can see over the crowd. Did everyone make it on?"

"I wouldn't worry about it," he said, holding firm to a red steel post while wrapping his free arm around Grace's waist. "The guys will do whatever it takes not to miss out on any kind of food. Throw in pie and they'll move mountains."

Grace laughed and leaned back into Andrew. Any confusion she felt when they were apart melted away when she was wrapped in his arms. It felt comfortable, warm, right. She moved against his chest in time with the rocking of the train and watched, in silence, as the blur of white subway tile and plastic covered advertisements glided by outside the windows. As the train slowed to its fourth stop, she motioned to Andrew that they needed to exit.

Exiting the Underground station, the winter wind sliced through them and they ran for the red awning marking the entrance of their destination. Inside the door, they were immediately wrapped in warmth and treated to the unmistakable smell that only a French brasserie could deliver. Grace inhaled deeply, taking in the scent of bread, butter and notes of rosemary.

"Have you been here before?" Andrew asked.

"I've been to the one in New York, but never here. It's remarkably similar."

Andrew pointed to the back where Brad was motioning the group over. They wove through brass rails and red leather booths to a long table draped in white linens and fall flowers.

The Thanksgiving feast didn't disappoint. There was indeed a turkey and all its trimmings, but there was also spiced butternut squash soup and a fantastic warm winter kale salad. And the pie. It was sublime. She looked at Andrew. And the company didn't suck.

"Did you enjoy the meal?" Andrew asked, catching her gaze.

"I did. Though I missed the cranberry jelly."

"Really? The ones shaped like the can?"

"It was a childhood tradition, and one I've never been able to give up. Your family must have some weird traditions?"

Sadness passed over his eyes. "It's been a long time since I've been home for Thanksgiving—or any other holiday, I guess." Andrew sighed, his shoulders dropping. "I'm thirty-five years old and love making music and yet I'm still letting my father keep me from my family."

Grace reached her hand across the table and placed it on top of Andrew's. He flipped his hand over and laced his fingers with hers. "Families are complicated," she said softly.

"It's why I was so terrible to you at first. Not being able to finish the songs freaked me out. I kept hearing his voice, telling me I couldn't do it, that I would fail. I was scared he was right. I thought needing help meant I already failed."

"You know that's not the truth, right?"

He nodded. "I'm not going to let him ruin this day." He flipped his hair from his face and gave his head a little shake.

"What's next?" he said, directing his question to the entire

175

table. Most of them wanted to explore Covent Garden before heading back to the hotel.

"I downloaded a copy of 'A Charlie Brown Thanksgiving' before we left the States," Grace announced over the din, "how about whoever is interested in watching it come to my suite at seven?" Heads bobbed in agreement and they stood to head off to their chosen afternoon activities.

"Ug," Matt said, patting his stomach, "I ate too much."

"It wouldn't be Thanksgiving if you didn't," Joe said, slapping him on the back. "Gluttony. It's what we Americans do best." They laughed and exited the restaurant, bracing themselves against the chilly London air.

"Joe and I are going to do a little Christmas shopping. You want to join us, Grace?" Julia asked.

Grace agreed. It would be the perfect opportunity to find holiday gifts for Annie's girls—and get a little space from Andrew. Just while she collected her thoughts.

"Can I come, too?" Andrew asked, stepping up behind Grace. So much for that plan.

"You hate shopping," Julia said, her eyes narrowing.

"But I like the company," he said, wrapping his arm around Julia's shoulders and pulling her into him with a tight squeeze.

"It's my company you're seeking, is it?" Julia asked with a wry grin. She pulled Andrew's hand off her shoulder, holding it aloft. "Grace, you want in here?" she said, motioning to space under Andrew's arm.

"No," Grace said, waving her off while pink blossomed under her cheekbones. "I've been carrying around his dead weight for a while now. I could use a break."

"Been there," Joe said with a laugh. He turned to his wife and threw his arm around her shoulder. "Jules, you want to pop into this shop?" he asked, pointing to a colorful window display of the latest bestsellers. "You guys want to join us?"

"Thanks, but I need to go to that toy store up there." Grace pointed to a rainbow-striped awning with twisting mobiles dancing underneath it. "You want to help me pick out Christmas gifts for Abbie and Ellie, Andrew?"

"Because I act like a child?"

"Your words, Cowboy. Your words."

Joe and Julia laughed before turning into the bookstore. "See you tonight," Julia called over her shoulder.

Grace pulled her laptop from her bag and plugged it into the TV. She wondered if anyone would show up to watch it with her—with them. Andrew was stretched out on her sofa, flipping through a book he'd purchased earlier.

They had shopped and laughed, all afternoon, gotten dinner and then returned here. He didn't ask if he could come to her room, he just followed her off the elevator. She watched him from the corner of her eye. Maybe—likely—she was making this too complicated. Perhaps she should enjoy this while she had the chance. They'd be together for the short balance of the tour and a few weeks following it and then they'd go their separate ways. A few more of those toe-curling orgasms and a little companionship, all with a prede-termined expiration date, sounded pretty good. Boundaries that guaranteed she'd never again vanish into another musi-cian's life.

A knock on the door sent Andrew from the couch to the door. Joe, Julia, Matt, Brad, and Brad's wife Ginny streamed over the threshold.

"Welcome," Grace said, opening her arms wide, happy to think about something other than Andrew and orgasms. "Are the others coming?"

"They're still at dinner and texted to say they'd try and meet us later," Brad answered. He lowered his large frame to the floor and leaned against the side of the couch.

"We're going to have to get cozy," Joe said, eyeing the two small sofas.

"That's what families do," Matt said, sliding down onto the floor next to Brad.

"I grabbed some popcorn from the store downstairs," Julia said, raising two brown bags in her hand.

"That's appropriate since that's one of the things Snoopy served at their Thanksgiving," Grace said, motioning toward the TV.

"And, Peppermint Patty was so mad," Brad added.

"Now I know why you two are friends," Andrew said with a smile. "You both seem to know a lot of useless information."

"It's not useless," Grace and Brad said simultaneously, and everyone laughed. Grace double-clicked the movie icon and when she turned around, every available seat was taken.

Andrew caught her eye and patted his lap. Grace's eyes grew wide as he hooked his finger at her. What the hell, she thought, what happens in London, stays in London, right?

Grace moved through legs and arms and dropped into Andrew's lap. He wrapped his arms around her middle and no one seemed to pay any attention as they cheered the Paramount logo appearing on the screen.

"This is the perfect, cheesy way to end an American Thanksgiving," Joe said.

"Cheesy?" Grace cried, "I'll have you know this little slice of Americana won an Emmy."

"Of course you'd know that," Andrew said softly into her ear and pulled her in closer.

Yes, a tour fling was an excellent idea, Grace thought as she settled back against his chest.

. . .

Grace's head slammed down onto her laptop's external keyboard sending discordant tones bouncing around the room. After staring at the home screen of GarageBand for nearly twenty minutes, she'd finally summoned the courage to click on Empty Project. She'd opened the software instruments, chose Steinway grand piano, plunked out a couple of notes, and then . . . nothing.

Nada. Zilch. Bupkis.

She'd like to blame yesterday's tryptophan. That it was simply a case of a brain tired from too much turkey. But that required more denial than even she could muster.

Frustrated didn't even begin to explain the emotions coursing through her. Since leaving New York, she thought she'd started to silence the doubts, the demons, the fears, but here she sat totally blocked once again, with lyrics and notes tangling up in her mind like a giant ball of hair in a sink trap.

The only words she heard were doubt's nasty ministrations: *maybe people only celebrate your songs because the great Jax Jensen sang them, not because they're any good.*

She needed Andrew.

Fuck. No.

She may want him. She may have eased into the idea of an affair with boundaries, but when she'd given into Ford's demands, she made herself a singular promise: to show everyone, including herself, they were wrong. That she could do this on her own. That she would never again stand in another musician's shadow. That she would and could—scale this mountain under her own power.

Except she wasn't. And it was pissing her off.

She slammed the lid of her laptop shut and pushed her chair back so quickly she nearly tipped it over.

She needed a change of venue. And coffee. And chocolate

croissants. Yes. That's what she needed. Coffee, butter, and sugar solved all problems.

She unceremoniously tossed her laptop into her bag and shoved her arms into her coat with a final reminder that she didn't need Andrew—or anyone else for that matter. She wrenched open her hotel room door and squealed, clutching her heart. Had she actually conjured him up? She'd only said his name twice. She was sure you had to say it three times for a proper conjuring.

Andrew smirked and flipped his hair back from his face. "Not used to finding good looking men lurking outside your door?" he said in that deep rumble that immediately made her forget her anger and annoyance. He leaned down and placed a gentle kiss on her lips and she couldn't recall why she'd thought it was a good idea to send him back to his own room last night.

She could invite him in now . . .

No. No more ignoring the reason she was here in the first place. She was here for the music, not for the sexy musician. *Pull it together*.

She rolled her shoulders and summoned professional Grace. "Why are you here? I thought you were spending the day with your mom and sister."

His smile faltered. "I'm seeing them later. Right now, duty calls. The guys and I are grabbing breakfast and then heading to tonight's venue for a quick run-through. I thought maybe you'd like to tag along. But," he said, leaning to look at her laptop bag, "it looks like you might have other plans?"

"I need to top off the coffee tank and then I'm going to try and get a little writing done." Try being the operative word. "I've been a bit distracted the past few days. It's time to get back to work."

Andrew waggled his eyebrows and slowly ran his hand down his chest. "Care to tell me what's been distracting you?"

Grace followed his hand with her eyes, her breath catching. "Oh, you know, sightseeing, turkey." She looked up into his emerald eyes. "Turkeys," she said, emphasizing the plural.

He smirked. "Very funny. But you're going to work on our songs? Without me? I'm not sure I'm okay with that."

She wasn't sure either and neither was the lump expanding rapidly in her throat. She bit down on her lip and swallowed. "Relax, Cowboy, my plan was to work on the new song, not muck about changing any of yours."

He leaned down to meet her eye-to-eye. "C'mon, Gracie, you know you don't really want to write without me. Come with us. We have plenty of time to work on all the songs. Together." He held out his hand to her and wiggled his fingers.

"Fine," she said, slapping away his hand and marching in front of him toward the elevator. A nagging voice suggested she'd given up on her promise to herself, but it was promptly and loudly shouted down by relief. Grace O'Connor proudly putting the "pro" in procrastinator.

After breakfast, they made their way to the evening's venue. The building manager unlocked the auditorium doors and flipped the stage lights on. "The lighting tech should be here shortly. Until then, I'll show you the backstage lounge," the manager said, leading the five men of Storyhill down the center aisle.

Having no desire to see yet another greenroom, Grace sat down in one of the padded, crushed velvet auditorium chairs. She closed her eyes and let her head fall to the back of the seat. She loved the silence of an empty theater. It was peaceful and held so much promise. Music and monologues seemed to whisper from the walls. Soon the room would be packed with people and the powerful energy performers brought to the stage, but now it was just her and the ghosts of performances past.

"Only old ladies nap before noon."

Grace jumped. Brad had slid, unnoticed, into the seat next to her. For the second time today, she found herself slapping a hand over her racing heart.

She swiveled her head, still propped up on the chair back, toward Brad and made a face. "Old ladies also have heart attacks when startled."

He chuckled. "Duly noted. I wouldn't want that on my conscience."

"Or be the one to tell Ford you need another songwriter because you killed the first one." Grace pushed herself upright in the chair and caught movement at the edge of the curtain. She turned to see Andrew, Joe, and Blake walk onto the stage. She nodded toward them. "You here to supervise the run-through?"

"Not really. Just wanted to make sure tech showed up and everything was okay with the venue. Why are you here?"

"Procrastinating."

"How are the songs coming along?" Brad asked without taking his eyes off the stage.

"Good, I guess?" Grace counted off on her fingers. "Six songs are ready to be arranged. Three more are nearly done and three have a strong hook, but not much else."

"That's great progress. Why don't you sound happy?"

Grace leaned forward and tapped her fingers along the chair in front of her, matching the beat of the song Storyhill currently sang. "It's lucky number thirteen—the extra song Ford demanded—that's getting to me. It's going to have to be written from scratch." Grace looked at her friend. Time to come clean. "And I've got nothing. Possibly less than nothing."

Brad shrugged. "I wouldn't worry about it. In case you

haven't heard, you're the great Grace O'Connor, a writer whose talent is as bright and shiny as all those Grammys she's won."

Grace grunted, folded her arms across her chest and sunk back into her seat. "I really wish people would stop saying things like that."

Brad finally took his eyes off the stage and turned his full attention on her. "Too much pressure?"

Grace nodded.

"Just remember that even a tarnished and dented Grammy is still a Grammy."

Grace laughed, the tension easing from her shoulders. "Wow. That was deep. You been scrolling through inspirational memes again?"

"Hey, that was a Brad Rodgers original, I'll have you know."

"You are truly a man of many talents—and hidden depths."

"Speaking of talented men, you and Andrew seem to be getting along better—some might even call it cozy." As if on cue, Andrew dropped into a deep, rumbling A ♭ 1, causing the sound tech to scramble to readjust the auditorium speakers— and giving Grace a breath before having to respond to Brad's comment.

Heat crept up her neck and spread across her cheeks. This so wasn't a conversation she wanted to have with Brad. "It's nice not to be at each other's throats anymore." Shit. Poor choice of words. "To not be fighting anymore," she quickly added. She might be ready for an affair, but she wasn't ready for everyone to know about it.

A wry smile pulled at the corners of Brad's lips. "You sure that's all it is?"

"Yes, of course. What else would it be?" *When did she become the woman who lied to all of her friends?*

"I've known you for over twenty years, Grace O'Connor. I was there when you got the diagnosis and I was there when Jax died, leaving you heartbroken. And, I've been here ever since, and this is the first time I've seen even a glimmer of happiness in your eyes since he passed."

Damn it, when did everyone in her life become so observant? She needed some air. And to escape.

She popped up. "I think I'm going to head back to the hotel. I need to email Ford an update."

Brad's eyes narrowed. "On a holiday weekend?"

Grace nodded a little too vigorously. "I'm hoping the tryptophan from the holiday turkey will have put him in a mellow mood."

"Okay," he said slowly. "Are you planning on coming to the concert tonight?"

She nodded and he dug a small card out of his bag.

"This is will get you in the side door."

Grace grabbed the pass and stepped over his legs into the aisle, already counting the number of steps back to the double doors.

"And Grace?"

Please don't ask any more questions about Andrew. She sucked in a breath and turned back toward him. "Yes?"

"He's a good guy, G, and while I know it's none of my business, I think you should give him a chance. You two seem to fit."

She nodded and fled up the aisle, not bothering to stop when she heard Matt call her name.

Andrew relaxed back into his chair. Tonight's concert had been nearly flawless. The lights worked, the sound system performed perfectly, and the audience sang along and laughed at every funny anecdote. And now the entire team was packed shoulder-to-shoulder around a well-worn pine table littered with all the usuals—several empty beer glasses and a nearly decimated basket of fries.

He looked around tonight's bar choice and took in the paneled walls cluttered with portraits, paintings, and other curiosities. It looked like something out of a movie set, complete with a bartender that appeared to have been pickled right behind the bar—Central Casting couldn't have done a better job. A centuries-old iron fireplace crackled and popped in the corner, burning real wood. Chipped oak barstools surrounded the carved bar. And, surprisingly, there was a little space cleared in the far corner where a few couples swayed together, foam sliding over the top of their pints as they moved to the music.

He looked at the woman sitting to his left, smiling and laughing with Joe and Julia. So much had changed in such a short period. They'd fallen into a rhythm and working side-by-side they'd generated music unlike any he'd ever written and created an amazing partnership.

Could he break through the last of her walls and convince her to give him a chance?

He leaned down to whisper in her ear. "Thanks for coming."

She turned and looked up into his eyes, her smile pulling wider. "Mattie didn't give me much choice. He told me that now that I am an official member of Storyhill, post-concert celebrations are not optional."

"That is true. Plus, with you sitting next to me, it helps keep all the other women at bay—on account of the fact that I'm so sexy."

She slapped him on the arm and shook her head. "Again, with the human shield thing?"

He laughed and gave her thigh a quick, gentle squeeze. "Seriously, it's been a great night and having you here makes it that much better."

Grace's smile fell and a hint of sadness passed through her eyes. "You're right, it has been a great night. And a great couple of weeks." Her gaze zig-zagged from his forehead, over his eyes and his lips. She inhaled a long, deep breath and placing both palms on the table, stood up.

Was she leaving? No, he wanted her here. He reached for her hand, tugging it toward him. She gave it a squeeze and tapped a fork against the side of her pint glass, quieting the table.

"I'd like to make a toast. When I was first asked to help Storyhill with their next album, I wasn't exactly happy about it." Titters of laughter cascaded down the table. "But now? Well, I want to thank you all for reminding me how much I love what I do. I've been drifting since my husband passed, and it has taken my time with you to remind me how much I love being part of this industry. Thank you. You might not realize it"—she turned to look directly at him—"but you've given me my life back, and I will be forever grateful. Cheers."

A thoughtful silence came over the table and everyone raised their glasses and clinked them together. Grace slipped back into her chair and turned to Andrew. "Did I just kill the mood?" she whispered.

He shook his head, words escaping him. The noise at the table built back to its usual deafening din, and he saw her lips move but couldn't make out the words. "What?"

"Dance with me," she called out a second time.

Matt overheard and laughed. "Good luck, Gracie-girl, Andrew doesn't dance. Unless you count those stiff moves he busts out in the occasional video. But, don't worry, I'll dance with you," he said, starting to rise from his chair.

"I've seen those videos," Grace said, laughing, "but it's okay, I'm a good teacher." She stood and reached her hand out again and raised her eyebrows. "You man enough to try?"

To everyone's surprise, he took her hand and allowed her to lead him to the miniature dance floor. Matt was right, he was a little stiff. She moved closer to him and put her hands on his hips. "You need to loosen up from here. Let me show you." She pushed him one way and then slid him back, keeping her hands on his hips. He moved uncomfortably, trying to match the driving beat of the song.

Grace chuckled. "That's not working. Try this instead. Imagine moving your hips in a figure-eight pattern." She cocked her hips from right to left and his gaze fell to follow the pattern. "The center of the eight is right here," she said, placing a finger right above his zipper, not breaking her movement.

"Grace," he said, his voice rough and ragged, "you need to stop that." He pulled her hand away from his waist and held it between them.

"Why?" she asked, mischief dancing in those beautiful blue eyes.

She knew damn well why he needed her to take her hands off him. His pants were already a little too tight and if she kept moving his hips back and forth, he wasn't sure they could accommodate what was happening. He took the hand pinned between them and twirled her away in a small circle. Before he reeled her back in, the song ended, and she started to move back toward their table.

He reached for her, but she ducked to avoid his arm. "How about getting me another drink?" she said with a smile over her shoulder.

He sighed and turned toward the bar. Ordering, he propped his forearms on the counter and dug his thumb into the space between his eyebrows.

"You sure you know what you're doing?" a familiar voice said as he set an empty pint glass next to Andrew's elbow.

"Never been much of a dancer, so no," he said, not turning his head to look at Joe.

Joe snorted. "I'm talking about the heart eyes and that post-coital glow you were rocking yesterday."

Andrew closed his eyes and fisted his hand in his hair. "I told her you'd notice. She thought I was kidding. Thanks for not saying anything in front of her."

"I'm right?" He slapped Andrew on the back. "I was just trying to yank your chain."

"You need to keep this to yourself—not a word, not even to Jules."

Joe leaned down onto the bar, mimicking Andrew's pose. "Seriously? You're sleeping with her? I thought maybe it was just a little harmless crush. What about your stupid rule about no relationships until Storyhill is bankable?"

The bartender slid two pints down the bar and Andrew sipped the foam off the top before it cascaded down the side. "It was always more of a guideline than a rule."

Joe grabbed his freshly filled glass. "Whatever you say, Captain Barbossa."

Andrew gripped Joe's forearm. "Seriously, not a word. She's skittish about the whole thing."

Joe waggled his eyebrows. "And you'd like to do it again?"

"You're such an ass. Surely, you have better things to do with your time than harass me."

Joe cocked his head from side-to-side and laughed. "Better, yes. More fun? Definitely not."

"Joe," Andrew warned.

"You know I'd never tell anyone, but be careful, Andy. This has an excellent chance of blowing up in your face."

"Thanks for the vote of confidence." Andrew looked over Joe's shoulder, his eyes washing over his bandmates—his brothers—and shuddered. Joe wasn't wrong. He had convinced himself that relationships were synonymous with taking his eye off the ball. Would giving into his feelings for Grace jeopardize everything they were trying to build?

He strolled back to the table and placed Grace's pint in front of her, sliding into his chair.

"You okay?" she asked, her eyes searching his face and her brow crinkling.

He nodded and tucked a curl behind her ear, reveling in the silky way her hair slid between his fingers. "Just lost in thought about tomorrow's concert in Dublin," he lied.

CHAPTER FOURTEEN

B lue lights hung overhead, coloring the smoky haze crawling across the stage. The din of noise from the house increased as audience members filled the seats. Grace's eyes washed over the stage. It was so simple. The complete opposite of Jax's stage shows.

Four black risers, five bar stools, and two simple rows of lights, changing color throughout the show. With everything stripped down, it allowed their voices to shine.

"Last show, G."

Grace turned to find Brad standing behind her. "It went so fast." She swallowed the unexpected melancholy burning in her throat.

"I'm sorry the schedule didn't allow time to see the sights of Dublin."

He'd misinterpreted her sadness. Thankfully. Grace reached into her mind to redirect the conversation into a space that didn't bring up more questions than it answered. "No worries. I understand how tours work."

"Of course you do." He nodded, gave her a small smile and threw his arm around her shoulders. "Thanks for everything. I know this wasn't easy for you, but you set aside your concerns and helped them meet an almost impossible goal."

"We're not quite there yet."

"True. But they are so much closer than they would have been without your help."

"I can't believe I almost didn't come." This trip had done more for her than she could have imagined.

"I need to rally the troops. Come with me to the greenroom?"

Grace shook her head. "I'll wait here."

She would watch the final show from the same place she watched the first—hidden in the wings. In the shadows. Where she'd always stood. Watching Jax command the stage and thrill the audience. Until this experience, she'd convinced herself that standing in the background was easy, comfortable. Now, she physically ached from playing second fiddle. She hungered for more. But, at forty-four years old, was it too late to change? Could she break through decades of conditioning? And, if she did, what then? Her eyes brimmed and a single tear fell over the edge.

A familiar staccato rhythm echoed behind her. Boots against wood. Warmth swirled around her spine as Andrew stepped up behind her. He turned her toward him, reaching up with his thumb and brushing away the wetness on her cheek. "Why the tears?"

Grace shook her head and choked out a laugh. "I'm just so worried you guys are going to screw it up out there."

"Well, then you better wish me good luck."

"Good luck."

"That all you got?" He twitched an eyebrow. "How about giving your sexy bass singer a good luck kiss?"

"Here?" She looked side-to-side, her eyes growing wide. "Joe's right there."

"He knows."

"You told him?"

"He's my best friend, Grace. He guessed the other night, and I didn't want to lie to him. There's really no reason to hide it, anyway. No one can say we aren't getting the work done. Lay one on me, pretty lady."

She knew she should say no. The goal was to keep this casual, not to want more, feel more. Not to openly flaunt their relationship in front of the entire band. But she couldn't. She couldn't deny him.

Her lips quirked upward, and she grabbed the collar of his jacket and pulled him down to her. As their lips met, Matt turned around, and his mouth dropped open.

"Knock 'em dead," she said, pulling away and giving his butt a little squeeze as the house lights dropped.

"Hey, Gracie-girl, does everyone get a good luck kiss?" Matt asked. She shot a look at Andrew and marched up to Matt and placed an exaggerated kiss on his lips.

"Good luck, Mattie," she said, patting him on the butt.

Andrew winced. "Enjoy that mate, it's the last one you're going to get."

Grace placed her hands on her hips. "You did not just tell me who I can and cannot kiss, did you?"

"Depends. You done flirting with Matt?"

"Flirting? He's not exactly my type."

"What is your type?"

She smirked. "Someone who wasn't in diapers when I was in high school."

Andrew nodded sagely. "I was at least in Pull-Ups by the time you got there."

Grace's eyebrows scurried up her forehead. "Drawing attention to our age difference might not be to your advantage, Cowboy. You sure you want to go there?"

Andrew walked up to her and rested his hands on her shoulders, pinning her with those emerald eyes that had captured her attention that first moment in the coffee shop. "As much as you like a good fight, this is not the time or place. Unless you believe in make-up sex?"

Grace pulled a face and Andrew laughed, palms out. "Okay, okay, no make-up sex, but I would like to take you out after the concert, just the two of us. Celebrate our final night before heading home. I have a surprise for you."

She opened her mouth to say she didn't like surprises, but he held up a single finger, gave her a wink, and strode up to the four other men. They stepped on stage to raucous applause.

"Where are we going?" Grace said to Andrew as he returned from the greenroom, jacket in hand.

"You'll see." He grabbed her hand and pulled her toward the stage door.

"Tell me where we're going."

"Nope. As hard as it is for you, you're going to have to trust me." He led her outside, stopping at the corner where a horse and carriage waited.

"Is that for us?"

"I know it's kind of cheesy and touristy, but—"

"Why should anything change now?" she teased, a grin pulling at the corners of her mouth.

He laughed and stepped into the red and white carriage, turning and offering his hand.

She placed her hand in his, letting him help her into the crimson crushed velvet seats. "Now, tell me where we're going."

"And people say I'm the stubborn one. We're going to the Ha'Penny Bridge. It's supposed to be magical at night."

"Magical? You going soft on me, Cowboy?"

"I find I'm rarely soft when you're around."

Grace snorted and fell against him as the driver snapped the reins and the horse lurched forward into the night. "How was the table tonight?"

Andrew smirked. "No cleavage requests."

"Are you losing your touch?"

"Naw, probably just thought it was inappropriate since it was a Christmas concert . . . or maybe they all sensed that I'm only interested in one woman's cleavage right now." His eyes dropped lower.

The carriage slowed and dropped them at the base of the curved bridge where each iron arch was topped with a glittering globe. Green and white lights illuminated the underside of the bridge, casting dancing pools of brightness in the river below. He chuckled as she stepped forward and grasped the white railing.

"Why are you laughing?"

"I guess I'm waiting for you to share a little-known fact about the bridge." A smile played across his lips, his eyes crinkling at the corners.

"Drum roll, please—it was a toll bridge when it was first constructed, thus the name 'Ha'penny'."

"And what is a ha'penny?"

"British half-penny, originally minted in copper, then in bronze. It ceased being legal tender in the late '60s."

He laughed. "You don't disappoint, do you?"

"What can I say, I have a brain for trivia, song lyrics, and commercial jingles. All taking up valuable space in my head and totally useless."

"Useless until you realize how much it charms certain men."

She snorted. "Walk with me—certain man." She held out her hand and he wrapped his fingers around hers.

"You cold?"

"A little." He put his arm around her shoulders, pulling her into his warm chest. She gazed into the river. Lights from the nearby bars and restaurants flickered and swayed over the river's rippled surface casting shadows on the many couples huddling together as they crossed the iconic bridge.

He placed a light kiss on her temple and ran his hand over her hair. "Now, how about we cap off the evening with a cocktail over there at Temple Bar? I hear all the cheesy tourists do it."

Grace laughed and they turned around and headed back toward the cobblestone street.

They wedged themselves in the front door of the historic red building and Grace spotted a couple leaving a table near the door. Squeezing her small frame through the throng of people, she jumped on a stool within seconds of the previous inhabitants' departure. The table was nothing more than a piece of glass resting atop an oak wine barrel and based on the number of rings on the glass, it had turned many times. Everywhere she looked, there was something new to see—the patterned tile floor, the flags hanging from the red ceiling, and paneled wood walls covered with prints of horses and the Irish countryside.

"I can't believe you found this table," Andrew said. "Impressive. How about you stay here and protect it while I get a couple of drinks." He eyed the crush of people at the bar. "Somehow. What would you like?"

"Cider," she said, reaching for her handbag.

"I got this one." He zigzagged through the crowd and positioned himself in front of a pretty bartender at the end of the bar. Leaning in, he said something that made her laugh, and within minutes, he was heading back to their table, drinks in hand.

"Must be tough for you."

A smile danced on his lips. "Tough?"

"You know, getting everything you want with just a smile and a wink."

"Is that all it takes?" He flashed her a wide grin and winked.

Ignoring the heat pooling between her legs, Grace put two fingers on the pulse point at her wrist. "Nope. I got nothing. Apparently, I'm more immune to your charms than . . ." She waved her hand toward the redhead at the bar.

"Emma. She's worked here three years and she's an Aquarius—and she gets off work at 2:30."

"Unbelievable." Grace rolled her eyes and took a draw from her cider. "This is good," she said, rotating the bottle in her hand and reading the label. "What did you get?" He turned his bottle toward her.

"Raging Bitch? Really? Have you ever noticed how it seems to be okay to name a beer something like Raging Bitch, but if the tables were turned and it was named, say, oh, Droopy Cock, we'd never hear the end of it?"

Andrew spit out his beer and wiped his chin, laughing. "I prefer the Flaccid Phallus. It's less hoppy. You really are an interesting woman, Grace O'Connor."

"I hope that's a compliment."

"Or?"

"Or this raging bitch will pour that Raging Bitch over your head."

"If you ruin my hair, it will slow down our service."

"Wow. Your conceit really knows no bounds, does it?"

He flashed his megawatt smile—again. "Is it conceit when it's the truth?"

"I think I preferred it when you hated me and grunted your responses."

His eyes softened and he placed his hand atop hers. "I never hated you."

"You sure about that?"

"One hundred percent."

Grace narrowed her eyes, suspicion dancing over her face.

"So, we fly home tomorrow," he said.

Grace's head snapped up at the abrupt subject change. "And in a couple of weeks, we'll have all this wrapped up, and I'll be a distant memory."

He looked down and drew a line in the condensation on his bottle. "Is that what you want?"

What did she want? When she'd decided to give in to her feelings, it was just for the duration of the tour. A safety bubble. "Isn't that what you want?"

Something flashed across his face. Hesitation? Apprehension? She couldn't quite figure it out. When he finally raised his eyes to hers, the look was gone, replaced with something closer to a resigned determination. "No. What *I* want is to take you on a proper date when we get back to Minneapolis."

Joy bubbled up. He wanted to keep seeing her? Fear beat it back with a big bat. Shit, he wanted to keep seeing her. "We have a lot of work to do when we return. It's probably best if we keep things professional." *Fear, 1. Joy, 0.*

"I think we moved beyond 'strictly professional' a few days ago, but it sounds like you need a little more convincing." He squeezed her hand. "I'll have to wear you down. But it shouldn't be too hard—according to you, women find me irresistible."

"You sure you're up for the challenge?"

"I'll do whatever it takes. Whether it's agreeing with you about the songs or buying sour gummy worms and expensive, high-maintenance coffees or providing more mind-blowing orgasms, I'm your guy."

"Why?" Grace murmured, her heart squeezing.

Pulling her close, he placed his lips on her ear. "Because you're worth every bit of effort it's going to take."

. . .

The door flung open. "Tía!" Abbie and Ellie yelled in chorus, colliding into her with affectionate hugs.

Ellie stuck out her bottom lip and clung to Grace's leg. "We haven't seen you in *for-ev-er*. You were gone soooooooo long."

Grace laughed and walked forward, pulling the dramatic little girl along with her. "Where's your momma?"

"Mami? Mom! Mamá! Where are you? Tía Grace is here!"

"Inside voices, ladies. That is a lot of yelling for so early on a Sunday morning," Annie said, rounding the corner, pulling Grace into a hug and squeezing tight. "I missed you."

Grace returned the squeeze. "We talked on Skype."

"It's not the same. You haven't been away that long since . . ." Annie looked up and caught Grace's eye. "Well, for a long time."

Grace followed Annie into the kitchen and plopped down onto a counter stool. Annie slid a steaming mug across the island to her and Grace reeled it in, grasping the coffee with both hands, letting the warmth seep into her and the deep rich smell fill her nostrils.

Annie moved from stove to dishwasher, rhythmically stowing the morning's dishes. Through the French doors, Grace watched a squirrel scurry up a snowdrift and jump onto the wooden banister surrounding the deck. It was good to be home. It might be lonelier and quieter than her time on tour, but things made sense here. She had her routine and routine meant stability.

"Girls, Tía Grace and I are going to talk a little bit. Go change out of your pajamas and find everything you need for karate."

Grace raised an eyebrow as the girls scurried down the hallway. "Karate?"

Annie shrugged. "I'm ensuring they never tell a therapist that I didn't expose them to enough things. But, enough about my obsessive need to overcompensate. Now that you're home, how was it?"

"Surprisingly, the songs are nearly finished."

"That's it?"

Grace shrugged. "That is the reason I went, isn't it?"

"Yes, but after our conversation, I thought maybe you'd be making more than just music."

"Well . . ." Grace hedged.

"Well, what?" Annie circled her hands, prodding for more.

"I don't know what to tell you. It's all so confusing. And overwhelming."

"Holy crap. You slept with him."

A small hand appeared on Grace's thigh. The sleek, modern stool Grace was perched on chirped as she turned to the soft, fuzzy creature smelling of bacon, sleep and fabric softener sidling up beside her. Abbie snuggled up and looked deep into Grace's eyes.

"Tia G, are you happy right now?" Abbie asked, dropping her Gi on the counter and cocking her head to the side.

"Why do you ask, honey?"

"Because your face looks kind of glowy—like Ellie looks after opening her Christmas presents, like all excited and stuff."

"From the mouth of babes," Annie muttered under her breath.

Grace shot Annie a look and Annie mouthed, "You totally slept with him."

Grace scowled and turned her attention back to the child. "Of course, I'm happy Abbie," she said, pulling the intuitive child into her lap. "I'm here with you, aren't I?" Annie gave a snort and turned back to the sink.

"I missed you so much." Grace squeezed her tight and tickled her fleece-covered tummy. Abbie giggled, gave her a sideways look, and squinted her eyes. It was a look Grace recognized; another question was coming. Grace cut her off with her own question.

"What did you ask Santa for?"

"Tía, you know I don't believe in Santa anymore," she said, dropping her voice to a whisper and moving her face to within an inch of Grace's.

"Okay, big girl, then what do you hope is under the tree for you?"

Her eyes lit up, and pulling out of Grace's embrace, she hopped down. "I'll go get my list and show you."

"Abbie, I asked you to get changed. Please do that before you come back," Annie shouted after the child. "She's not wrong, you are kind of glowy and stuff. Want to tell me what's going on with him?"

Grace sighed and dropped her head into her hands. "I don't know. I like him, I do. He makes me laugh. He's so damn good-looking it makes my eyeballs hurt, but he's a musician—been there, done that, got the t-shirt—and, oh yeah, he's like a decade younger than me."

"And, he's great in bed," Annie said, repeating her previous assertion, clearly fishing.

"Yes," Grace answered, barely over a whisper, not lifting up her head.

"You did it! You did sleep with him!"

"Shhh." Grace's head popped up, looking around for Will and the girls. Annie's eyes were open wide, and her mouth hung slack in a perfect O.

"You're the one who told me to have a fling."

"I didn't think you'd actually do it. It's so unlike you." Annie leaned across the island and got inches from Grace's face. "Was it good?"

Grace closed her eyes and pressed her thumb and forefinger

into the bridge of her nose. "Let's just say Santa brought my gift early. And he *really* delivered."

A huge smile spread across Annie's face. "Hot damn. So, what happens now?"

"We have an album to wrap up."

"And?"

"And he wants to take me on a proper date, apparently."

"That's a bad thing?"

"Somehow a little fling when you're thousands of miles away seems totally different than having dinner three blocks away from your own home."

"I get that you're scared." Leave it to Annie to get right to the heart of the matter. "It's been a long time since you've been out on a date."

"It hasn't been a long time, it's been a lifetime—twenty-two years, to be exact, since I've been on a first date. I don't know how to have a first date in the twenty-first century. Do you just sit across the table from each other texting emojis back and forth?"

Annie threw her head back and laughed. "Oh my god, Grace, when did you become an old lady?"

"When I started having sex with a thirty-five-year-old musician."

"Stop it. Having sex with a younger, hot man doesn't age you—just the opposite actually. Get over yourself and go on the date."

Grace tipped her head back and stared at the ceiling. "Why?"

"Why not?"

"I can think of a lot of reasons."

The corners of Annie's lips pulled up. "None that I can't refute. And, you might as well tell me how many times you slept with him. You always crack under cross-examination."

Grace scowled. "I need a new best friend who's not a lawyer."

"How many times, *chica*?"

"Here's my list," Abbie yelled, coming back down the hallway, waving the paper in her hand.

Grace let out a sigh of relief.

CHAPTER FIFTEEN

ndrew's plan had been to sleep late, give his body some additional time to recover from the concerts and the overseas flight, but Grace had a different idea. Forty-eight hours was more than enough time to recover, she'd told him. They were due at Unstrung Studios this morning at 9:00 a.m. Who started work that early?

Grace was picking him up at 8:30. A shower only took ten minutes and if he didn't shave, he could lay in this big, comfortable bed for another half-hour. It was a great bed, but he was alone in it. He'd hoped—assumed, even—that Grace would invite him to stay with her, but no.

He thought about being invited into her bedroom, wrapping himself around her, and holding her every night. A deep and desperate yearning flooded through him.

Did she know she'd done the impossible? Did she realize she was the first person to make him feel whole? She'd broken down his walls with nothing more than a smile and the words, "I believe in you." No sledgehammer required.

On the flight from Dublin to Minneapolis, he'd watched her from his seat two rows back. At one point or another, all four of his bandmates had walked by her, stopping to talk with her. They'd laughed and joked, comfortable with one another —even Joe.

By the end of the flight, an undeniable certainty settled within him. His relationship with Grace—whatever it was— would not adversely affect the band. She was far too professional for that. And he certainly didn't need to push her away to accomplish his goals. It had never been more apparent that she was his partner, not his adversary.

But despite all that, she was still a puzzle he couldn't quite piece together. Tough and guarded one moment. Scared and vulnerable the next. They'd stopped fighting. They laughed together. They'd made love. Yet, every time he felt like they grew closer, she closed down.

He tried to understand. She was still grieving. Probably always would be. She was nervous about getting involved with another musician because every part of her life had been scrutinized by the press. Rubbed raw and taught to be cautious through life's hardest lessons.

He needed to show her she was safe with him. He could do that. Take her hand and help her step forward and when she tried to step back, he'd hold her, telling her through his touch that there was nothing to be afraid of—especially not him.

His phone vibrated on the nightstand. He reached for his glasses, sliding them on, bringing the screen into focus—which really wasn't necessary, there was only one person who would text him this early.

You up, Cowboy?

He propped himself up on the pillows and snapped a selfie —a shirtless selfie. Yes, he'd help her feel safe, but he wasn't above using other tactics—especially those that were already proven winners.

I'm awake, but not up. Want to come over and help me with that part?

Ignoring your seventh-grade humor. Put on a shirt. I'll meet you outside in fifteen minutes. Driving a silver Nissan Leaf.

The speech bubble appeared again.

And, before you think about getting cheeky, put on pants, too. Shirt, shoes and pants. All required.

He laughed and rolled out of bed.

Andrew zipped his jacket up to his chin and moved through the revolving door. The December Minnesota air hit his lungs and, he kept on walking right back into the hotel. He'd wait inside.

He sat on a chair near the windows and poked through the magazines littering the coffee table until five words splashed across a dog-eared cover stopped him. He picked up the magazine and flipped through to the article when a silver flash caught his attention as Grace's car pulled up to the curb. He stood, rolled up the magazine, and slid it into his back pocket to read later.

He folded his long legs into Grace's small car and placed a gentle kiss on her temple. "Good morning, beautiful."

"Sorry about the lack of legroom. I'm not used to transporting oversized humans. It's only about a thirty-minute drive."

He alternated between rubbing his hands together and rubbing them down his thighs. "It's okay, at least it's warm. I don't know how you do it. It's so cold."

She met his gaze for an instant before turning back to the road. "First, we know how to dress for it. That little leather jacket is not going to cut it. And second, we're not whiners. It's going to be thirty-five degrees today."

"Heatwave."

"Hey, it could be minus ten."

"C'mon now, we all know thermometers don't register nega-
tive numbers."

Grace laughed. "After we're done today, we'll get you a
winter coat and some gloves—maybe I'll even throw in one of
our fancy, new-fangled, all-temperature thermometers."

"You sure you want to do that? That doesn't exactly fall into
the 'strictly professional' category."

"If you're frozen stiff, you can't help finish the songs."

"Of course. Another example of Grace O'Connor covering
every angle and anticipating every need."

Grace's smile faded and she flicked on her turn signal,
tapping the lever a few times before moving her hand back to
the steering wheel. "I'm organized, but I learned the hard way
that you cannot begin to be prepared for all the things life is
going to throw at you."

*Great. He'd attempted a joke and inadvertently touched a
sore spot. Not the way to make her feel safe.*

"How did you do it, Gracie? How did you move on after
such a big loss?"

"God, I hate that saying. You don't move on. Moving on is
something people uncomfortable with grief want you to do. The
whole concept is ridiculous."

She stared out the windshield, neck stiff, eyes pinned
straight ahead. He smoothed his hand over her thigh. "What do
you do? Gracie," he said, his voice a whisper, "explain it to me.
Teach me."

She drove in silence, not looking at him, but also not
refusing his touch. He waited, not asking again. Minutes later,
she pulled into the driveway of a luxury home and killed the
engine. She turned to him, placed her hand over his and ran her
fingers lightly over his knuckles.

"You move *forward*. 'Moving on' asks you to pack everything
up in a neat little box and store it on a shelf. Like it was just

something that happened to you once. A series of memories, nothing else. Jax and our life together is not just wispy visions that pop up once in a while. Our life, our experiences, our love, will forever be sewn into the fabric of my being. It makes me who I am. So, you walk forward, carrying that person with you, not putting him in a box on a shelf. He may no longer be with me physically, but he is always at my side."

"Christ, you're amazing. I can honestly say I've never met a woman like you."

Grace wiped a tear from the corner of her eye and smiled shyly. "Yeah, all that and a great rack."

"And, the jokes are back."

Grace shrugged. "We all gotta find a way to cope." She pointed at the looming house in front of them. "We should go in."

He stepped out of the car, rounded the front and opened her door, offering her a hand. "Can I ask you one more thing?"

"Do I have to give a serious answer?"

"Yes."

She closed her eyes and sucked in a deep breath. "Hit me."

"Does that mean you don't have room for more love in your life?"

She studied his face, eyes moving rapidly, and murmured, "No, it doesn't mean that."

It was only a tiny sliver of light sneaking through an even smaller crack in her walls, but to Andrew, it felt like the heavens had opened, the sun illuminating a giant heap of hope. She wasn't against love in general. Now, if he could convince her to get into the specifics—the specifics of a guy who was losing the ability to picture his life without her in it.

"Ready?"

Hell yes, he was. Knowing he was answering a different question than the one she asked, he nodded and followed her up the winding sidewalk, taking in the clean lines of the dominating structure. "Apparently, business is good."

"You should see it in the summer when the lake isn't frozen. It's stunning."

Andrew followed the voice to the man standing in front of a pair of giant frosted glass doors. Dark skin against the creamy European-style stucco, bald head, heavy-rimmed glasses and a full beard made for an indomitable presence.

"There's a lake out there? Looks like a pile of snow to me," Andrew said.

The man's stern face broke into a smile and a deep belly laugh escaped. He walked down the steps and extended his hand. "Chris Cooper."

"Andrew Hayes."

"Nice to meet you, man. And, if you're the person responsible for getting this crazy-talented lady back in the studio, I owe you a debt of gratitude." He turned and opened his arms. "Gigi."

"Chris," Grace said, wrapping her arms around the man, delivering a crushing hug. "So good to see you."

"Not as good as it is to see you. I'm so fucking excited to have you back in the studio." He pulled back from Grace and squeezed her shoulders before opening the door ushering them inside. Grace immediately turned to the sweeping staircase and started down.

"Are you ready to be blown away?" Chris asked Andrew as they followed Grace.

"Sorry?"

"Grace." He pointed at her retreating back. "She's the best producer I've ever worked with—present company excluded, of course. I've tried to convince her to start her own company for years, but she keeps downplaying her skills. Watch. She'll take over in the studio and then give me all the credit. I've never been able to figure it out."

At the bottom of the stairs, Grace held the door open to the most extraordinary studio Andrew had ever seen. State of the art . . . well, everything. This might be the best day of his life—this studio, the music they created together, and her—he couldn't imagine needing anything else.

Grace pulled the magazine out of his pocket as he ran his hands over the mixing board. "What's this?"

Andrew tried to pull it back, but she held it out of his reach. "I didn't take you for a rag reader." She scanned the cover and her bright smile faded. She flipped to the middle of the magazine.

"Jax Jensen's widow is apparently done mourning," she read aloud.

"Grace, c'mon, give it back to me." Andrew reached for the magazine again.

She spun from him and continued. "Jensen's widow has been spotted out and about with a younger man. A new partnership is rumored, but *Gossip* can't help but wonder if this is more play than work." A picture of the two of them leaving Temple Bar stared back from below the headline.

"I'm not that much younger than you, Gracie."

She shook the magazine at him. "You think that's why this bothers me? Because the world can't get over its cougar complex?"

"What then?"

"I'm a person. I'm not just an extension of Jax Jensen. The article didn't even mention my name. Again," she said, muttering the last word. She launched the magazine into the armchair in the corner of the studio. "When will it end?" She looked between the two men. "When?" She paced back-and-forth in front of the console. "I guess I should be happy the headline didn't read, 'Jensen's widow found herself a new muse.' Because, of course, my skill only appears in the presence of sexy men."

Andrew smirked.

She stabbed a finger at him and pursed her lips. "Don't even think about it, Cowboy. I am not in the mood for your arrogance right now." She ripped the binder from her hair, shaking it out, and forcefully pulling it back into a messy bun atop her head. She slapped the side of the console and then shook her hand out with a grimace. "I'm so over the rumors and the accusations."

Chris put his arm around her. "Start your own production company, Gigi, and that'll end that. Step up. Show the world your stuff."

She stilled, her eyes closing and her lips twitching. Andrew watched her as she buried her feelings—again. When she opened her eyes the anger and hurt were gone.

She slapped Chris on the chest. "You couldn't handle the competition."

"Might make me step up my game."

Andrew scratched his chin. "Frankly, if anyone should feel bad, it's me."

Grace's eyebrows crept up her forehead. "You?"

"Yes. I'm nothing but a boy toy in that article. Not a single mention of the immensely talented bass singer from the country group, Storyhill. I feel cheap."

Grace laughed and raised her hands, palms out. "I got the message, boys. Loud and clear. No letting these hacks ruin my day. Let's get these songs arranged so we can get the individual parts sent to the guys."

Andrew stretched his arms over his head and rolled his chair away from the mixing board. They'd been at this for hours, not even breaking for lunch. Food had mysteriously appeared on the table behind them around noon, and they'd eaten while recreating Joe's beats with a synthesizer until they could work with the real thing. Between the two of them, Andrew and Chris had recorded each of the other four parts so they could get the mix exactly right.

"Great work today," Chris said, rubbing a hand over his smooth head. "Grace, I have a call in thirty. Can you close everything down?"

"Sure. Same time tomorrow?"

"That works. Have a great night. Again, cool to work with you, Andrew—you and Grace make a good team."

"I agree." Andrew glanced at Grace who quickly averted her eyes and powered down the computer, screens, speakers and board.

"Speaking of being a team, Gracie, how about dinner tonight?"

"I can't tonight."

"Can't or won't?"

"Can't, Andrew. Ellie has a dance recital. I promised her I'd be there. And, Annie invited me over for dinner beforehand."

"Is your calendar clear tomorrow night?"

"Yes."

"Good. I'll make reservations. Do you have a favorite?"

Grace's lips pulled up at the corners. "That depends."

He couldn't help but smile back at her. "On what?"

"You buying?"

"I asked, so yes."

"If that's the case, I choose Belle Nourriture."

"That sounds fancy. Do they serve cowboys there?"

Grace smirked. "Since you only play a cowboy on TV, it should be okay. But you might want to brush up on what fork goes with what course."

"You've met Sylvia Hayes. You can't believe for a moment I'm not versed in cutlery and proper etiquette?"

"Maybe I'm the one who's not fancy enough."

"Don't worry, she also taught me to be a gentleman. I won't make fun of you when you mess it up."

"That's generous of you."

Andrew smirked and tapped a finger to his chest. "Gentleman."

"Okay, okay, that's enough from you. Up the stairs, out the door, and get in the car."

"Grace," he wrapped his fingers around her wrist, "about what happened earlier—with the magazine—I thought you'd want to see it—as a head's up. I was wrong. I'm sorry. But you know you can talk to me if—"

"Thanks," she said, cutting him off, "but there's nothing to talk about it. The past is the past. There's no use talking about something that can't be changed. I'm over it."

He nodded and placed a soft kiss on the tip of her nose. He let it go, but he seriously doubted she was anywhere near over it.

"I'm having dinner with Andrew tomorrow night." Grace slipped around Annie and dropped a handful of pasta into the boiling water.

Annie's eyes shot wide. "Is this the proper date?"

"I guess so."

"Where's he taking you?"

"I suggested Belle Nourriture."

"Nice. Not stuffy yet totally romantic."

Grace gave the pasta a stir, raising her hand to rub her fore-head, letting water drip all over the stovetop. "What the heck I am supposed to wear?"

Annie laughed and shook her head. "I like this new Grace."

"What does that mean?"

"You're usually so collected and controlled. It's fun to see you a little undone—I didn't know that was possible."

"If you think I seem anxious on the outside, you should see what is happening inside."

"I'm not sure why you're so nervous. All the boxes have been checked."

"Meaning?"

Annie held up four fingers, lowering each one in turn. "Nice guy, gainfully employed, good kisser, fantastic lover." Annie pursed her lips and tapped her chin. "I think you might be on to something, Grace. Maybe the correct order is to test all the equipment *and then* go on the first date."

"You're incorrigible."

"What's in-core-gerbil?" Ellie asked, walking into the kitchen.

"It means your mom is impossible." Grace winked at Annie.

"Oh, my dad says that all the time," Ellie said, climbing up on a barstool and shrugging her shoulders.

Grace grinned. "What was that you said the other day?" Grace snapped her fingers and pointed at Annie. "Out of the mouths of babes?"

Annie furrowed her brow and turned back to the stove, stirring the sauce—and ignoring Grace's comment. "I've been telling the girls about New Year's resolutions. Ellie, why don't you tell Tía yours?"

"I have mine," Abbie said, joining in. "I'm going to buy dog beds for at least four shelters."

"I'm still trying to pick," Ellie said, screwing up her face, thinking hard.

"How about getting your yellow belt in karate or starting to learn a petit allegro in ballet?" Grace asked, trying to guide her young companion.

Ellie nodded emphatically and crossed her arms. "Both. Papi says I can do anything I think really hard about."

Annie stifled a smile. "You mean, 'set your mind to'?"

Ellie rolled her eyes. "Same, same, Mami."

Grace laughed and shot Annie a look. "Pretty early to already be rolling her eyes at you."

"What your resolution, Mama?" Abbie asked.

"For you, and Ellie, and Papi and me to be happy and healthy all year long."

Abbie pulled a face. "That's boring." Annie looked at Grace. They both knew a wish for health was not boring at all— it could be taken in a moment's notice.

"Tía G, you haven't told us yours," Ellie said. "What is your reso-blu-tion?"

Grace steepled her fingers, tapping them together, trying to buy a little time. What did she want? To keep writing? For sure. But, should she start a production company like Chris suggested? Or throw all caution to the wind and fall in love?

"Tía, why is your face red?"

Grace forced out a laugh. "Probably because I'm thinking too hard." Annie cleared her throat, but Grace had no intention of looking at her. She didn't need to. She knew Annie would be standing with one hand on her hip, head cocked to the side, with a perfectly waxed eyebrow shooting up her forehead.

"I don't know what my resolution should be, Ellie. Probably to finish all the songs I'm writing right now."

Ellie seemed satisfied and jumped over into her lap. "I missed you." She placed her hands on Grace's cheeks and patted them softly.

Grace chuckled and wrapped Ellie's hands in her own. "I was just here a few days ago, little one."

"But before you were gone for a *very* long time. And I was worried you were lost."

"Lost? Because I was across the ocean?"

"No, 'cause Mami said you were trying to find yourself." A bowl clattered on the countertop, sending splatters of sauce across the counter.

Grace massaged her temples. "What else did your mom say?"

"Eleanor Grace, why don't you show Tía what Abuela sent you for Christmas?"

"She sent me a ballerina puppet and Mami let me open it early!"

Annie audibly sighed as Ellie jumped down from the stool and turned toward her bedroom. Before reaching the hallway, she stopped and turned to Grace. "And, I heard Mami telling Papi that she hoped you finally got some."

Grace coughed, wiping a trickle of wine off her chin.

"I asked her some of what and she said, 'back rubs,' but that didn't make any sense to me, 'cause I give you back rubs all the time. I'll go get my puppet now," she said, skipping down the hallway.

Annie handed Grace a napkin. "Nice spit take."

Grace turned, eyebrows raised. "Wow."

Annie had the decency to look embarrassed, but still whispered, "You still haven't told me how many backrubs you got."

"In-core-gerbil," Grace muttered. "You need to get a life." She tried to sound stern, but the corners of her mouth twitched upward.

Grace draped her coat over her arm and scanned the restaurant. She sucked in her bottom lip and bit down lightly as her eyes came to rest on the beautiful man sitting at the bar. Apparently, she wasn't the only one who was early. So much for a quick cocktail to calm her nerves.

"Is this seat taken?" she said when she came up beside him.

He looked over his shoulder and grinned. He lazily took her in, and his eyes went from amused to something else, something that sent a lightning bolt of heat straight through her. When his gaze fell to her feet, he laughed. "Nice boots."

"Early Christmas gift from Annie," Grace said, lifting a full-on western boot, stitching and all, turning it in the air. "She thinks she's funny. And, I thought they'd make you feel more comfortable in this fancy French restaurant."

"You're always looking out for the simple folk, aren't you?"

She nodded solemnly. "I do what I can."

He stood just as she stepped toward him, causing her to collide with his chest. She put a hand up and stabilized herself, but instead of removing it, she drew a finger around the outside of his pec.

"Gracie," he growled, "if you actually want to eat dinner, you need to stop that right now."

She looked up through her lashes at him. "What this?" She let her finger drop down his chest, taking a slow path to his navel. "I'm simply admiring the softness of your sweater. It is cashmere?"

He took her hand in his and placed it gently at her side. "Let's see if our table is ready."

The hostess seated them at a secluded table for two in the back corner of the restaurant. Before they opened the menus, the server arrived at the table. They placed their drink orders and a comfortable silence fell between them.

He ran his thumb over her fingers. "You were amazing in the studio today," he said, breaking the silence. "Your production and arranging skills are phenomenal. Remind me, why don't you do more of it?"

She looked down at the table, straightening her knife and fork. "Writing —and traveling—with Jax was a full-time job."

"Grace," he said, his deep voice filling the space between them. "Grace, look at me." She raised her head, shook her hair back and looked into his eyes. "I think it's more than that. What's really holding you back?"

She chewed on her bottom lip. Should she—could she—tell him? She sighed. She held it in for so long. She wanted to tell someone. No, that wasn't right. She wanted to tell *him*. "Jax is the only person who's ever performed any of my songs," she whispered.

He didn't say a word, he simply wrapped his fingers tighter around hers, giving her the time she needed.

"And, every time someone approached me to write or produce, he'd say, 'why bother, we have enough money.' At first it made me feel special, like he wanted to keep me all to himself. But then, doubt started to creep in. I wondered why he was so insistent that I not work with anyone else. It made me question whether I had the skills to work with other artists. And strangely, the higher Jax's star rose, the lower my confidence sunk. It was easier to just disappear into the background than challenge him. And then, after his death, the media confirmed my biggest fear—that I was nothing without Jax Jensen. That's why I got crazy over the magazine article yesterday."

"Baby." He tipped her hand over and placed a single kiss in the center of her palm.

"But, that's not really the worst of it. The worst part was I started to question his love. Too many times I wondered if he was in love with me or in love with the songs I wrote for him." Grace blew out a giant breath. "I'm sorry to unload on you. I've never said that stuff out loud before."

"No need to apologize. I'm honored you trust me enough to share it."

A sad smile passed over her lips. "Not exactly first date conversation, though."

"We haven't exactly gone about this in a conventional way. Why start now?"

"Can we please talk about something else?" she asked when the server returned with their drinks.

Andrew lifted his glass. "Let's put the past in the past and celebrate the future. What should we toast to?"

"Awkward first dates that aren't really first dates?"

"Nope. Try again."

She pointed at her feet. "To finally getting a city girl into country boots?"

"I prefer getting city girls *out* of their boots," he said, winking at her, laughing at his own joke. "How about to women who are smart, funny, and talented as hell?"

Grace reddened and lightly clinked her glass against his. She squirmed in her seat and a look of pure relief washed over her face as their entrees arrived. "Tell me about your West Coast tour dates."

"Sylvia's Rules of Etiquette state the proper response to a compliment is 'thank you.' Changing the subject to avoid said compliment constitutes a major rule infraction."

"And here I thought those only applied to cutlery and not talking with your mouth full."

Andrew laughed. "Us Hayes' are full of surprises."

Grace nodded and took a large gulp of her drink. *Yes. Yes, you are.*

Grace licked the last of the chocolate soufflé from her fork. "I'd say that was a pretty successful first date."

"Agreed. Think you might like to go out with me again?"

"Aren't you supposed to wait at least twenty-four hours before you ask me out again, so you don't look desperate?"

"Conventional wisdom goes out the window once you've shared an orgasm."

"Andrew!" Grace said, looking around to see if anyone had heard.

"What? You don't agree?"

"No comment. Annie is hosting her annual Christmas party in a week. Does that qualify as a date?"

"I don't care where we go, just as long as I'm with you. And, now I'm going to walk you to your car to prove to you I'm a gentleman and not just some guy after hot, sweaty orgasms."

"Why is everyone in my life impossible? First, Annie and now you."

"Why? Does she want hot, sweaty orgasms as well?"

"Enough!" Grace said, trying to sound tough, but unable to hide a smile. He threw his head back and laughed, guiding her to the exit, his hand at the small of her back. Grace pointed left at the corner and they turned on to a side street.

"This is me."

He pulled her close and dipped his head, kissing along her jawbone before finding her lips, starting gently, then pushing for more. Grace let out a small gasp when he pushed her up against the car.

"Nice car. I meant to tell you that the other day." He ran a finger along her neck and down her collarbone.

"It's electric."

The corners of his mouth pulled up. "It's not the only thing that's electric."

"The man with all the lines."

"What can I say, you bring out the best in me."

"How did you get here?"

"Uber."

"Do you want a ride home?"

"Depends," he said, tucking a curl behind her ear. "Your home or mine?"

"I thought you weren't after sweaty orgasms."

"I lied." He tipped her chin up and brushed the hair from her face. He leaned in and placed a kiss on her temple. He dropped his gaze from her eyes to her mouth and traced a finger across her lips. She opened her mouth and sucked his finger inside, rolling her tongue around it. His eyebrows shot up.

Grace winked and pulled his finger out with a pop. "My place."

CHAPTER SIXTEEN

G race inspected the tree, heavy with gold, mercury glass, and champagne-colored ornaments. Natural kraft paper wrapped boxes embellished with ribbons of gold and silver, one for each party guest, covered the tree skirt. The neutral colors, considered untraditional by many, created a chic and elegant look. The tiny lights sprinkled throughout the room glistened off the silver and gold making the space soft and inviting.

She spun in the center of the room, impressed with her efforts. In a matter of a few hours, she had transformed Annie's great room into a festive Christmas wonderland. Only one thing was missing. She reached into her bag, pulled out a wrapped package, and placed it under the tree.

A gift for Andrew.

"I'm here! What can I . . . wow, Grace, this place looks amazing," Will said, rushing through the doorway and stopping short.

Grace pushed thoughts of Andrew to the back of her mind and forced her focus back to the room and the people around her.

"You pulled out all the stops. Old Grace really has resurfaced."

Annie cleared her throat. "Excuse me?"

Will reeled her in and placed a kiss on top of her head. "I love you, honey, but we both know this is all Grace. Now, how can I help?"

Grace lightly punched him on the arm. "You can start by not calling me 'old Grace.' And then you can help me carry the food in here."

"You cooked, too?" Will asked.

Pinpricks of pink dotted Grace's cheeks. "If you think I got carried away with the decorations, wait until you see the food. Curtis would be proud."

Annie threw an arm around Grace's shoulder. "We're all proud, G. Christmas wasn't the same without you."

Grace frowned. "I've been here every year."

"Maybe physically, but this Grace"—Annie pointed around the room—"she's been gone for a while. Can't help but wonder if a certain sexy singer might have something to do with her reemergence?"

Grace's heart bumped against her chest. She could deny it. Tell Annie it was simply grief running its course. But she owed her best friend more than half-truths. From the day she had stepped into that Manhattan studio, Andrew had impacted her life in every way possible. Hard as she tried to convince herself, it wasn't the work that had breathed life back into her. It was working with *him*, spending time with *him*. And she knew that when the album wrapped and they went their separate ways, her heart would sustain damage. She looked into Annie's chocolate eyes and blinked back tears.

Annie met her gaze and furrowed her brow. "You okay?"

"Not even a little bit."

"Will wine help?" Annie always sensed when to push Grace and when to let her be.

Grace laughed. "Wine *always* helps."

By seven o'clock, everyone had arrived. Everyone except Andrew. Grace surveyed the room. Conversation and laughter filled the space and the Christmas tree trembled.

Wait, the tree was shaking?

Grace approached it and found two sets of feet poking out from underneath the branches. She bit back a smile and swallowed her laugh. "Ladies, care to tell me what you are doing under the tree?"

Ellie slithered out on her belly and flipped over—not a trace of guilt on her face. "Tía G, I can't find any presents under the tree for me," she said, sticking out her bottom lip and crossing her little arms.

"Your mom hid yours—I wonder why?" She cocked her head at Ellie and grasped Abbie around the ankles and tugged. "And I'm bringing your presents on Christmas Day."

Ellie's eyes lit up. "Ooooh, what are they?"

"You'll have to wait and see," Grace said, mimicking zipping up her lips.

"But," the little girl continued.

"No, buts," Grace said, directing both girls toward the food table. "How about a candy cane cookie? They're delicious."

"Mama said no more sugar," Abbie replied, expression serious.

"Then we won't tell her."

Ellie giggled and Abbie looked wary.

Annie met them at the buffet and laced her arm through Grace's. "I heard that."

Grace handed each of the girls a cookie and grabbed a mini

quiche for herself. "I'm only a bad influence around the holidays."

A sequin-clad woman sidled up to Annie and piled a plate high. "Annaliese, you must give me the name of your caterer. Everything is amazing. Do you think she'd be available for the New Year's party at the firm?" Grace looked away, popping two goat cheese stuffed dates into her mouth and subtly slicing her hand across her throat.

Annie's lips twitched. "She's very exclusive. I have to book her months in advance. And, frankly, she's terrible to work with." Grace choked on her mouthful and Annie slapped her on the back.

"Regardless, please let her know—holy cow, who is *that*?" Annie and Grace followed the woman's gaze across the room. Andrew. He'd arrived without her noticing. "Merry Christmas to me," the woman said, sashaying over to the tall singer.

Annie sucked a breath in through her teeth. "Is that Andrew?"

Grace nodded. Words seem to have abandoned her.

"Oh, *chica*, the pictures did not do him justice. But"—Annie chuckled—"you may want to go rescue him. Ramona is not known for her subtlety."

A nervous giggle escaped from Grace's lips as an unsettling combination of joy and uneasiness bubbled up. "Let's see how he does on his own. He's always bragging about his prowess with female fans. I'd like to see how he does without a stage or signing table between them." She was happy to admire him from a distance for a bit—and let her nerves settle.

Annie laughed. "You're just a little bit horrible, you know that?"

They watched as Annie's co-worker busily babbled and Andrew politely nodded. When the woman paused to sink her teeth into a salmon rillette, he lifted his head and met Grace's gaze. Her chest tightened and her stomach shimmied past her diaphragm and climbed into her throat.

Annie waggled her fingers at him, and Grace hauled Annie's hand down, holding it to her side.

Andrew flashed a smile and Grace nearly melted into the floor. His five o'clock shadow had five o'clock shadow and his long sleeve t-shirt strained against his broad shoulders and the well-defined muscles of his chest.

She touched the corners of her lips to make sure she wasn't drooling.

Andrew said something to the woman and strode over to them. "You must be Annie," he rumbled, soft and smooth. Grace teetered in her heels and touched Annie's elbow for balance. Seriously, that voice. It would be her undoing.

"And you must be the reason my best friend is smiling again."

"Annie," Grace warned.

Andrew ignored Grace. "I don't know about that, but she's quickly become the best part of my day."

"Oh, holy hell, G, marry him, marry him now."

Grace reddened and pinched Annie's elbow.

"Ouch. What the . . ."

Ellie ran up to Andrew, grabbed his hand, and thrust a package at him. "I found this under the tree for you. It's from Tía."

Andrew turned his full attention to the little girl, and she giggled. It seemed he could charm women, no matter their age. "Who is Tía? And how did you know it's for me?"

"I thought it said 'Abbie' on the tag—she's my sister—but she said it said 'Andrew' not 'Abbie' but she didn't know who that was, so I asked Papi and he said, 'Tía G's new boyfriend.' And, I said, 'Papi, Tía doesn't have a boyfriend' and Papi said I should give it to the tall man in the corner—and ask if you are Tía's boyfriend."

Andrew chuckled. "That was a lot of information." He took the package from her. "Thank you for this."

"Ellie," Grace admonished, "I thought we talked about not digging under the tree."

"You said I couldn't look for presents for myself. You didn't say I couldn't look for presents for other people."

"Can't tell she's the kid of a lawyer, can you?" Grace grumbled.

"Andrew"—Ellie pulled on his hand— "are you Tía's boyfriend? If not, can you be my boyfriend?"

"I think you might be a little young for a boyfriend," he said, patting her head. "And, as far as your Tía goes, I'd love to be her boyfriend if she'd let me." Andrew turned his green eyes on her, and she let out a slow exhale—trying to quell the explosion of butterflies threatening to let loose in her stomach.

"Will you let him, Tía?"

"Ellie, I think I'm too old for a boyfriend."

"Nonsense, you're never too old for a boyfriend," Annie piped in. "Andrew, don't listen to her. She needs one. Wants one. She's just confused."

"Um, standing right here. And I think I know what I want."

Andrew locked his eyes on hers. "Do you?" And with two words, every ounce of air and every thought in her head whooshed out. He didn't drop her gaze until they heard a faint knocking.

Ellie was tapping on Andrew's gift. "Open it."

"Ellie," her mother warned.

"Open it, *please*."

Andrew flipped the gift in his hands. "I wonder what it is?"

Ellie let out a giant sigh. "Open it and you'll know. Duh."

Andrew laughed and ripped the paper. Inside the package

was a beautiful leather-bound notebook with pages evenly divided between lined, blank, and staffed.

"It's just like yours," he said, running his thumb over his initials inscribed in gold in the bottom right corner. "Thank you." He leaned in and gave her a chaste kiss on the lips.

"Ewwww." Ellie scrunched up her face. "Adults are gross."

Grace gave one of her long braids a tug. "I thought you wanted him to be your boyfriend, Ellie? Boyfriends kiss their girlfriends, you know."

"No, no, no. I take it back. I don't want a boyfriend."

As the little girl ran across the room, Grace laughed and turned back to Andrew. "I thought you should have one, too." She smirked and knocked her shoulder into his. "Maybe then, you'll stop digging around in mine."

"I can't make any promises. That journal is a front-row seat to the depths of your talent. And your talent is one of the sexiest things about you." He dragged her into his chest and gave her a kiss that was light years away from chaste.

"Ewww," Annie said, "adults are gross."

Exhausted, Grace flopped down next to Annie on the over-stuffed sofa, removed the clip from her hair, and let it tumble down. The last of the guests had left ten minutes ago and there was hardly a crumb left on the buffet table. Dishes, though? They were a different story. Packed high and tight in the sink, they tumbled out across Annie's granite countertop.

Annie kicked off her shoes and tucked her legs underneath her. "Thank you. That was a great party. And your *boyfriend* is pretty great, too. Where is he, by the way?"

"I sent him back to the hotel. I need him sharp in the morning."

"He's not staying with you?"

"No."

"Why not? If I were single, I'd never let that man leave my bed."

"It's better this way."

"Really? That man looks at you like Will looks at the double bacon maple-glazed donuts from Angel Food Bakery. I don't get it, Grace. Why are you holding back? Is this about Jax? Because, honey, he would want you to be happy. He would never expect you to live the rest of your life alone."

Grace sucked in a ragged breath. "It is about Jax, but not the way you think."

"Explain it to me."

Grace hesitated, letting her gaze drift from the buffet table to the tree, avoiding Annie's gaze. "I'm scared of repeating history."

"Huh?"

"I'm terrified of getting involved with another musician—getting sucked into his world—and losing my identity all over again. I will not go from Mrs. Jax Jensen to Mrs. Andrew Hayes. It's time for me to be Grace O'Connor."

"Do you really think that will happen?"

"I don't know. Maybe. I'm not sure I'm willing to take the risk."

"I sense a 'but'."

Grace extracted a small black box from her pants pocket.

"MacAllisters, Dublin," Annie read from the lid. "What is that?"

"It's a Christmas present. For me. From Andrew. He gave it to me before he left tonight."

"You're looking at it like it might explode."

The box creaked as Grace opened it. She swiveled it toward Annie. In the center of the soft green velvet was a small rose gold ring with a single stone nestled inside two prongs.

"Is it a wishbone?"

Grace funneled her fingers through her hair. "It's a tuning fork."

"Is that a diamond in the center?"

"It appears so."

Annie's eyes grew wide, darting between Grace's face and the ring. "Whoa. What do you think that means?"

Grace cringed. "I have no idea, but based on your expression, I'm guessing you're going to tell me."

Annie slipped the ring from its box and rolled it in her fingers. "I think it's pretty clear that while you might not want to risk it, someone else does." She handed the ring to Grace. "That's not a gift you pick up on a whim."

"No, I suppose not," Grace whispered. She slipped the ring on her left ring finger and immediately pulled it back off, putting it on her right hand.

Annie chuckled. "Now, that was a Freudian slip if I've ever seen one."

Grace sprang from the sofa, rubbed her hands down her thighs, and moved toward the kitchen. "We should do the dishes."

"Denial ain't just a river in Egypt."

Grace smirked and turned back toward Annie. "Really? That's what you're going with? An ancient overused pun?"

"If the shoe fits."

Grace groaned. "You're killin' me, Smalls."

Annie shrugged. "You're the writer, not me."

"Clearly. Now, that dishwasher isn't going to load itself."

"Grace . . ."

"I hear you, Annie. I do. But I prepaid for this boat cruise down the deNile and I have a few hours remaining. I'd hate to waste it."

. . .

229

"It's clear you guys are burnt out," Chris said, as the clock struck four the following day. "Andrew, when do you leave for your West Coast tour dates?"

"January fifth."

Chris closed down his laptop.

Grace gulped. "What are you doing?"

"You both need a little distance from the work. I'm sending you away on holiday break."

"No," Grace pleaded, "we're so close."

"Exactly. We picked the bonus song and sent it to the rest of Storyhill and Ford, which will get him off your back for a while. We've completed ten of the other twelve songs, eleven is almost there, and you're blocked on the last one. Go," he said, motioning them toward the exit. "Have some eggnog, spend some time with your families, and I'll meet you back here on January second. That will give us three days to finish arranging song eleven and, maybe after some time off, you'll have some ideas for twelve."

Grace pivoted toward Andrew. "Can you come back to Minneapolis after New Year's?"

"If that's what it takes to get this done, I'll be here."

Chris powered down the rest of the equipment. "Worst case scenario, we work on the last song remotely while Andrew's in California."

"You sure?"

"Grace, get out," Chris said sternly, but a smile danced at the corners of his lips. He yanked their coats off the hooks flanking the door. "I'm sick of both of you." He flipped off the lights and opened the door, ushering them out.

"Chris . . ." Grace said as they arrived at the front door.

"Trust me on this, Gigi. It's the best thing. Andrew, can you please remind this woman what fun looks like?"

"But . . ."

"See you on the second." He shut the door.

"Now what?" Grace asked.

Andrew grabbed her elbow and led her off the front step. "You heard the man, Gigi. It's time to have some fun. What do you want to do?"

"Write music."

"Survey Says . . . no. Try again."

"But you leave for Nashville in less than two days!"

Andrew ignored her comment, pulling her down the sidewalk and opening the car door for her. "Let's go to your condo. Do you have flour?"

"What?" Grace said, buckling her seat belt, not following the non sequitur.

"White powdery substance, usually comes in five-pound bags."

She pushed the ignition button and pulled out of Chris's driveway. "I know what flour is. Why do you want it?"

"How do you feel about pizza for dinner?"

"So, the flour is for the delivery guy? Unusual tip."

Andrew snorted. "I'm making the pizza, Grace."

She signaled left and turned to him. "You cook?" she asked, astonished.

"Growing up, I spent a lot of time with my grandmother and she taught me how to make bread. I make it whenever I'm home —in Nashville—not New Orleans. I find it relaxing. Pizza crust is just an extension of that."

"I gotta say, Cowboy, you keep surprising me."

"I have a lot of talents you've yet to see." He smiled with an indecent amount of charm and ran a finger down the length of her thigh. Her body begged her to abandon all remaining threads of self-control.

"Promises, promises," she said, her voice distant and breathy.

. . .

Grace had barely closed the door to her condo when Andrew swept her over his shoulder in a fireman's carry and ran up the steps.

"Which door?" he said when he reached the top.

She tried to wiggle out of his hold. "Put me down."

"Nope. Can't have you believe I don't follow through on my promises. Which door?"

"Second one."

He turned the corner into her bedroom and threw her on the bed, following her down. He buried his face in her neck, planting hot kisses from her earlobe to her collarbone.

"Andrew."

"Not now baby, I'm busy."

"Andrew." She pounded on his back. "Stop"

He pulled up, bracing himself on his forearms. "This not your idea of fun? I'm simply trying to follow the directions of our esteemed producer."

"Get off."

"I'm trying . . . for both of us."

She slapped him playfully on the chest. "Andrew, while there might be some merit to angry sex, nothing good comes from hangry sex."

Andrew laughed and ran his finger along her jaw, sending shivers through her body. "So many rules, Gracie. Coffee before work. Food before sex. No kissing in front of Joe. Any others I should know?"

"One more. 'Grace O'Connor' should always come before 'Andrew Hayes' in the liner notes." He stiffened and something dark passed over his eyes. She reached up to cup his cheek, but he turned away from her. Before she could speak, he stood and walked out of the bedroom.

Andrew shoved his hands in his pockets and stared out the window. Thick gray clouds hung heavily in the sky while snowflakes the size of quarters fluttered past, quickly accumulating on the sill. His first white Christmas. He glanced at the stairs leading to the second floor—looking for the first person, in many years, that made him want to celebrate it.

Yet, he'd left her alone. Abruptly. Because he was still acting like a petulant child. He thought he'd moved past this. They were partners. Listing him second in the writing credits didn't mean he was less essential to the process.

She'd taught him that.

He sensed her before she wrapped her arms around his waist and laid her head on his shoulder. "I'm sorry," she said softly. "I didn't mean to upset you. I was just trying to make you laugh. You know I didn't—"

He spun in her arms, kissed her forehead, and smoothed the lines pulling her eyebrows together. "I know, Grace. I'm sorry. Old habits die hard. I try to silence his voice, but occasionally it still sneaks up on me."

"You know we're partners—equals—right?"

"I do." He laughed at her wary expression. "Really. Rationally, I do know that."

She cinched her arms tighter around him and rested her cheek against his heart. "Then maybe, in the spirit of the season, it's time to let it go. Carrying all that around has to be exhausting. It's time to forgive him."

He pulled out of her embrace and shoved his hands back into his pockets. "You want me to suddenly be okay with him maligning my career—every chance he gets?"

"No. I want you to be free of the power it has over you.

Forgiveness is not about excusing his behavior. It's about deciding to release your resentment."

He nodded and grabbed her hand. He only had two days to spend with her before their holiday break. He didn't want to fight. And he certainly didn't want the specter of his old man getting in the way. He pulled her toward the kitchen. She pulled back.

She squeezed his fingers and waited until he turned toward her. "Andrew, tell me you'll at least consider it."

He stared up at the ceiling and let his eyes drift close. He refused to make her a promise he had no idea if he could keep. He placed a kiss on her temple and whispered, "Considered." This time when he took a step forward, she followed. "Now, how about you take me to your flour, and we get this pizza started."

She narrowed her eyes but didn't say anything further. She pointed at the large cabinet to the right of the refrigerator. "Second shelf."

Andrew pushed his hands through the dough, stretching it as he rolled it over onto itself. Nothing like a little kneading to work out some residual frustration.

"You cook," he said, looking across the island at her. "But you don't make bread?"

"Never learned."

He motioned to the lump of dough in front of him. "Want to?"

"Sure," she said, reaching for the dough.

"No, come over here." Despite their previous conversation—or maybe because of it—he wanted her close. He needed to touch her. Needed her in his arms.

She rose from her stool and walked around the vast island.

He motioned for her to step between him and the counter. His eyes traveled to her hand and followed the motion as she slowly pulled the ring from her finger. The ring he'd given her. The ring neither had mentioned.

"Do you like it?" he said, motioning to the spot where it rested on the marble countertop.

"Yes." A light pink spread across her cheeks and she cleared her throat. "You got it in Dublin?"

"I did." He turned his attention back to the dough and rolled it over twice more.

"Why?" she said quietly.

"Because I thought you'd like it." Because the minute he saw it in the store window, he knew it belonged on her hand. Because he hoped it would say the things he was too scared to say out loud. "I'm glad you're wearing it."

Grace was watching him when he looked up. "Of course," she said, searching his face. "Andrew . . ."

He sucked his bottom lip under his teeth and slapped the dough against the counter, making her jump. "Let's get on with this lesson." Though it might be more appropriate if they were making chicken instead of pizza because that's what he was—a giant chicken.

She placed her hands on the dough and lightly poked at it. "Like this?"

He placed his fingers over hers and pushed them through the dough. The minute he touched her all thoughts of forgiveness and rings melted away, replaced by the ever-present electricity that arced between them. "More like this." He felt her body relax against his. Strands of her hair fell in front of her face and she blew them away.

"Do you need help with that?" He stroked her hair back and trailed kisses down her neck while still guiding her motions. He was pretty sure it was criminal to have skin this soft.

"I don't think this is the way your grandma taught you."

"True. I've improved on her techniques." He unbuttoned the top two buttons on her shirt and dipped his fingers under the fabric, drawing small circles from her neck to her cleavage.

Grace elbowed him in the ribs, and he jumped back with a chuckle. "Keep that up and we'll have to order pizza after all."

"I think the dough is good." He spun her toward him and brushed his flour fingerprints from her chest. "Find me a bowl and a towel and we'll let this rest for a little bit."

"I'm a little trapped here. Bowl is in the cabinet to the left of my knee. The towel is in the drawer above it." Andrew pulled out the towel and bent to retrieve the bowl. Wrapping an arm around her knees, he hoisted her onto the counter, sending a cloud of flour into the air and the bowl clattering across the countertop.

"Oof. You could give a girl a warning."

He reached around her and plopped the dough into the bowl, keeping his gaze on the sweet curve of her mouth. "What should we do while the dough rests?"

"Hmm, what did you and your grandma do while the dough rested?"

"Certainly nothing I'm thinking about right now." He ran his hands up the insides of her thighs, moving to cradle her head. He kissed her forehead, her cheeks, finally connecting with her lips. He ran his tongue over her bottom lip. She moaned, letting her lips fall apart and he slid his tongue inside, circling it around hers.

Her fingers left a trail of heat down his body and his restraint snapped. He ripped through the remaining buttons on her shirt and covered her breasts with his hands. She arched into him, her nipples hardening under his touch.

"Grace," he half groaned, half growled. It was becoming abundantly clear he may never be able to get enough of this woman. He brushed the hair back from her face thinking about that first day in the label's conference room. He'd been such an ass. What if she'd left that day? He'd have lost the opportunity to work with her, to see her talent firsthand. He'd almost missed out on all of it.

He pulled her closer and a puff of flour bloomed behind her. He leaned in and nipped at her ear and then soothed the spot with his tongue.

"Shouldn't we check on the dough?" she said, her voice wobbly.

"It's not rising as fast as me. I think we need to deal with me first."

Grace laughed and pulled his head back up to meet her lips. "Very well." She reached down and popped the button on his jeans. She stared into his eyes as she slid his zipper down, pushed a hand inside, and wrapped her fingers around him. He sucked in a ragged breath and swayed into her. He inched her even closer and they both jumped.

A sharp buzzing came from the video panel near the front door. She pushed a finger into his chest, and he immediately missed the heat of her body. A familiar face stared out of the screen. Annie.

"Any chance she'll go away?" he said, trying to tuck her back against his chest.

Grace laughed and kissed the tip of his nose. "If I don't answer, she's likely to call the paramedics and then we'll have an even bigger problem on our hands."

Andrew groaned as he stepped back and watched her button her shirt. She threw a look back over her shoulder and pointed at his crotch. "You should probably punch that down."

He laughed. "I'll never look at dough the same way again."

Grace depressed the intercom button. "Hey, Annie."

"Hey. I was nearly ready to call 911." Grace turned back to

Andrew and winked. "Will has Daddy Night with the girls and I was in the neighborhood, so I thought I'd stop by. I might have stopped by the liquor store." She waved a bottle of wine in front of the lobby camera. Grace hit the buzzer to release the door and allow Annie into the building.

She turned to him as he was buttoning his jeans. "I'm sorry. I'm afraid she's gotten too used to me being alone." Confirming Grace's statement, Annie pulled open the door without knocking.

"I hope you feel like a big red tonight. It seemed like it would be . . . oh!" Annie stopped short when she caught sight of him. Her eyes widened as she took in Grace's swollen, red lips. "I'm so sorry. I didn't know you had company. I'm such an idiot," she said, madly shaking her head. "I'll just go now," she added, motioning back to the door with her bottle of wine.

Andrew walked over to Annie and took the wine from her. "No need. We're making pizza and a bottle of red will make it perfect. Join us?"

Annie swiveled her head, looking at Grace before turning to him. "Are you sure?"

"No man in his right mind turns down an evening with two beautiful women."

Annie looked at Grace and stage-whispered, "Good lord, Grace, what more do you want? Charismatic, kind, and clearly good with flour." She reached behind Grace, brushed the remaining flour smudges from Grace's jeans, and winked.

"Andrew was teaching me how to make bread," Grace stammered.

"Mm-hmm," Annie hummed. "Did you knead it with your butt?"

Grace's mouth opened and closed like a fish out of water and her face heated to five-alarm fire level.

Andrew stifled a laugh and grabbed Annie around the

shoulders. "You know her," Andrew said, pointing at Grace. "She's the master of meeting any objective, by any means necessary."

Grace rolled her eyes at them. "Remind me why I introduced the two of you?" She slunk into the kitchen as the laugh he'd been holding rumbled from his chest. God, he was going to miss this woman—and they'd only be apart for a week.

CHAPTER SEVENTEEN

A ndrew opened the door to his apartment and was nearly knocked over by the smell wafting from it. What the hell? It smelled like a cat had eaten a dead rodent and then died too. Not that he knew what that smelled like, but he could imagine.

Breathing through his mouth, he walked into the tiny kitchen and found the culprit—a bag of trash, propped up against the cupboards, oozing a greenish-brown goo. Shit. He'd been so distracted and stressed when he'd left for Manhattan, he'd forgotten to grab the garbage on his way out.

Thank god he'd come home before the bag fully decomposed.

No, that wasn't true. He'd gladly hand over his security deposit to still be on Grace's couch with his arms wrapped around her while he kissed the spot under her ear that drove her crazy.

But he was here now. And the bag had to go. Yanking a second bag from the roll, he held it open and maneuvered the oozing one into it. Almost. The radioactive bag split as he lifted it and covered him waist to knees in something that could only be called sewage.

Having to leave Grace and soaked in sewage all in one day. Yep. Frickin'. Fantastic. Day.

Staring at the offending bag, his phone chirped, reminding him of dinner at Joe and Julia's in an hour. "I've got places to be, bag. And I will win this battle. Best to surrender now." Andrew chuckled. Not only was he talking to garbage, but he was trying to reason with it. Clearly, the noxious fumes were getting to him.

Shaking the sludge from his hands, he doused the offending mess with air freshener, stepped into the hanging cloud of scented mist, and wrangled the garbage into a third bag. Gingerly lifting the bag, testing for leakage and seeing none, he moved it as quickly as possible to the dumpster outside. He contemplated throwing his clothes in after it, but Mrs. Cheng, the octogenarian self-appointed building security manager, was sure to be watching out her window. At best, streaking would earn him an interesting conversation with the cops and a ticket for indecent exposure. At worst, it would rattle Mrs. Cheng's already weak heart. No need to push his luck on an already crappy day.

He plugged his nose, headed inside, and stripped next to his washer, dropping in the offending jeans and t-shirt. He couldn't remember a time he'd been happier for a shower.

"Whoa," Joe said, leaning away from him, after opening the door. "Why do you smell like rotten cabbage and lilacs?"

"Nice to see you, too," Andrew said.

"Seriously, dude, what is with the smell?"

"I got into a fight with a bag of garbage and a can of Glade."

"You clearly, did not win."

"Hello, Andrew. Merry almost Christmas. I've missed you," Julia said, coming up behind Joe. "Why are you standing outside?" She stepped toward him and held out her arms for a hug—and dropped them. Quickly. She crinkled her nose and turned her head. "Please know that I'm only saying this because I love you like a brother—you need to start showering more often."

Andrew sighed. "I did shower."

"In garbage?" Joe asked, fighting a smile.

"It must have gotten on my boots. I'll leave them out here on the porch."

"Were they expensive?" Joe said.

"Not particularly. Why?"

"I'm thinking the masked bandits of greater Nashville may take a shine to them."

Julia laughed as Andrew pulled the boots off. "Even raccoons have their limits," she said, pushing them further away from the front door with her foot. "Now, come in. I have dinner set up in the kitchen, and I'm dying to hear about your time with Grace."

"Usually, it's Joe who harasses me about the album," Andrew answered, following his best friends down the hallway.

"Oh, silly boy, I'm not interested in the songs," she said, waggling her eyebrows. "Have a seat." She pointed at the table. "And tell Jules everything."

"How about a beer first?" he asked, walking to the refrigerator and ducking his head inside. How was he supposed to explain something he didn't fully understand?

Cracking the bottle open and sliding into his chair at the table, he watched as Joe placed a soft kiss on his wife's temple as they plated dinner. She turned toward him and rested her hand on his cheek.

Andrew's gut twisted. He wasn't a jealous person. He'd

never longed for the comfortable love Joe and Julia shared. Until today. A vision of standing in Grace's kitchen flashed in his mind. Nothing extraordinary, just him washing dishes while she dried them. He was beginning to understand why people made a lifetime commitment—because merely being together made everything better.

"Remind me. How long have you guys been married?"

Joe set a plate in front of him. "You don't remember? You were standing right next to me."

Andrew smirked. "So, you don't remember, either?"

Joe's eyes grew wide. "No, of course, I remember. Um," he said, peering at his wife from the corner of his eye, "almost twelve years?"

Julia laughed. "Yes, Joe, almost twelve years." She slipped into the chair across from Andrew. Her eyes narrowed and she cocked her head to the side, examining Andrew's face. "Why do you ask? Are you thinking about—"

"It just occurred to me that you've put up with him for over a decade," Andrew said, cutting her off and slicing into his pork chop.

"Uh-huh," Julia said, tapping a finger on her lips. She opened her mouth to speak and he braced himself for any number of probing private questions, but instead, she turned to Joe and placed her hand over his. "It's not always been easy, that's for sure."

Andrew looked at her expression and realized she wasn't teasing Joe, she was serious. She turned to Andrew and pinned him with a penetrating stare. "Marriage—any long-term relationship—takes work. It's more than romantic love. It's a commitment to compromising, trusting, and forgiving—and it works best if you don't bring a lifetime of baggage into the relationship." She cocked a single eyebrow at him.

Joe snorted around a mouthful of glazed carrots. "Truth.

Remember that girl I dated before Jules? The one that was sleeping around on me? I had some real trust issues. Jules made me talk to a therapist about it."

Andrew's eyes widened. "You went to a therapist?"

Joe shrugged. "You don't know everything about me. I'm an onion. Layers and layers."

Julia laughed and patted her husband's hand. "Let's not get carried away." She held up her empty glass. "Joe, honey, can you top me off?"

"Oh, I brought a bottle of Prosecco." Andrew turned and looked at the kitchen counters. "I must have left it on the porch." He started to rise, but Julia placed her hand on his. "Joe can go get it. You're our guest, Andrew."

Bullshit. When had he ever been a 'guest' here? She was clearly separating her prey from the herd.

Joe shuddered. "Out where Andrew's boots are?"

"You'll be fine. Plug your nose." She watched her husband walk to the front of the house before turning to Andrew. "I know you, Andrew Charles Hayes," she hissed. "You don't make small talk. You asked that question for a reason. And I meant what I said. If you're thinking about what I think you're thinking about, sort your shit first."

He pushed the tip of the table knife she was pointing at his face toward the table. "And what exactly do I need to sort?"

She rolled her eyes in a way that clearly said, *You wildebeest, me cheetah.* "You need to figure things out with your dad."

"That seems to be a popular sentiment," he muttered under his breath.

"Whew," Joe said, returning to the kitchen. "I didn't breathe while I was out there, and my eyes still watered. Andy, those boots are a total loss."

Julia held his gaze for a beat longer and stabbed a single

finger at him before turning to Joe and holding out her glass. "Thanks, baby."

Andrew soundlessly set his suitcase down on the marble entry tile and dug deep, searching for the hidden reserves of patience he was sure to need over the next few days. Apparently, he had some forgiving to do, or in Jules' less poetic words, some 'shit to sort.'

After dinner at Joe's, Grace's request and Julia's words had replayed over and over in his mind. He'd come up with every imaginable excuse for not talking with his father, but none of them held enough weight to counteract their reasoning. But how to start? An email? A phone call?

Go home for Christmas, a little voice had whispered. And before he could over-analyze the thought, he opened his phone and booked a flight to New Orleans.

And, so, here he stood.

The house was unusually quiet. Did he get lucky enough to arrive when no one was home? He slipped his shoes off—Sylvia's Rules—and padded into the formal living room. A massive Christmas tree reached the peak of the vaulted ceiling and stockings hung from the mahogany mantle. He ran his fingers over his name, stitched on the sock furthest to the left. He remembered the year his grandmother had sewed them and proudly hung them for the first time.

"She knew how to do Christmas right, didn't she?"

Andrew spun to find Bridget standing in the doorway. He nodded and she closed the gap between them, encircling him in a hug. "What are you doing here?" she whisper-gasped into his hair. "Mom is going to lose it."

"Where is she? The house is so quiet."

"Last time I checked, she was icing cookies in the kitchen with her headphones on, dancing badly."

Andrew laughed and then sobered. "And dad?"

"He's picking up Colin."

Andrew snorted. "The wunderkind couldn't manage the ten-minute drive from Tulane to the Garden District?"

"His car's in the shop."

"And he couldn't lower himself to take the train?"

She shrugged. "Dad offered."

Andrew shook his head. "Of course, he did."

Bridget placed a hand on his arm. "Do you think you can play nice, just for a couple of days? Think of it as a special gift to Mom."

He nodded. If he had any hope of this succeeding, he needed to lose the attitude. Easier said than done. He was going to need a mountain of Christmas miracles—maybe a whole range.

"Bridget, I need your opinion on something. Can you come in here?" his mother called from the kitchen.

Andrew smirked. "May I?" he asked Bridget.

She met his smile. "Be my guest."

Andrew rounded the corner into the kitchen. "Bridge's got terrible taste. How about I do one better?"

His mother gasped and the cookie in her hand fell to the floor, shattering into a thousand pieces. "Andy?" She stood, staring, unmoving. "What are you doing here?"

"Somebody told me it was Christmas. Did I get some bad information?"

"No, no, no." She rushed around the kitchen island and hauled him into a hug.

A spot above his pec grew suspiciously wet. "Ma? Are you crying?"

She sniffled and pulled back. "Of course not."

He laughed. "O-kay."

A door banged behind them and his mother jumped out of his embrace.

"Andy? Holy shit," his little brother said, crossing the kitchen. Colin slapped him on the shoulder and his mother dissolved into sobs.

"All my babies are home."

"Sylvia, what is all the ruckus?" Andrew stiffened at the sound of his father's voice. Charles Michael Hayes stopped short as he entered the kitchen and his eyes landed on his eldest son.

"Look, Charlie, my Christmas wish came true. Andy came home."

His father stared at him for a beat before giving him a single nod. "Andrew."

"Dad."

"We didn't expect you."

Didn't expect me or didn't want me? He caught the thought before it leaped from his mouth. No need to piss the old man off in the first five minutes. He broke his father's penetrating gaze and turned to his siblings and mother, forcing a smile. "I brought everyone presents from London. Should I put them under the tree?"

"Yes, do that," his mother said, releasing a giant breath and wiping away her tears. "Then come back and we'll have a Christmas toast." She turned to her husband, still standing in the kitchen doorway. "Charlie, go down to the cellar and pull a good bottle of wine. I feel like celebrating."

Andrew sighed. She was sending them to their corners. Like always.

. . .

Andrew passed the mashed potatoes to his sister while watching his father across the table. Over the past thirty-six hours, he tried, several times, to get his father alone. The couple of times he'd succeeded, his father had 'suddenly' remembered something he had to do. Leaving Andrew with absolutely no idea what to do next.

"Andy, will you be able to come back for your dad's sixtieth birthday party in two weeks?" his mom asked, slowly slicing through the Christmas ham.

There was a party for the old man's birthday? News to him. "No, I'm sorry, Mom, but in two weeks, Storyhill will be back on the road, on the West Coast."

"You haven't given up on that ridiculous dream yet?" his father said, causing everyone at the table to stiffen.

It took everything in him to dial his expression to neutral and maintain an even voice. "You taught us to figure out what we do best and then go all in. That's what I'm doing."

"I meant getting a good education and being a doctor, like your brother, or a business executive, like your sister. Not to fritter away your life in entertainment."

Shot across the bow. Andrew balled his fists, bouncing them on his thighs. Everything in him screamed, *give up, leave, this will never work.*

"Charlie, please, it's Christmas," his mother said, her voice breaking. "I've dreamed of all of us around this table for so many years and now it's happening. Please let me have this."

Andrew relaxed his fingers and unclenched his teeth. He would not ruin his mother's holiday.

But his father apparently did not share his sentiments.

Charles threw his napkin on the table and pinned his eyes on Andrew. "This is why you shouldn't come here. You stir everything up and upset her." He stood and, without a look back, stormed out the side door and his car revved to life.

Sylvia laid a trembling hand on top of Andrew's. "He didn't mean that. You're always welcome here."

The fight drained from Andrew, leaving him feeling limp and boneless. He'd come here to clear the air, to bury the demons—and he couldn't even get his father to talk to him. He turned to his mother and placed his other hand over hers. "Thanks Mom, but I'm exhausted. I'm tired of the fighting. I can't do it anymore." Andrew started to rise from the table.

"Andrew, sit down."

Andrew turned, startled by his mother's tone and use of his full name, and dropped back down into his chair.

"Bridget, Colin," she said, addressing his siblings, "go cut the pies in the kitchen. And pull the doors shut when you leave. Andy and I need a moment."

Sylvia watched her children leave and waited for the snick of the dining room pocket doors coming together before turning to him. "You know I support you, right? Every mother wants their children to follow their dreams."

Andrew rubbed the back of his neck, trying to loosen the tension and not take his anger for his father out on his mother. "You haven't always felt that way."

"That's true, but not for the reasons you think. I've been keeping something from you. And I see now that I shouldn't have. I thought this thing with your father would resolve on its own."

"Mom?"

"Your father is a difficult man."

Andrew laughed humorlessly. "That's like saying an elephant is a little bigger than a squirrel."

His mother ignored his comment. She stood and walked to the bay window and stared out into the yard. "Haven't you ever wondered where your musical ability comes from?"

Andrew furrowed his brow and shrugged. "I've always assumed it came from Grandpa George."

His mother moved to the antique sideboard flanking the dining room table, opened the far right, bottom drawer and pulled out a faux leather photo album that he'd never seen. She flipped it open to the third yellowed page and placed it in front of Andrew. "Look closely," she said, barely over a whisper.

Andrew scanned the photos and then quickly flipped the page, and the next, and the next. The album was full of a young man playing guitar, singing, and smiling.

His father.

It felt like someone had siphoned all the air from his lungs.

His mother sat down next to him and pushed his hair away from his face. "The two of you are so much alike. So handsome. So talented. So stubborn," she added, with a smile playing at her lips. "And, once upon a time, chasing the same dream."

"I don't understand."

She looked at the photos, running her hand lovingly over her husband's face. "He was so good. Just like you. I wish you could have seen him perform."

"This doesn't make any sense. If this was Dad's dream, why has he spent the last fifteen years making my life miserable? Is he jealous? Is that it? I have something he wanted but couldn't get? If that's supposed to make me feel better, it doesn't."

"It's not jealousy."

"Then what?"

She looked up into his eyes, a pleading look in her own. "It's fear."

"Fear? What is he afraid of?"

A single tear traveled down her cheek. "I'm so sorry I kept this from you. But when he gave up performing, our agreement was that we'd never speak of it again."

"What happened?"

"You aren't our first child, Andy. I got pregnant in graduate school, and your father and I planned to marry. We moved into a tiny apartment and your father insisted I stay in school. He made enough money from his gigs to pay rent and buy food, but just barely."

Andrew looked around the luxury home he'd grown up in and couldn't picture the two of them nearly broke in a studio apartment.

"When I was about six months along, I started having contractions and miscarried the baby. Your father was devastated, we both were, but he took it especially hard. He convinced himself if he'd had a proper job with health insurance, we wouldn't have lost that baby. Much as I told him it wasn't true, it changed him. He packed away his guitar and applied for college scholarships the very next day. That's why his constant refrain to you is to 'get a job that can support a family'."

Andrew raked his hands through his hair and looked down at the photos again. His father looked happier than he'd ever seen him. "Why am I just learning about this now?"

"I made a promise to him. I didn't want to betray his trust. And, when this became more than a hobby for you, when you became financially stable, I thought he'd come around. There have been signs. Like when he thinks I'm out of earshot, I hear him listening to Storyhill's YouTube videos."

His father was watching their videos? Why? Was it simply a matter of gathering more ammunition for his next round of insults? Or was he curious? Maybe even interested?

He sighed and his shoulders sagged. Did it even matter?

"That's great, I guess. But is it too little, too late? So much damage has been done."

"I know, honey. And that's on me."

"And him."

"Let me talk to him. Tell him you know the truth."

Andrew pushed himself up and out of his chair. He didn't know exactly what to do with this information, but he knew he needed some space.

"Andy, don't you want to stay for pie?" his mother asked.

He turned to look at her. Was she serious? She'd just dropped the bomb of a lifetime and now she wanted him to eat pie? He shook his head. "I'm going to my room for a while."

He climbed the stairs, but instead of entering his childhood bedroom, he walked to the end of the hall. The thin white door creaked as he pushed it open. Light streamed through the port-hole window at the top of the unfinished stairs. Dust motes rose and danced in the sunlight as he climbed higher.

He brushed by Lego sets, paintings his mother had relegated to the attic, and doll carriages filled with naked babies who'd clearly seen better hair days. Awards from spelling bees, dance contests, and debate competitions filled an old bookcase.

He spun three hundred and sixty degrees, searching the corners. And there it was. He pushed aside a Tiffany floor lamp and pulled out the black case. He wiped the dust from it and unsnapped the gold buckles. Grandpa George's guitar. Except it wasn't. This was the guitar his father had held in the photographs.

He sat on an ancient trunk and strummed. He adjusted the tuning pegs and played a chord. And then another one. "Why didn't he ever say anything?" he whispered.

"Because he didn't know how."

Andrew's head snapped up. His father stood at the top of the stairs, his eyes fixed on the guitar.

"You told me this belonged to Grandpa George. Just one of your many lies, it seems."

His father scrubbed his hand over his head. "I didn't lie about that. That guitar was his before he gave it to me."

Andrew knocked his fist against the pickguard on the guitar. "Why not just tell me?"

"When your mother lost that baby, I'd never experienced pain like that. I had to bury that part of my life to survive the grief. And I never wanted you to feel that kind of pain. I get that it might not make sense to you."

"Ya think?" Andrew stood up and swung the guitar as he paced back-and-forth in the dingy attic. "I thought . . . I thought so many things. I thought I embarrassed you. You made me think I had no talent." He rubbed his chest, soothing the pain blooming behind his heart. "You've belittled my career, practically pushed me out of this family, and apparently, lied to me every day for thirty-five years." The tears that were threatening to fall burned behind his eyes. He squeezed his eyes shut. He would not give the old man the satisfaction.

Andrew stopped pacing and met his father's gaze. "You know why I chose to come home this Christmas?" He didn't wait for an answer. "I came home to try and make things right. To figure out how we might be able to be in the same room without fighting—to figure out how we might be a family again. But this," he waved his hands in the air, "I have no idea what to do with all of this."

Andrew marched over to the older man and shoved the guitar into his chest. He turned and started down the stairs.

"Andrew," his father called.

Andrew stopped, drew a long breath in through his nose, and turned his head in the direction of his father. "Yes?"

"Don't waste your trip."

Andrew nearly faltered on the stair; his father sounded almost . . . broken.

"Over there, in Bridget's old Barbie house, there is a bottle of whiskey."

Andrew turned, his eyebrows inching up his forehead. It

was Colin's Barbie house, but that didn't seem pertinent to the conversation. "Excuse me?"

"Your mother doesn't like me to drink hard liquor, something about my blood pressure, so I keep a small stash up here, you know, just in case of emergencies. Join me for a glass? Feels a bit like an emergency, doesn't it?"

He wanted to leave. But a refrain reverberated through him, building in volume. *Sort your shit.* Crap, when did Julia become the voice of his conscience?

Andrew turned, stepping back onto the attic landing. His father took that as a yes and pulled the bottle from the pink mansion. "I'm sorry. I only have one glass."

From the bookshelves behind him, Andrew grabbed a plastic lavender teacup just the size for two fingers of whiskey. He wiped out the inside with the edge of his shirt and held it out to his father.

His father filled their glasses, flipped open a folding chair, and motioned for Andrew to do the same. "They don't sprinkle magic dust on you in the delivery room, making a guy into the perfect parent. I wish they did. And I'd like to say that given the chance I'd do it differently, but those are empty words, and probably not true. I can't change the past, but I can try and do better going forward." His father smiled the tiniest of smiles. "Though it has been mentioned, a time or a hundred that I'm kind of a son of a bitch. So maybe I should stay away from making any specific promises."

Andrew's lips twitched and raised his teacup, clinking it against the side of his father's glass. "And I've been told I may have inherited that bit of DNA."

His father smiled and then sobered. "Can you forgive me, Andrew?"

Andrew's chest tightened and he forced out his answer. "I'd like to." He tipped his head back and emptied his cup. Could they actually do this? Could they start over? Get to know each other as adults? He'd never realized how badly he wanted that until this moment. "I'm going to try."

"It's gotten quiet up there. Are you okay?" His mother yelled from the base of the stairs, making both men laugh.

"We're both alive if that's what you're asking," Andrew yelled back to his mother.

"I guess that's all I can ask. And, Charlie?"

"Yes, dear?"

"Don't think for a moment that I can't smell that whiskey all the way down here."

Andrew's father tipped his head back and let out the first real laugh Andrew had heard from him in over a decade. "That woman will be busting my chops until the day I go to the great beyond."

Andrew laughed. "Probably longer." He twirled the teacup in his hand, watching the remaining drops of alcohol circle the cup. "But there is something pretty fucking amazing about strong women, isn't there?"

"Is that why you're here? Because of a woman?"

Andrew's first instinct was to deny it. It'd become ingrained to hide his life from his family, but if he wanted a real relationship with his father, that would have to change. He nodded. "Yes."

His father poured another shot into each of their glasses and stared down into his. "Tell Grace thank you from me."

Andrew's head shot up and his mouth dropped open. "How did you—?"

They stared at each other for a moment. "Bridget," they said simultaneously, laughing.

CHAPTER EIGHTEEN

Grace's phone vibrated and a purple crayon flew out of her grasp. Abbie and Ellie giggled, making the elf hats adorning their heads jiggle. The girls had burst into the guest room this morning, insisting it was time to get up and play with their new toys. Grace had tried to feign sleep. Yesterday— Christmas Day—had been filled with squealing little girls ripping packages open, demands for AAA batteries, and way too much food. She really needed another hour of sleep. She'd even tried faking a snore, but when Ellie had pried open one of her eyes and got very close to her face reeking of sugar and peppermint, she'd accepted the inevitable—the bed would soon only be a distant memory.

That is how she ended up sitting here, at Annie's island, entertaining two overstimulated, over-sugared Christmas elves while a bleary-eyed Will stuffed the wrapping paper wreckage into the recycle bin and Annie moaned softly, dragging a sponge over the sticky counters.

Grace flipped the phone over to find Andrew's picture flashing in front of her. It was a selfie taken in front of Big Ben.

When had he managed to get his photo on her phone? She must remember to check her security settings.

Ellie looked up and grinned. "It's my boyfriend!" Apparently, she had reconsidered her stance on significant others—again. She pushed her coloring book aside and hit Accept and speaker. "Hi, Andrew! Merry Christmas! Are you coming to my house today? Me and Tía are coloring in the new books Santa brought. Tía's coloring a unicorn and I'm coloring Ruth Bader Ginsburg."

Andrew's laugh flowed out of the phone's speakers and Grace felt her pulse kick against the cuff of her shirt and an unexpected warmth rocket toward her core. Huh. Was she also reconsidering her stance on significant others? Unclear. But one thing was utterly unambiguous, her body was on board for more of his magic lips and talented hands.

"Merry Christmas, Ellie," he said. "You need to keep an eye on your Tía, I'm not sure she knows that all unicorns have rainbow-colored manes. Is she doing it right?"

Ellie nudged closer to Grace and gasped. "Andrew, her unicorn has a purple mane. You're right, she doesn't know." Ellie looked up at her and shook her head, clearly disappointed.

"Well then, you better let me talk to her."

"Hey, Cowboy. I'm assuming you called for something other than to micro-manage my coloring skills. How's Nashville?"

"It was good when I left it."

Grace stopped coloring and turned toward the phone. "You're not in Nashville?"

"Nope. I'm at the hotel. I got on an earlier flight . . . from MSY."

"MSY?" She was sure Nashville's airport code was BNA. And then it clicked. "Wait. What?" Grace sucked in a breath and replayed his words, making sure she'd heard him correctly.

"You flew in from New Orleans? Did you spend Christmas with your *family*?"

"I did."

"How? What? *Why*?" Grace stumbled.

Andrew laughed. "Said the woman who makes her living by putting words and sentences together."

"How was it?"

"That is not a story for the phone. I'll tell you later, but right now I need a favor. The hotel seems to have lost my reservation. They claim they don't have any more rooms and I don't have it in me to battle with them. Can I stay with you?"

Grace cut a look over at the girls. "Like a slumber party?"

"Yep, in that giant bed where we . . ."

Grace grabbed the phone and jammed a finger on the audio button, silencing it. "Andrew, you were still on speaker," she hissed into the phone. "It is not my goal to be the one to teach the girls about the birds and the bees."

He snorted—and ignored her comment. "What's your answer, Gracie? Am I on my way to your place or to Booking.com?"

Grace sighed. "Give me an hour and I'll meet you at the loft." She ended the call and looked up, finding Annie smirking at her. "What?"

"You're leaving," Annie said, slamming the dishwasher door shut with the heel of her foot and draining the coffee pot into her mug.

"Andrew had a hotel mix-up, so I guess he's staying with me for a little bit."

"So I heard." Her smirk broke into a full grin. "You didn't put up much of a fight. So un-Grace-like."

Grace ducked her head and shoved crayons back into the box with a little too much force. "What was I supposed to do? Leave him out on the street?"

"And he came back early." Annie waggled her eyebrows. "I wonder why?"

Her bestie was clearly getting far too much pleasure from Grace's discomfort. "I should go."

"Yes, yes, you should."

Grace rolled her eyes.

"Here, Tía," Abbie said, handing Grace her hat. "You can wear this when you meet Andrew."

Grace opened her mouth to tell Abbie she didn't need the hat as Ellie blurted out, "Mami, what are the birds and the bees?" Annie spit coffee across the counter. "And do I need to know about them before *my* next slumber party?"

Annie's grin vanished and Grace shrugged, biting back a smile of her own. *Justice served.*

Grace walked off the elevator and missed a step, nearly tripping over her own foot. Andrew was leaning against the wall, glasses on, eyes closed—and damn if he didn't take her breath away. She spun the tuning fork ring around her finger. Wasn't attraction supposed to be fun, and not exhausting? This tug-of-war between, what was quickly becoming genuine affection, and the constant refrain of, *'He's a musician'* was wearing thin. Very thin.

She slid her key into the lock and pushed the door open. "Coming in, Cowboy?"

He cracked open his eyes and his face broke into the smile that never failed to send a rush of awareness through every inch of her body. Had he really only been gone a few days?

He pushed off the wall and placed a soft kiss on her cheek before rolling his suitcase in and propping it against the stairs. "I missed you, Gracie."

"That's why you came home early?" She stiffened at her

unconscious use of the word 'home.' "Because you missed having someone to fight with?"

"Did you miss the part where I told you I went to New Orleans?"

Grace winced. "Did you fight with your dad again?" She opened the refrigerator and slid in the left-overs Annie had sent home. "Andrew?" She turned to find an empty apartment. "Where did you go?"

She wandered forward, scanning the room, and turned to find him sprawled on the couch, an arm over his eyes. She came around the edge and kneeled, gently lowering his arm. Upon closer examination, his eyes were bloodshot and deep, dark circles hung under his eyes. She frowned and swept the hair back from his face, pulling his glasses off. He leaned into her touch and his hand brushed her lower back.

"Do you want me to let you sleep for a while?"

His fingers dug in as he lifted her, in one smooth movement, on top of him. "No," he said, his voice low and rough. He searched her eyes for the briefest moment before lifting his head to press his lips against hers. His lips didn't move, didn't push for more, a gentle gesture that was both comforting and disconcerting. He pulled back and stroked his fingers over her cheeks. "So beautiful."

She wanted to unbutton his shirt and run her hands over the planes of his chest, tangling her fingers in the soft hair that dusted his pecs, but she knew the difference between satisfying lust and seeking comfort. The look in Andrew's eyes was definitely the latter.

She placed a palm on either side of his chest and levered up. "So, New Orleans, huh? What brought about the change in plans?" She rolled off of him and moved to the end of the couch.

He slowly dragged himself into an upright position and scrubbed his hand over his face, scratching against at least three days of stubble. "It was time." When Grace narrowed her eyes and pinned him with a suspicious look, he added, "And apparently you're not the only one who thought I needed an intervention."

"Julia?"

Andrew laughed and nodded. "She told me, and I quote, that it was time to 'sort my shit.' Said my 'family drama,'" he flexed his fingers in air quotes, "was keeping me from the things I really want in life."

"Getting the album done."

He pinned her with a look that did funny things to her insides. "Among other things."

Grace squirmed and cleared her throat. She wasn't ready for this conversation. "And did you? Sort your shit, that is. Were you able to talk with your father?"

He bit down on his bottom lip and nodded almost imperceptibly. Her re-direct was not exactly nuanced and it was clear he knew exactly what she was doing. She braced herself, waiting for him to call her out, but instead, he moved toward her and laid his head on her shoulder, absently playing with her fingers, rubbing over the top of the ring.

"We talked."

"And?"

His body stiffened and his hand wrapped tighter around hers. "I found out the reason he's always been against my chosen career."

She placed a gentle kiss on his forehead. "Want to tell me about it?" She wouldn't force him to talk about it. She'd been in that situation too many times herself.

He turned his head, his eyes running over her face and preceded to tell her the story, without stopping and seemingly without taking a breath. When the words stopped, she wrapped an arm around his shoulder and squeezed. "Wow," she breathed out. Even with her vivid imagination, she'd never have come up with that story. "Where did you leave things?"

Andrew shrugged. "I think in a better place, but I'm not sure. He seemed genuinely sorry, but I can't shake the feeling that a simple conversation, years ago, would have saved a lot of pain and uncomfortable family moments. I've never lost a child, so I have no idea what kind of pain that causes, but it seems through all of this, he nearly lost another one."

"You've had a difficult relationship for years. One conversation won't make it easy. It'll take time. But, at least, it's out in the open now."

"I hope so. Being there, especially for Christmas, made me realize how much I've missed being part of the family."

"So why come back early? Why not stay and enjoy a little more family time?"

He shifted and turned to face her. He tucked a piece of hair behind her ear and dragged a finger across the line of her jaw. The way he was looking at her made her feel intensely uncomfortable and her skin prickled with understanding that he was about to say something that would put all the longing looks and gentle touches into actual words. She turned away and got immensely interested in the fringe on her couch pillows.

He picked up her hand, flipped it over and placed a single kiss in the middle of it. "Grace, look at me." He put a finger under her chin and turned her head back to face him. "For the past fifteen years, I've buried myself in the music. I've had no long-term relationships, and the Storyhill guys became my only friends. I thought I was focused and driven, but really, I was just trying to get my dad's approval. I've pushed too many people away trying to get one person's attention. And, the minute I found out the truth, I knew I didn't want that life anymore. I needed to get back to you. To tell you how I feel before this album is complete and it's too late."

Grace shimmied under his intense gaze. "Andrew, I think . . ."

"No, let me finish, Grace. I know we've only known each other for six weeks. And, I know you might not be ready, but I have *really* lost my taste for secrets." He collected her hands between his. "I am in love with you, Grace O'Connor. Hopelessly, utterly, in love with you."

Panic crept up her spine and twisted its tentacles around her lungs. Air rushing out, nothing replacing it. She had to move before she passed out. She walked to the windows, taking small breaths, black spots dancing in her vision.

Andrew walked up behind her but didn't touch her. "This cannot be a complete surprise to you, Grace."

It wasn't, but seeing it in his eyes, starting to feel it in her own heart, was entirely different than hearing it said out loud.

He placed his hands on her shoulders and she startled. He turned her slowly toward him.

She shook her head, "Andrew . . ." she managed to squeak out.

He placed a finger over her lips. "The last time we stood in this very spot, you asked me to 'at least consider' your request. And now, I'm asking you to do the same. Consider me, Grace. Consider us."

Didn't he know? Didn't he see that she'd been 'considering' him since the day he strode into Ford's conference room, full of anger, attitude, and arrogance?

She searched his face. The full spectrum of emotions—fear, hope, longing, love—dancing in his beautiful eyes nearly brought her to her knees. Right now, she couldn't do anything about the fear, hope, and love, but she could do something about the longing. It wasn't fair. It was the coward's way out, but she pulled her t-shirt over her head and pulled him toward the couch and pushed. She climbed into his lap, slid her arms around his neck, and placed a few nibbling kisses under his ear before pulling him to a deep, engulfing kiss.

Right now, this would have to be enough. Right now, this was all she could give.

Grace stretched and rubbed the small of her back. Not the best choice to spend the night on the sofa. She cracked an eye and blinked from the sunlight streaming in the windows. She rolled over and tried to shake off the last vestiges of sleep. She ached in ways she'd hadn't for years. When was the last time she'd made love anywhere but in a bed?

She sat up, pulled the blanket tighter, and tried to focus on the room. Boots. Shirt. Boxers. But no sign of the man to which they belonged. She listened for the sound of the shower but heard nothing.

She reached for his shirt, pulled it over her head, and breathed in his delicious smell. She padded over to the kitchen and pushed start on the coffeemaker. He'd probably snuck upstairs to her bed. It wasn't like the sofa was comfortable for someone his height.

She poured cream into her favorite blue and white earthenware mug and leaned against the counter, waiting for the coffee to finish brewing. His words from last night reverberated through her mind. He loved her. He loved her? Damn it. This was supposed to be a fling—a way to crawl back into the land of the living.

Too bad her heart never got the message.

She might not be able to say the words. But that didn't mean she wasn't falling. Hard.

But was it enough?

"Grace?" he called from upstairs, interrupting her thoughts. *Get real, Grace, he's interrupting your obsessing and over-think-*

ing. "Once you've had your coffee, can you please come up here?"

She walked over to the stairs, nearly tripping on his boots. She wasn't ready to deal with his proclamation just yet and his boots gave her an idea—a little distraction for him and a whole heaping load of denial for her. She bent and picked them up. At the top, she slipped her feet into them and tried her best not to trip down the hallway. She nudged the door to her bedroom open, but the room was empty, bed still made. *Where did he go?* She turned to see the door to her office slightly ajar.

"Andrew?" she called, moving down the hallway.

"In your office, baby."

She pushed the door open to find him sitting at her desk, scratching away in his new journal. "What are you doing?"

He winked. "Got inspired. Been writing since 3:00 a.m."

She tromped over to the desk and picked up the papers in front of him. "You finished the eleventh song?"

"Yes, and I'd like your take on . . . wait, are you wearing my boots?"

She shoved the chair back and straddled him, losing one boot in the motion. "Yep," she said, the 'p' popping hard. "Do you approve?"

He grabbed her hips, pulling her closer. "Are you also not wearing any panties?"

She sucked her top lip under her teeth and shook her head slowly side-to-side. "Nope." She looked up at him through her lashes while sliding down his zipper.

"Think we should take this to the bedroom?"

"No time," she said, rubbing up against him.

"Um, why?"

"I texted Chris and told him you were back early. He says we can come over today."

"Before New Year's?"

"Apparently, he is more than happy to have a break from his mother-in-law. I told him to expect us in about ninety minutes. You've proven you're good at slow and gentle, but how good are you at fast and hard?"

He gripped her bottom, pulling her up and settling her back down over him. She gasped as he filled her and started moving. "I'm a satisfaction guaranteed kind of guy. I'll do my best, but if you're not one hundred percent pleased, I'd be happy to make it up to you later."

"This is really good, Andrew," Chris said, flipping through the music and lyrics for the eleventh song. He picked up a guitar and started strumming. "Adding the female vocal makes all the difference. Finally, the lyrics make sense." The producer turned to Grace, pinning her with his gaze. "How about it, Gigi? Fancy getting in that booth over there and singing it with him?"

Grace spun in her chair so quickly she needed to grab the console to stop the rotation. "Um, that would be a hard no."

"C'mon Grace," Chris pressed, "you don't have to be on the final track, I just want to hear it. See if it works."

"Please." Andrew leaned in and whispered in her ear. "I did what you wanted when you were pleading with me earlier. One 'please' for another?"

He looked at her with an expression of pure sin, and she couldn't summon a single excuse. "Fine. But, just to help us finish the song." She strode into the booth, interlacing her fingers to try and stop the shaking, and slapped on the headphones. It was official. She'd lost her mind. Chris was recording her—and then she'd have to listen to the playback—over and over again. A tremor ran down her spine. And as usual, she had no idea if it was fear or excitement.

Chris turned his back to the window separating the control

room from the recording booth. "I don't know what you said to her, but good work. I haven't been able to get her behind a microphone in years. You clearly have special negotiating skills."

"I heard that. Talkback is on. If you'd like to have a private conversation about me, it's the big green button."

"Gigi, you're feisty today."

"Today?" Andrew looked through the window and smirked at her. "Try every day."

Entering the booth, Andrew dropped the music onto the stand and situated one headphone over an ear, pushing the other back into his hair.

Chris' voice boomed through the headphones. "I'm ready when you are."

Andrew lifted a single headphone from her ear. "You sure you know how to do this *a cappella* thing, Gracie? There aren't any instruments to cover up your mistakes."

Grace cocked an eyebrow. "You know I don't have to do this, right?"

Andrew trailed a single finger up her spine, eliciting an involuntary shudder. "You want me to beg?"

Grace snorted. "Let me know if you need help figuring out all those black dots on the page. They're called notes, by the way."

Andrew smirked. "Do you sit and think these things up or does busting my ass come naturally to you?"

Grace shrugged. "What can I say? It's a gift."

"Getting paid by the minute here," Chris said sternly, but there was amusement in his voice.

"Anything more you need to get out of your system?" Andrew asked.

Grace raised a single finger and looked thoughtfully up at the ceiling. She cocked her head to the left and then the right.

"Nope, I think that's all for now." She turned to face Chris. "Count us in, Mr. Cooper."

Andrew moved through the intro, dropping the base beat to set the tempo. Grace watched the music, preparing for her entrance in the fourth stanza. Three, two, one, she took a breath and—nothing. Not a single sound came out of her mouth.

Stopping after reaching the chorus, Andrew covered the mics and turned to her. "You okay?" he whispered.

Heat crawled up her neck. "I just wanted to hear it before I jumped in," she lied.

He didn't buy it, not even a little bit. "It's just you and me." He squeezed her fingers. "Not any different than when we sing together as we write. Forget about everything else."

She nodded and pulled his fingers from her mic. "Chris, let's take it from the top." This time when her part came up, she forced out the notes, rough and ragged at first, growing louder with every syllable until she was at full power.

The song stopped. And silence. Both men were staring at her. Was it that bad?

She looked at the floor. "I'm sorry. It's been a long time."

"Damn, Grace," Chris said into their ears. "I'd forgotten the pure power of your voice."

Andrew laughed, a deep belly laugh, and picked her up and spun her around. "Welcome back, Gracie." He dipped his lips to her ear and whispered, "Welcome home, baby. Welcome home."

She swiped at her cheek, catching the single tear that escaped at his words. How did he know? How did he know that she'd come to back to herself . . . that somewhere in the final verse she'd indeed come home?

. . .

"Where's the seat adjuster in this thing?" Andrew asked, legs nearly pinned to his chest.

Grace laughed. "It's on your left." The car never felt small to her, but with Andrew behind the wheel, it resembled a clown car. "You regretting your offer to drive?"

He shook his head. "No, but is there anything I should know about driving this electric contraption?"

"Go is on the right and stop is on the left—and don't get distracted by everything that lights up on the dashboard."

He pulled out of Chris' driveway, easing onto the road. "Wait, is that a tree on the upper left of the dashboard?"

"I told you not to worry your pretty little head about all that." She punched Home on the GPS and dropped her head to the headrest, closing her eyes. She wasn't so much tired, as unnerved.

Despite the men's earlier reaction, Grace tensed as Chris' finger had hovered over the playback button. It had felt good, but that didn't mean it sounded good. She braced for disappointment, but the instant sound flooded the studio, a rush shot through her body.

Her voice sounded strong and her throaty alto melted into Andrew's deep bass effortlessly. They sounded good together—like they'd been singing with each other for years.

She'd spent a lifetime telling people that she was a writer, not a singer—that she could sing well enough to help someone hear the song, but not well enough to perform publicly. After today's session, she didn't need a Ph.D. in psychology to know that belief was just another way she justified shrinking into Jax's shadow.

"You realize, that after your superstar performance today," Andrew said, breaking into her thoughts, "we only have one song left. Twelve down, one to go. Hardly seems possible."

She rolled her head to face him. "And it only took two dozen high maintenance coffees and three bags of sour gummy worms."

Andrew laughed. "I'm proud of us, Gracie. If you'd have told me two months ago what a great team we'd make, I'd have laughed at you."

"Or at least spilled your coffee on me."

He slid a hand from the steering wheel and squeezed her fingers, running his thumb over the ring, twisting right to left. "That coffee turned out to be the best four dollars I've ever spent. How about we go out tonight and celebrate?"

"Do you think we should? Before the last song is done? We've only got a few days before you leave for California—a song in that amount of time is virtually impossible."

"Not if you share a song you've already written."

He was persistent, she'd give him that. She tried to see his request for what he thought it was, a way to help his bandmates.

"Let me think about it."

His eyes swung away from the road and went wide. "Really? I know just the one!"

"I didn't say yes. I said I would think about it. Don't get your hopes up. We need to keep tossing ideas around."

"Sure. Sure. But tonight, let's celebrate."

"Andrew, I need to know you heard me. I did not agree to give you one of my songs. I only said I'd think about it. Do you understand?"

He pulled into the underground parking at her condo and killed the engine. "I got you, Grace. I heard you."

"You promise? The decision on whether or not I give a song to Storyhill is mine to make. Alone."

"I promise, Gracie."

"Good. And while I think a celebration is premature, let's still go out tonight. I don't have one ounce of creative energy left in me. Did you have something in mind?"

"How about someplace that doesn't require three forks, and everything comes with a side of chili cheese fries?"

Grace snickered. "Only home for a couple of days, but got enough of Sylvia's Rules?"

He leaned over, kissed her on the temple, and winked. "Yes, and I recently read an article that said cheese sauce is an aphrodisiac. We could eat and do research."

"How very scientific of you, Cowboy. Though something tells me the beans in your chili cheese fries would negate the stimulating effect of the cheese."

Andrew laughed and put the car into reverse, backing out of the parking space. "That's why an exhaustive experiment is necessary."

"And, how do you plan on proving your thesis?"

Andrew turned toward her, heat smoldering behind his eyes. "I think by your third orgasm, we'll know."

"Three?" Grace said, swallowing hard. "That's ambitious."

He ran a single finger up her thigh and up and over the tip of her breast. "We need conclusive proof."

Grace's core clenched. Hard. And suddenly she didn't care, even a tiny bit, about what this man did for a living.

CHAPTER NINETEEN

G race stared at the man sleeping next to her. His long hair fell over his eyes and his mouth was slightly turned up at the corners like he was having a lovely dream. She placed a light hand over his heart and felt the gentle beat.

She'd been awake since 4:00 a.m., staring at the ceiling with thoughts rumbling through her head with the subtlety of a wicked spring thunderstorm. Andrew's declaration of love. Her own deepening feelings. The way her voice sounded emanating from Chris' speakers. Her vow to steer clear of musicians. Chris' suggestion she start her own production company. And Andrew's persistent request for one of her songs. She tried to pick the thoughts apart, take them and their ramifications one-by-one, but she couldn't, they were all knotted up. Tight.

Ugh. She couldn't lay here a moment longer.

She slithered out of bed, careful not to wake Andrew, and dressed in her dark closet. At the bottom of the stairs, she bundled up for the winter wind and snuck out the door. She'd grab a coffee at the corner shop and bring back some of the pastries he liked so much.

Avoidance? Her? One hundred percent.

"You're early today, Grace, we only opened five minutes ago," the barista said from behind the counter as Grace entered the shop and kicked the snow from her boots.

"Work calls early today," she lied. "Can I have my usual for here and two coconut cream cheese Danishes boxed to go?"

"Sure thing."

Grace retreated to a worn cocoa-colored leather chair in the corner. She picked up the folded newspaper from the fireplace hearth and mindlessly flipped through it. The headlines blurred as her mind kept returning to Andrew. They made incredible music together and the sex was off the charts. She thought about him all the time, and she'd willingly opened her life to him. He'd met Annie and Curtis. She'd told him her secrets and her fears.

But love? Maybe he wouldn't bring it up again. He was leaving in a few days. They'd be on the West Coast for three weeks. That would give her time to think about things—give her the space to see if she missed him. Her heart plummeted. Who was she kidding? Right now, he slept in her bed two blocks away and she already missed him.

But she'd been serious when she told Annie she wouldn't allow herself to be swallowed up again. Could she give him her whole heart and still shed the mantle of supporting character? Or would she always wonder if she'd sublimated herself and her dreams again?

"You left this on the counter," the barista said, setting her coffee on the table and handing her a ringing phone.

Grace laughed softly, extracting her phone from his outstretched hand and silencing it. "Thank you. I'm a little out of it today, I guess."

"That's what the coffee is for," he said, giving her a little smirk and a wink as he returned to his station.

She twisted the lid from her drink, letting the steam escape, and flipped her phone over. A missed call from Chris. Followed by the briefest of text messages—*Call me ASAP.*

A bright yellow wooden bird wobbled out from the kitschy cuckoo clock behind the counter, warbling an out-of-tune announcement of the hour. 7:00 a.m. Apparently, Grace wasn't the only early riser this morning.

She tapped on Chris' number and waited for the producer to answer.

"Did I wake you up?" her friend said in place of a greeting.

Grace laughed. "A little late to ask that now, isn't it?"

"Suppose so. But I have a client waiting for an answer. And as soon as the call came in, I thought of you."

A tremor of anticipation snaked up her spine. Did someone need a song written? Six weeks ago, this would have sent her into a fear spiral. Now, it kicked up a zing of excitement.

Chris cut into her silence. "I need you to hear me out—and really think about this—before saying no."

"Okay," Grace said slowly. *Maybe not a song then?*

"I got a request from an artist that I can't fit into my schedule, but they're a longtime client and I don't want to send them somewhere else."

"And this has something to do with me?"

"I want you to produce the project, Gigi."

Grace squeezed the paper cup in her hand, sending coffee gurgling over the edge. "What?"

"It's perfect. You can use the studio during my off-hours. The client gets what they need, and you jump start the next logical step in your career. It's win-win."

"You want me to produce it *on my own?*"

"You're more than ready, Grace."

Grace set the cup down and placed a hand over her racing heart. Sixty seconds ago, she was thrilled at the idea of adding to her songwriting credits, but now . . . Producing? By herself? "So,

I'd work for you?" How did that fit into her goal of proving she could do this on her own?

"No. You'd be my partner."

Partner.

Without warning, tears flooded her eyes. He believed in her that much? She swiped a hand over her eyelashes, dislodging the tears before they could fall. "You want to partner with me? Why?"

Chris chuckled. "Only the best for Unstrung Studios."

"And that's me?" She knew she was good, but the best?

"I wouldn't even consider trusting my clients with anyone else. But, honestly, Gigi, it's also a selfish move on my part. I'd get to expand my business while you did the same. And, imagine the press I'm going to get when Unstrung announces they've partnered with the incomparable Grace O'Connor."

When did she become the 'incomparable Grace O'Connor?' Didn't the press think she was just a washed-up widow? Maybe not, if Chris was willing to give her this shot?

"I can practically hear the wheels turning through the phone, Gigi," Chris said with a laugh. "I told the artist I'd get back to them by tomorrow morning. I'll email you the details. Think about it. Talk to Andrew about it."

Wait. What? Talk to Andrew about it? Memories of conversations with Jax roared to life, exchanges that always ended with her turning down opportunities to work with other artists. Not happening again. "Why would I talk to Andrew about this?" she said between gritted teeth. "He has no say over my career."

"Of course not. I just figured he'd be a good sounding board. I gotta run, but I'll check in with you tonight. Okay?"

Grace slipped her fingers under the candy-cane-colored twine tied around the white box filled with Andrew's pastries and sucked in a breath. "Fine," she said, trying to steady her voice. Chris disconnected and she slugged down the remains of her coffee, wishing it was something stronger. Coffee, the tequila of the morning, she thought, marching back to her apartment.

She tromped up the stairs, replaying the conversation with Chris. He offered to partner with her and yet she couldn't stop obsessing about his comment to discuss it with Andrew. She slapped her hand against the stair rail. *Enough.* She wasn't going to let her past dictate her future. Not anymore. She didn't need to talk to Andrew—or anyone for that matter—this opportunity was a no-brainer. She'd fight through the last dregs of her fear and prove to everyone she could do this. On her own.

Decision made. No need to wait. She'd email Chris right now.

She turned right at the top of the stairs, instead of left toward her bedroom. She stopped short when she heard Andrew's voice coming from her office. She placed a hand on the door, pushing it open a crack. He was bent over her desk with his phone pressed to his ear and her writing journal open in front of him.

"I haven't told her." Pause. "Yes, it's what I want." She stilled at the words. He laughed. "It's my talent. She may be reticent, but I'll talk her into it. And, if not, I'll just do it." Pause, pause.

He'd talk her into it or just do it? Oh, hell, no. This new, decisive, more confident Grace was not about to let another man —another lover—co-opt her talent and manipulate her career. She powered through the door and he looked up and smiled, until he saw her expression.

"I gotta go," he said into the phone, "I'll call you back." He hung up and rounded the desk, trying to draw her into his arms.

"No way. Don't touch me."

"Grace?"

"I've been crystal clear. You cannot strong-arm me into giving you a song."

"What are you talking about?"

"Why is my journal open?" She marched around the back of the desk. "And to the very song you've been begging for? You thought, if she doesn't give it to me, I'll just take it?"

His eyes narrowed and he took a step back. "Grace, where is all this coming from? I don't understand."

"The hell you don't. I heard what you said on the phone just now. Have you been manipulating me all along? Was all your talk of love just part of your plan? Pretend to care for the poor widow and get the song you need—and get laid a few times as a bonus?"

"Grace, this is sounding crazy. I don't have a plan. And, if I did, falling in love with you certainly wasn't part of it."

She crossed her arms and turned to the window. She would not cry. She wouldn't break. "You need to leave Andrew."

He gingerly wrapped his fingers around her shoulder and coaxed her gaze back to him. "I'm not leaving until I have a chance to explain." His voice quieted, but strength and determination flashed in his eyes.

She met his steely gaze with one of her own. "I'm not interested."

"Too bad. I was talking to Brad and it had nothing to do with the final song. I asked him to help me convince you to come along on tour so we could finish the album."

Grace snorted and pulled her phone from her back pocket. "If I called Brad right now, would he tell me the same story?"

Andrew sighed and dropped his hand from her shoulder. "I can't believe we are still dealing with trust issues but go ahead and call him if you need to, he'll tell you the exact same story.

But, once he does, you're going to have to own up to what's actually happening here."

"And what is that?"

"That you're blowing this—us—up intentionally."

Grace's eyes widened and she stumbled back a step. "I am not."

"Then what is going on? And don't give me any bullshit reasons like you're nine years older than me, or we're co-workers and should keep a professional distance, or your favorite, that I'm a musician."

"That's not an excuse!" Grace's voice rose a decibel or two. "Getting involved with another musician complicates everything."

"It doesn't, Gracie. It's just an easy excuse. You know we make a great team—personally and professionally."

"Maybe I don't want to be a team. Did you ever think of that?" Tears were burning the backs of her eyes, but she wouldn't give in. Andrew was wrong. She was not blowing this up on purpose. She was finally standing up for herself. Finally going after what she wanted. Finally putting herself first.

She pushed her shoulders back and stuck out her chin. "Chris made me an offer this morning. To be his partner. To produce music. And I'm going to do it. On my own."

"That's great, Gracie," Andrew said, moving to the other side of the office and leaning against the wall. "I'll stand beside you and cheer every step of the way."

Grace funneled her fingers through her hair and tugged softly at the roots. She took a deep breath and forced her voice into something calm and level. "You're not understanding me, Andrew. I have to do this alone. Prove I can do it . . . by myself."

"Prove what?" Andrew sneered, ceding the patient, slow voice he'd been using. "That you're finally brave enough to stop hiding your astonishing talent?"

Grace sighed and dropped into her chair. "I'm not hiding. At least I won't be once I partner with Chris."

"Just because you're finally willing to step out of Jax Jensen's shadow doesn't mean you're not still hiding."

Grace slapped a hand on her desktop. "Don't you dare bring Jax into this!"

Andrew pushed himself off the wall and leaned forward on her desk. "Why not? He's been here, with us, the whole time. He's the specter that you throw between us when things get too hard for you. Aren't you getting just a little bit tired of blaming him for all your issues?"

Grace reared back like she'd been slapped, but apparently, Andrew wasn't finished.

"News flash, Grace. I'm not Jax. No one wants you to spread your wings more than me. I have zero interest in placing limits on you. I love you. I look at you and I forget to breathe. I hold you in my arms and wonder how I ever managed to live without you. You astound me. Strong, beautiful, smart, funny—everything a man dreams about. You've made every part of my life better, but to borrow from Julia, you've got some shit to sort, too."

The tears finally fell, running down her cheeks in thick rivulets. She loved him, too. But it didn't matter. She had to do this on her own. She. Had. To. "I guess that's it, then," she said, between gulping breaths. "I'll honor my commitment to finishing the album and I'll call Chris and let him know that he'll be your point person from this point forward."

Andrew kneeled down beside her and wiped the tears from her cheek. "That's not what I meant, you maddening woman." His voice modulated back down into his deep, calming, dulcet tones. "I'm not giving up on us. I'm just going to give you some space. I leave in two days and for the three weeks we're on tour I won't text you, I won't call you. I told you before that I'd wait as long as it took for you to be ready and I meant it. But, when the tour is over, I'm coming straight back here and we're going to work this out. Together."

Grace placed her hand on his face, running her thumb over his stubble. "Andrew, I'm not changing my mind."

He stood and tucked a strand of hair behind her ear. "Neither am I, Gracie." He walked to the door, stopped and placed a hand on the doorframe. "I'll see you in three weeks," he said, without fully turning around, and left.

Andrew got to the lobby and collapsed into the sofa flanking the door. What the fuck just happened? He held himself together in front of Grace, but it felt like a knife was lodged in his chest. It wouldn't surprise him to look down and see blood splattered all over the glossy foyer floor.

He'd given her his heart and she'd thrown it back at him because she believed she couldn't have love and a career? He rubbed his hand over his heart and spit out a mirthless laugh. Wasn't that ironic? She'd shown him relationships weren't a liability and he'd, somehow, convinced her they were.

The elevator doors started to open and for a moment relief flooded through him. She was coming to find him, to tell him she'd made a mistake. Despair quickly doused his flicker of hope as an elderly lady hobbled out pulling an empty shopping trolley. He nodded at her and she gave him the stink-eye before moving out the door to the garage. Zero for two with women today.

He closed his eyes and tried to clear his head, tried to figure what to do and where to go, but it was useless. Behind closed lids all he could see was her. Sitting at the piano in the New York studio. Standing in the wings at the concerts. Laughing at

Matt's jokes. Naked, eyes full of lust, urging him on. Singing in Chris' studio like she was born to it.

Damn it. He'd always fought for what he wanted. And he wanted her. He was going to march up there and tell her, *again*, that she didn't need to do this alone.

He stood up, took a single step, and sunk back down into the sofa. His plan was to demand she love him? Might as well admit he'd never listened to her. She didn't need someone else telling her what to do, what was best for her. That was precisely what she was fighting against, wasn't it?

He may need and want her, but this wasn't about him. It was about her.

If he truly loved her, he'd give her the space she needed— the space he'd promised her.

Which meant he had to find somewhere to stay until he left for California. He dug his phone out of his back pocket to call Brad, but before he could tap the number, his phone vibrated with an incoming call. He stared at the screen, confused.

"Dad?"

"Hi, Andrew."

"Is Mom alright?" He couldn't handle any more bad news today.

"She's fine."

"Bridget? Colin? They okay?"

"Everybody's fine, Andy."

Andrew bristled; his father hadn't used his nickname since high school. "Then why are you calling?"

His father cleared his throat. "I'm just making sure you got to Minneapolis okay."

Andrew pulled the phone away from his ear and stared at it. "Dad, I've been here for three days. Did Mom make you call?"

"No. I guess I just wanted to say I'm sorry—again."

Clearly, everyone around him had lost their minds today.

"Okay, thanks." What he supposed to say? He felt like he'd been dropped into upside-down world. Grace didn't want a relationship with him, but his father did?

"Well, I guess that's it," his father warbled, "you'll let me know if you need anything, okay?"

"I'm good, Dad." Biggest lie ever. "Actually, Dad, there is something." Clearly, he'd lost his mind too, he was about to ask Charles Hayes for advice.

"Yes, son?" his dad asked with a rush of excitement.

"Got any advice for a guy who's just gotten his heart stomped on?"

His father laughed. Actually laughed. "You sure you don't need money? That's more my area of expertise." His tone sobered and he continued. "I didn't date much before your mother and she's had my heart for over forty years. But," he said, humor sliding back into his voice, "she's not always the easiest woman. I learned the hard way that going in with a bulldozer is always a bad idea. We've lasted this long because I learned to be patient."

Andrew nodded and rubbed the spot over his heart again. "Thanks, Dad."

"Andy, are you in love with Grace? I'm assuming it's Grace."

"Yes, and yes, Dad."

"Then be patient. If for no other reason than your mother seemed quite taken with her and we both know how likely that is to happen again."

He said goodbye and hung up the phone and ordered an Uber back to the hotel that had turned him away three days ago. With a final glance back toward the elevator, he whispered, "I told you'd I'd wait for as long as it took, and I'm a man of my word, Grace O'Connor."

CHAPTER TWENTY

Grace smoothed a hand over the paper fresh from the printer, letting the residual warmth seep into her fingers. A new list. This one wasn't about an ending, but a beginning—a bulleted outline for taking back control of her life. A familiar vibration tingled up her spine. This time she didn't need to wonder if it was fear or excitement. She knew it was both. And she was totally okay with that.

Picking up her favorite neon pink pen, she drew a steady line through item number one. She shuddered, emotion crawling into her throat, her breath catching behind the clog. She'd just wrapped up her first video call as Producer, capital 'P.' Chris had kicked off the call and then sat back and let her run the meeting. She'd shared her ideas and the artist had loved all of them.

She did a little chair dance, shimmying her bottom in celebration. Grabbing ahold of her future felt fucking fantastic. She did this. Herself. Not alongside Jax Jensen. Not because of threats from a music executive. Not with Andrew Hayes.

Andrew Hayes. There was no use in lying, she missed him —ached for him. But she'd made the right decision. She needed the shakeup. Despite what he thought, she absolutely had to take this next step solo. But before she could officially close the book on Andrew Hayes and Storyhill, there was one final thing to do. Number two on her list.

She opened her email and clicked on 'compose new message.' She typed Ford's address into the 'to' line.' She stared at the subject line and her fingers quivered as she typed 'Final Song.' She pointed her mouse at the paper clip icon and clicked.

"You can do it, Grace. Attach the file. It's the right thing to do. It's the next step toward your new future."

She dragged the document over, closed her eyes and hit 'send.' The whoosh alerted her it was gone.

With a whisper of a sound, she brought her time with Storyhill to an end. It didn't matter that it had been two of the best months of her life. Yes, Andrew had left the door open for more, but she had to close it. Now, while her resolve was still strong.

She crossed the second item off her list. No chair dance this time. No satisfaction, just a hollow emptiness. *Shake it off, Grace. A pity party is not on the list.* She picked up her phone to check the time and it vibrated with an incoming text.

A: I've left you alone long enough. Meet me at the coffee shop in an hour.

She'd texted Annie last week, told her that she and Andrew had decided to go their separate ways and that she needed a few days alone—at least that was her version of the story. Andrew likely would tell Annie something else entirely. And she was nowhere near ready to dissect their final conversation with Annie.

G: I'm working. Have a new list to get through.

A: What???? There's a new LIST? Now I know something is up. No more dodging me.

G: I'm fine. Said no woman, ever, when she was actually fine.

A: But I'm not. I don't understand what happened. One minute you're exchanging Christmas gifts and getting kinky with flour and the next it's done?????? Something is rotten in Denmark.

G: Hamlet? Really?

A: Methinks the lady doth protest too much.

G: Well, I'll admit to this being the winter of my discontent. But much as I'd love to continue swapping Shakespeare quotes with you, I gotta get back to work.

A: I'm not going to stop texting until you agree to meet me. Give in.

G: In Core Gerbil. Common Grounds in an hour. But if you make me cry in public there's going to be hell to pay.

A: You don't scare me.

Grace ambled over to the table, careful not to spill a drop of her latte. She hadn't been sleeping and every drop of caffeine was precious. She settled in her chair and examined the paneled walls and antique thermoses lining the high shelves. Was it only eight weeks ago when she sat here with Annie telling her about Ford's ultimatum—and praying Annie would give her an excuse not to do it?

Grace flinched as Annie's handbag landed with a thump on the chair opposite her. She extracted her wallet out of her big pink designer bag and waggled a finger at Grace. "I'm getting my coffee and then you're telling me everything."

Grace watched her best friend elegantly move through the tables and make conversation with the barista. Within moments, she was back with a steaming cup.

"That was fast."

"Frequent customer benefit—they start my order when I

walk in the door. Now enough small talk. Start explaining how you let a hot, talented, charming man get away."

Grace toyed with the idea of concocting a story, but she knew Annie would see through it in an instant. Grace ran her finger around the rim of her coffee.

Annie stilled her hand. "That's your tell."

"Pardon?"

"When you're nervous, you run your fingers around the top of your cup." Annie narrowed her eyes. "Sad, I get, but nervous? What's the story?"

Grace stared into her cup, worried what Annie would see in her eyes if she looked at her. "It's time for me to carve my own path."

"The producer thing?"

Grace nodded.

"And that has something to do with breaking it off with Andrew?"

"When Chris made me the offer, I realized it was time to get my life sorted." She conveniently left out the part about accusing Andrew of stealing one of her songs. Her best friend didn't need to know she had acted like an unhinged crazy person.

Annie's eyebrows squeezed together, and she cocked her head to the side. "And reading between the lines, you think you need to do that alone?"

"Yes. After everything I told you about Jax, why is that so hard to believe?"

Annie blew out a puff of air that sent ripples across the top of both of their coffees. "Because it's stupid."

Grace finally looked up from her cup, eyes wide. "Wow. Tell me how you really feel."

"Grace, honey, you know I love you like a sister, but you sound ridiculous."

Grace's spine straightened and she tightened her fingers around her mug. "It's ridiculous to finally believe in myself and put myself first? I thought you'd be the one person who'd understand."

"You're going to wear a hole in that cup." Annie stilled Grace's fingers again. "Of course, you should believe in yourself —recognize what the rest of us have known all along—but you don't need to do it alone. Will and I parent together, that doesn't make either one of us less capable. I have a team helping me on every case and that doesn't make me a less effective member of the bar."

"You sound just like Andrew," Grace mumbled and yanked her cup to her mouth.

Annie leaned forward on her elbows and pinned Grace with her prosecutor stare—never mind that she wasn't a prosecutor—she'd mastered the look to make defendants sweat.

"I thought your split was mutual?"

Annie strummed her manicure on the table and Grace knew she wouldn't stop until Grace broke.

"Fine," Grace said, pushing back in her chair. "I told Andrew it was over, and he said, and I'm paraphrasing here, that he'd be back after this next leg of the tour and we'd work through my 'issues,' Grace flexed her fingers in air quotes, "together."

"Dammit, Grace," Annie slammed her cup down with a clatter that caused several sets of eyes in the shop to dart their way.

Grace settled the teetering cup. "You don't have to get so mad."

"You know what," Annie retorted with fire in her voice, "I think I do! I'm not going to tell you how to live your life, because god knows I've made my share of mistakes, but you are letting one of the best things to happen to you slip away. I think you're making—or made—a huge mistake."

Grace reached for her coffee and missed, flipping the cup over and spilling coffee over the tabletop and onto the floor. "Grab your bag," she instructed Annie, "and I'll go ask Bart for something to wipe it up."

The barista met her halfway. "Looks like it's time to cut you off, Grace." He winked and handed her the bar towel, and she burst into tears. He froze and stared wide-eyed at Annie. "I know how important your coffee is to you. Don't worry, I'll make you another one."

Annie took the towel from Grace, put her arm around her shoulders and guided her back to the table. "Thanks, Bart."

Annie wiped up the spill and pulled her chair over to Grace.

Grace stared at her lap, twisting the tuning fork ring around her finger. She hadn't been able to bring herself to take it off.

Annie tugged a tissue from her bag and handed it to Grace. "You have some mascara on your cheeks."

Grace forced out a garbled laugh. "I specifically told you not to make me cry in public."

"I think Bart did that, not me."

Grace shook her head and let out a real laugh. "I've probably traumatized him forever."

"He does keep looking at you out of the corner of his eye. Do you love him, Grace?"

Grace sniffled and rubbed the tissue over her cheeks. "Bart? I'm very fond of his coffee, but love? Seems a bit over the top."

"Grace."

"Yes, Annie, I love him. Stupid heart and stupid girl parts railroaded my brain."

"Do you think he loves you?"

"I think his quote was, 'I'm in love with you. I look at you and forget to breathe. I hold you in my arms and wonder how I managed to live without you.' Not that I memorized it."

Annie bit back a laugh. "Of course not." She pulled out a second tissue and swapped it for the one mangled in Grace's grip. "Please don't misunderstand me. It is time for you to step out of the shadows and embrace your gifts and talents, but I suspect there is something else going on—at least where Andrew is concerned."

She grabbed both of Grace's shoulders and stared into her eyes. "You can't possibly believe Jax only wanted you for the music. That man thought the moon and sun set on your ass, anyone with eyes could see it. And, in case you've forgotten, you were a writing team before you were a couple, he didn't need to marry you, he was already getting the music."

That wasn't true. Was it? Andrew thought she was blaming her issues on Jax and now Annie was intimating the same thing? Grace shook her head, trying to quiet her swirling thoughts. No, they were both wrong and she would prove it. She squared her shoulders to Annie. "But he never wanted me to work with anyone else."

"How do you know that?"

"Because he said so!"

"Did he? Did he use those exact words?"

Grace dug into the memories, trying to find the times he'd told her not to take other gigs, but they didn't materialize. Yes, he'd said they didn't need the money, that he wanted her with him as much as possible, but she realized he'd never, ever, explicitly told her not to write for anyone else. She'd mangled his words, and his memory, to protect herself. Unshed tears burned behind her eyes and she looked at Annie, who was patiently waiting her response. "No," she whispered, "never."

Annie reached across the table and laid her hands atop Grace's. "What are you really afraid of, *amiga*?"

"What if something happens to Andrew?" Grace whispered. "I don't think I can survive that again. I barely survived it the first time."

"There we go. There's the truth." She pulled the second tissue from Grace's hands. "Let me ask you this, if you had to do it all over again, would you choose not to love Jax? Would you forfeit those years just so you never had to experience the pain of losing him?"

"No."

"And, you did survive it—it brought you here—to the place where you're ready to embrace your talent, to share it with the world, to help others share their musical gifts with the world, and, I think, to love again. To open your heart and love another man, not despite Jax, but because of him."

"Move over Oprah, here comes Annaliese Santos, lawyer by day, motivational speaker by night."

"Make all the jokes you want, but you know in here"—she tapped a finger over Grace's heart—"that I'm right."

"Oh god, Annie, I've blamed Jax for so many things. I questioned our marriage because it was easier than admitting my own fears. I made him the bad guy so I wouldn't have to own up to my own confidence issues. And," she paused, a shudder running through her, "I pushed Andrew away for all the same reasons. I've made a giant mess of things."

"Yes, you have," Annie said.

"Whoa, don't try and soften the blow or anything."

"It's called tough love, mama. And here's another bit of it: you're going to have to make the first move."

Grace's shoulders slumped and she looked up at Annie from under her eyelashes. "I can't just wait until he comes back in three weeks?"

Annie closed her eyes and shook her head. "Grace."

"I know, I know. No more hiding. But he did say no talking or texting while he's gone."

Annie snorted. "*He* said he wouldn't talk or text. Did you say the same thing?"

Grace laughed at the superior look on Annie's face. "Ever the lawyer."

Annie shrugged, a smirk playing at her lips. "What can I say? I got an A+ in Loopholes 101."

Grace sighed and the smile slipped from her mouth. "I was a giant ass, Annie. I can't just text him, 'Sorry, my bad.' I need to show him that I'm sorry and I'm serious about giving our relationship a go. What should I do?"

Annie arched a single eyebrow. Grace really had to figure out how she did that. "Do what you do best."

"Are you leading the witness, counselor?"

"I think you're actually the perp."

"Ouch, again." Grace pointed a single finger at her best friend. "That's enough tough love from you for one day."

Annie bit back a smile and held her hands up, palms up, just as Bart set a fresh latte in front of Grace. He turned to go, stopped, and pushed the cup into the center of the table. Grace dissolved into giggles. She felt lighter than she had in years.

"Thanks Bart, I promise I won't spill a second one."

Annie nodded sagely. "Can't waste second chances, can we, Grace?"

Grace nodded and hoped Andrew was still willing to give her one.

Andrew stood at the window. The Space Needle punctured the low-hanging clouds and small white caps rolled across the Sound. Cold and gray, it matched his mood. His only reprieve came each night as the stage lights dropped. By the third song, he'd get lost in the performance. But after the final applause, his mind immediately flashed to Grace and how much he missed her. He missed the way she blushed every time he winked at her and the way her skin pebbled every time he touched her. But mostly he missed talking to her and making her laugh.

Fuck this, he was going to call her. Screw the promises he'd made. Beg, grovel, he'd do whatever it took to release the knot in his chest. He reached for his phone as Joe slammed a FedEx envelope into his chest.

"This came for you."

Andrew turned the package over in his hands and sucked in a ragged breath. He knew that address. He pulled the tab, slowly revealing two pieces of paper held together by a glittery blue paperclip.

"Andrew, you want to join us?" He turned and blinked. All the guys were staring at him and Brad was motioning at the table. He nodded and sunk into the nearest chair, trying to focus on Brad and not the envelope tucked beside him. What was she sending him? *Don't get your hopes up, it's likely just the final song.*

Brad opened his leather portfolio. "As a reminder, we're meeting at the venue at three o'clock for a run-through and soundcheck." Brad held up a hand as Matt's mouth dropped open. "Before anyone asks, no, we cannot skip it. The stage is a funky shape and we'll have to re-block a couple of numbers.

"And, before I let you go"—Brad looked around the room and pulled a bottle of champagne and six plastic glasses from under the table—"I know it's a bit early in the day, but we need to celebrate." He popped the cork and began filling glasses. "Congratulations to Andrew and Grace for finishing the album."

Joe's head whipped to Andrew. "Andy, I thought you said

only twelve songs were done. Why didn't you tell us you'd finished it?"

Andrew sat straight up in his chair. "Because I didn't know."

Brad slid a glass in front of each man. "I got an email from Ford this morning, saying he had received the thirteenth song and the label was pleased. He even used an exclamation point . . . I worried for a moment that he'd had a stroke. Seemed so ebullient of him."

"Brad, what's the title of the last track?" Andrew asked, fingering the envelope.

Brad ran his finger down Ford's email. "*No Hesitation*."

"Shit. She did it. That's the song I've been asking for," he whispered, rocking his head side-to-side.

Brad bent, bracing his hands on the table. "Andrew? You really didn't know?"

"No." And he didn't know what it meant, either. Did she submit the song out of guilt or something else? Could he hope it was some sort of olive branch? A message that she'd reconsidered sharing her life with him? Maybe there was a note in the FedEx package. It took everything in him not to rip the pages from the envelope, but better to look at them without an audience.

"Huh." Brad looked over Andrew with a puzzled expression before shaking it off and turning to the rest of the men. "Well, regardless, it's done." He lifted his glass in the air. "To Storyhill's newest album."

They all cheered and threw back the champagne—everyone except Andrew—he was still reeling from the announcement and its implications.

"And, that means I will need all of you in Minneapolis, at Unstrung Studios, on March fifteenth. Now, get out of here and get some rest before this afternoon's call."

• • •

Andrew watched everyone leave the hotel conference room, except Joe. He sat at the other end of the table, fiddling with his phone. Andrew couldn't wait any longer. He slid the papers out of the envelope. A sticky note was affixed to the top page. His breath hitched when he saw the first two words. *Hey Cowboy*. She'd addressed it using her nickname for him. That had to mean something, didn't it? It wasn't cold and professional. It was warm and personal. His eyes slowly drank in the rest of the words.

Hey Cowboy,

I've been working on a new song. I've got the verses, but I'm a little stuck on the chorus. I figured you'd be the best person to help me out. When you've got time, find a piano, play it, and see what comes to you.

Grace

"Joe," he nearly yelled, causing his best friend to jump and send his phone airborne. "Have you seen a piano in this hotel?"

"Andy, what the hell? You scared the shit out of me."

"Joe! Piano?"

Joe's eyes widened and he looked at Andrew like he'd finally lost his last marble. "Best bet would be in the ballroom—most hotels keep a grand in there."

Andrew jumped from his chair and darted out the door, Joe at his heels. "Dude, should I worry? You're acting really weird. Did you get a sudden inspiration for a song?"

"Something like that," he shot back at Joe as he skidded to a stop in front of a hotel employee. "Ballroom?" he asked the startled teenager. The young man pointed to a door across the hall.

"Is there a piano in there?"

The guy bobbled his head, saying nothing.

Andrew threw open the door and scanned the room. A black baby grand sat tucked into the far corner. He pulled out the bench and set Grace's pages on the music rack. He played the first six measures before stopping, his entire focus moving to the lyrics.

For so long now I've lived my life in the wings
Afraid to step out of the shadows
Protecting my heart was all I knew
Until I stumbled into you

You found me and pulled me into the light
But I pretended not to see
A heart, cold and broken, began to beat
Love was all you asked of me

You gathered my shattered pieces
And gave me a new place to belong
You opened your heart and welcomed me in
While loving me like a love song.

"Whoa," Joe said, from behind him. "Is that Grace's work?"

"Uh-huh," Andrew said.

"I thought you weren't working together anymore."

Andrew mindlessly plunked middle C. "Yeah, she made that pretty clear before I left Minneapolis."

"So, what is this?" Joe said, waving at the music.

Andrew pulled the post-it note from the piano's shelf and handed it to Joe. "She needs help."

Joe paced behind the piano bench. "Seems like more than that to me."

Andrew spun on the bench, catching his best friend's arm. "It does, doesn't it? I'm not just seeing what I want to see, right?"

"No, I see it, too. If she was trying to send a cryptic message, she failed. Epically. That's pretty much laying it all out there."

Andrew grabbed the sheet music, shoved it back into the envelope, and pulled his phone from his back pocket. "I need to talk to her."

"Right now?"

Andrew fisted his hand in his hair. "Yes, now."

"You promised her no texts and no phone calls." Joe slid the phone from Andrew's grasp. "Show her you keep your promises. Women like that."

Andrew grunted. "Now you're the expert on women?"

"Hey," Joe said, tapping the phone against his chest. "Twelve plus years with the same woman." He tapped the phone against Andrew's chest. "Zero years with the same woman. I think that gives me an edge."

Andrew waved the package in front of Joe's face. "Okay, genius, don't you think this changes things?"

"Nope. A promise is a promise. It's in her court right now, let her finish out the set."

Andrew sighed and dropped his head to his chest. "Fine," he grumbled. "But if she hasn't reached out by tomorrow, promise or no promise, I'm calling her."

"Such amazing restraint you have."

"Shut up, Joe."

"Maybe you should give me your phone, you know, as an extra insurance policy."

Andrew grunted, shoved his phone back in his pocket, and stomped toward the door.

"See you at rehearsal," Joe called.

Andrew flipped him the bird from behind his back and let the door slam behind him.

CHAPTER TWENTY-ONE

Grace waited until the crowd quieted and Matt sang the opening bars of the first number before stepping up to the edge of the curtain. Her stomach somersaulted and she pushed her hand into her abdomen to quiet the butterflies. When she had pulled out of the FedEx parking lot, she realized just sending the song wasn't enough. She'd run into her condo, took the stairs two at a time, flipped open her laptop, and clicked 'select this fare' before she could change her mind.

As the first song ended, she turned her attention to center stage and the men who occupied it. The stage lights dropped and a single spotlight washed over the singer on the end. *Andrew*. The butterflies in her stomach exploded into a full zoo. Dark hair that just kissed the tops of his broad shoulders, a chiseled jaw blanketed in five o'clock shadow, and that well-worn leather jacket that pulled tightly across his biceps and ended at a pair of perfectly fitting jeans—it was like she was seeing him again for the first time. Except this time, it wasn't lust that flowed through her veins, it was so much more.

He'd stolen her breath in that first coffee shop—her body clearly understanding something it would take her heart and her mind weeks more to realize. She only hoped her realization hadn't come too late. He'd said he'd wait . . . but she'd behaved so badly.

"Grace?" a man whispered in her ear, making her startle. "What are you doing here?"

She turned to find Brad standing behind her. She shrugged. "I had some frequent flyer miles that were about to expire."

He chuckled silently and pulled at the lanyard around her neck. "How did you get backstage?"

Grace waited for the applause for the second song to subside before answering. "Apparently the beat boxer likes me," she said, pointing at Joe.

Brad's eyebrows shot up his forehead. "It's the beat boxer that likes you, is it?"

She stifled a nervous laugh and slapped Brad in the chest with the back of her hand. Andrew must have caught the movement because his eyes flashed to the wings—and he missed a step, nearly running into Blake. She smiled and offered a tentative wave. He held her gaze for a beat, but she couldn't see the expression in his eyes, the stage lights were too bright. Evidently, Joe had managed to keep her secret. Andrew was clearly surprised, but she couldn't ascertain any other emotions.

"Seriously," Brad whispered as Andrew tried to cover for his stumble and pick up the bass beat, "what is going on with the two of you?"

"Shhh," Grace said and pointed to the stage, "there's a show going on. If you can't be quiet, I'm going to have to ask Story-hill's manager to remove you."

Brad rolled his eyes and opened his mouth as Grace held up a single finger. "I owe Andrew the first explanation."

Brad crossed his arms but didn't ask any more questions. They stood in silence until the final note of the set reverberated through the auditorium and Nick announced they'd be back in fifteen minutes. Brad squeezed her elbow. "I'm headed to the greenroom. You coming along?"

Grace shook her head. Suddenly her shoes were cement. She couldn't move even if she wanted. Maybe this hadn't been such a good idea. But before she could go into full panic mode, Joe walked past her, and whispered, "You look like you're about to pass out. Don't do it. I'll forever be hearing stories about how women fall at his feet. Please save me from that."

Grace laughed, releasing the tension that held her frozen in place. Matt, Nick, and Blake ambled by each offering some version of 'Hey, Grace' until the final member of the group approached her. His greeting was a bit different.

"What are you doing here?"

"Um, well, uh," Grace stuttered and stammered. She'd practiced this exact moment at least 1,437 times on the plane. It had been so much easier talking to the seatback than looking into the green eyes that melted her in every way possible — her heart, her panties, and apparently, her ability to speak. She cleared her throat and tried again. "I won a back-stage pass," she blurted out. *Where did that come from? Seriously, Grace.*

The corners of Andrew's mouth twitched. "Did you? I wasn't aware that we were running any contests for this particular performance. What, exactly, did you have to do to win this?" He tapped a finger on her backstage credentials.

Think, Grace. You make up stories for a living. "I wrote an essay."

Andrew moved a step closer and her heartbeat jumped from allegro to allegrissimo. "An essay, huh? I think that's a new one for Storyhill. What exactly did it say? Must have been impressive to get you backstage."

He was not letting her off the hook. She squared her shoulders and plowed forward. "You had to pick your favorite member of the group and explain what you like about that person. So, naturally, I picked the sexiest singer."

"Joe?"

Grace smirked and shrugged. "You'd think so. I mean, he does have that whole post-sex-hair thing going on. But no. I chose the bass singer and wrote about his finer qualities."

He reached toward her but pulled his hand back. "And what are those?"

"Well, he's handsome, smart, stubborn, exceptionally talented, kind, immensely loyal to his friends, and . . ." Grace placed a hand on Andrew's arm. "And, forgiving."

"Andrew," Blake said, walking past, "we're back on in sixty."

Andrew's head twitched in the direction of Blake's voice, but his eyes never strayed from Grace. "Forgiving, huh? I'm not sure anyone else would agree with you."

"Andy," Joe said, pushing a mic into Andrew's chest, "we gotta go. Sorry, Grace."

Andrew's gaze washed over her face, his eyebrows pulling together.

"Andrew. Stage," Brad said, giving his shoulder a gentle nudge.

Andrew nodded and spun toward the stage as the house lights dropped.

Grace shuddered and sighed out a long breath.

"You okay?" Brad asked, slinging an arm around her shoulders.

She nodded. Surprisingly, she was okay—better than okay. He hadn't forgiven her, but he didn't ask her to leave, either. And that was enough for Grace 2.0. This new version of Grace fought for what she wanted—and she wanted Andrew.

～

The final applause rang through the auditorium, marking the end of the longest set of Andrew's life. He'd done his best to focus on the performance, but his eyes kept wandering to the wings. He needed constant reassurance she wasn't a figment of his imagination.

The last man off stage, Grace held out her hand for his mic, slipping it into the final foam slot in the molded microphone case.

His eyes followed her fingers. "You know we pay people to handle the gear, right?"

She dragged her hand along the edge of the case, not looking at him. "I asked everyone to give us some space."

"And they listened? Even Joe?"

Grace laughed, breaking the tension arcing between them. "Even Joe. Though I'd put money on him leaving the greenroom door open, in the hopes of hearing our conversation."

He smiled and nodded. "You'd win that bet every time. I'm assuming he had something to do with your backstage pass?"

"You didn't buy the essay contest, huh?"

He laughed and then sobered. "Grace, why are you really here?"

She shifted from one foot to the other and stared down at his boots. "You said no calling and no texts, and I have some things to say."

He placed a single finger under her chin—he had to touch her—and tipped her head up. "Your song said a lot."

"You liked it?" she whispered.

"I did."

"I'm glad. But you deserve more than some words on paper. I owe you more than that."

She wove her fingers into his and the heat that erupted in his hand was almost painful, but he would not let go of her, not again. "You don't owe me anything, Gracie."

"I do." She pulled her hand from his and started to pace in front of him. "I need to apologize for how I acted." She stopped and turned to him, placing both of her hands on his chest. "And, I figured the first time I told you, 'I love you,' it should be in person."

He covered her hands with his own. "You love me?"

"I do, Andrew. So much."

"What about needing to do things on your own?"

She nodded somberly and bit her bottom lip. "I absolutely need to step out of the shadows and chart my own course. All of that is true, but it's not the reason I let you go. I got scared. My heart broke into a million pieces when Jax died, and I didn't think I could survive that again. But what I realized after you left, was that my heart was already breaking."

"Grace," Andrew said, raking his fingers through his hair, flipping it away from his face.

"Let me finish, Andrew. All I could do was think about you, the way you look at me, the way it feels to write with you, the way I feel when you wrap your arms around me and if my heart was going to break anyway, I'd rather have it happen with you beside me."

"Wow," he said, drawing her in close. "You're really good with words. Ever think of trying to make a living with that talent?"

"Way to ruin the moment, Andy," Joe yelled from deeper backstage.

Andrew placed a soft kiss on her forehead, and she dropped her head to his chest, laughing. "Good thing I didn't take that bet."

Grace lifted her head and ran a finger over his jaw. "Am I forgiven, Cowboy?"

"I'm in love with you, Grace, and I told you I'd wait until

you were ready. There's nothing to forgive. I do have one question, though."

"Shoot."

"Why did you send the last song to Ford?"

She locked her eyes on his. "I sent it because it would link us forever. Even if you'd changed your mind and didn't want to see me again, every time I heard Storyhill sing that song, I'd know a piece of me was with you."

"Damn, Andy, she *is* good with words."

"Joe!" they yelled simultaneously before dissolving into laughter again.

He brushed the hair back from her face and dipped his head, pressing a kiss to her cheek. "I love you, Grace O'Connor."

"I love you too, Andrew Hayes. Now, how about we go to the afterparty?"

His eyes widened in surprise. "That's what you want to do right now? Spend time with Joe and Matt?"

Grace smiled and winked. "I was told post-concert drinks are not optional for members of Storyhill. That rule still standing?"

He grinned and placed a trio of kisses on the shell of her ear. "You do realize that I have a hotel room just blocks away, right?"

"I was banking on that. I didn't make a reservation of my own."

Andrew cocked an eyebrow. "Pretty certain of yourself, huh?"

"Just unwilling to give up until you agreed to give me another chance."

"Did I ever tell you that your backbone is one of the sexiest things about you?"

"Rumor has it, that I've been underselling that part of

myself. But not anymore. From now on, I believe in myself—and I believe in us."

"Just kiss her, Andy, so we can leave for the bar. On the lips this time," Joe called out.

Andrew sighed. "That man is a nuisance, but his idea is a good one." He pulled her to his chest and kissed her, trying to tell her with his lips how much he'd missed her and how much he loved her.

She pulled back, her eyes still closed. "That all you got, Cowboy?"

He laughed. "Still busting my ass, Gracie?"

Her lids popped open and she stared into his eyes. "Until we are old and gray. Or for as long as we get."

He kissed her cheekbone. "I'm not sure if that's a threat or a promise, but I'm in either way."

She gave him a slow smile and touched her nose to his. "Either way, we figure it out together?"

He nodded. "Together."

She could write him a lifetime of songs and nothing would mean as much as that single word.

GET A FREE NOVELLA!

Ready to dive into your next love story?

Then I've got great news! Follow the link below to subscribe to my readers' community and **I'll send you 'Friday at the Blue Note' for free!** (If you are already a member of my readers' community, don't worry, you won't be subscribed twice — you'll just get a great bonus read!)

'Friday at the Blue Note' is a best-friends-to-lovers story featuring Curtis and Megan.

Remember them? When Grace sits with her childhood best friend, Curtis, after his restaurant closes, she wonders about the true nature of his relationship with his business partner, Megan.

Inside 'Friday at the Blue Note' you'll get the answer to that question and be pulled into a story about resilience and enduring friendship.

Get your novella —> www.annmarieboyle.com/blue-note

DID YOU ENJOY THIS BOOK? HELP OTHER READERS FIND IT.

Reviews are one of the most powerful tools in an author's tool-box. Honest reviews of books help capture the attention of potential readers and open many other opportunities.

If you enjoyed this book I would be grateful if you'd leave a review on your preferred reading platform, Goodreads, or Bookbub.

Thank you!

ABOUT THE AUTHOR

Annmarie Boyle is a connoisseur of yoga pants, Sharpies, fancy coffee drinks and a sucker for happy endings. After two decades in the marketing and copywriting game, she decided to jump into the deep end of the pool and follow her dreams — to write stories that make you laugh a little, cry a little, and are always entertaining.

Annmarie lives in a sleepy Midwestern town overlooking a lazy river with her husband, who after 20+ years still makes her believe in happily-ever-afters.

She'd love to hear from you. You can find her on Instagram and Facebook.

instagram.com/annmarieboyleauthor
facebook.com/AnnMarieBoyleAuthor

ACKNOWLEDGMENTS

While writing a book can often feel like a solitary endeavor, nothing could be further from the truth. I am deeply grateful for every person who played a role in bringing this book to life. It's been a long, sometimes uphill, journey and I can't thank you enough for your unwavering support.

To the early teachers, Ami Silber, Brian Malloy, Angela Foster, and Shelia O'Connor, I thank you for taking this copywriter and teaching her the lyrical language of fiction.

To my first readers, Abbie Haug, Becka Rahn, Tami Enfield, Sandra Marine, and Kimberly Ford, I so appreciate you! Not only did you take the time to read this manuscript at various stages and offer feedback, but you helped me get past the fear of sharing my writing with the world. As a thank you, each of you has a character named after you in the book.

To Samantha Bohrman, who edited a very early version of the book and Jolene Perry, who helped me bring the final version to life, I am grateful for your patience and keen eye. This book would not have been the same without your efforts.

To my family and friends: my career path has never been a straight line and yet, when I announced I was going to try my hand at writing fiction, none of you blinked an eye (not to my face, anyway!). I appreciate your interest, questions, and patience as a rambled on about all the things I was learning along this journey. I am lucky to have each and every one of you in my life.

And, finally, to the people who purchased and read this book, you took a chance on a debut author and I cannot begin to express my gratitude for your leap of faith. Thank you.

This is a work of fiction. Names, characters, places, and incidents are products of the author's imagination or are used fictitiously and are not to be construed as real. Any resemblance to actual events, locales, organizations, or person, living or dead, is entirely coincidental.

Edited by Jolene Perry

Cover by Damonza

Copyright © 2020 by Ann Marie Boyle

All rights reserved.

No part of this book may be reproduced in any form or by any electronic or mechanical means, including information storage and retrieval systems, without written permission from the author, except for the use of brief quotations in a book review.

ISBN 978-1-7359351-1-9

CPSIA information can be obtained
at www.ICGtesting.com
Printed in the USA
LVHW031631230521
688267LV00003B/770